Lestrade and
the Magpie

Lestrade and the Magpie

Volume X in the
Lestrade Mystery Series

M.J. Trow

A Gateway Mystery

REGNERY
PUBLISHING, INC.

Since 1947 • An Eagle Publishing Company

Library of Congress Cataloging-in-Publication Data

Trow, M.J.
    Lestrade and the magpie / M.J. Trow
       p.   cm. — (A Gateway mystery) (Lestrade mystery series ; v. 10)
    ISBN 0-89526-289-4
    1. Lestrade, Inspector (Fictitious character)—Fiction. 2. Police—England—London—Fiction. 3. London (England)—Fiction. I. Title. II. Series.
PR6070.R598 L477 2000
823'.914—dc21   99-059915

Published in the United States by
Regnery Publishing, Inc.
An Eagle Publishing Company
One Massachusetts Avenue, NW
Washington, DC 20001

Distributed to the trade by
National Book Network
4720-A Boston Way
Lanham, MD 20706

Printed on acid-free paper
Manufactured in the United States of America
Originally published in Great Britain

10 9 8 7 6 5 4 3 2 1

Books are available in quantity for promotional or premium use. Write to Director of Special Sales, Regnery Publishing, Inc., One Massachusetts Avenue, NW, Washington, DC 20001, for information on discounts and terms or call (202) 216-0600.

The character of Inspector Lestrade was created by the late Sir Arthur Conan Doyle and appears in the Sherlock Holmes stories and novels by him, as do some other characters in this book.

For Jenny
who can always put her finger on it

The blackbird flies with panic,
The swallow goes with light,
The finches move like ladies,
The owl floats by at night;
But the great and flashing magpie
He flies as artists might.

'Magpies in Picardy',
T. P. Cameron Wilson.

1

He watched him wandering the horse lines. Heard his boots crunch on frozen tufts of grass. He saw him stop by one tall grey and fancied he whispered something in the animal's ear.

A weak sun was struggling through the hedgerows, dancing silver on the cobwebs, the spider's night of industry. He saw him glance once at the sun, then pull his fur collar closer. He saw the firm jaw, the tired eyes, the ramrod back and he felt, despite the numbing cold, his own left arm jerk up to catch the rifle. His woollen mittens struck his forehead, the best he could do by way of salute after a night's watch.

'Mr Dacres,' his breath snaked out in the morning. 'Welcome back, sir.'

'Flight-sergeant,' the officer returned his salute. 'How've you been?'

'Better, sir, thanks.'

'Hun kept you busy?' Dacres tugged a packet of Whiffs from his tunic.

'Now and then, sir. They say there's a big push coming. You haven't heard anything? At Headquarters, I mean?'

Dacres smiled. 'There's always a push coming, isn't there?' He offered the flight-sergeant a cigarette and lit up for them both.

'I've got a flask here, sir,' the man said, 'something for a cold morning.'

The officer accepted the khaki-covered bottle and winced as the contents hit the back of his throat.

'That'll put hairs on your chest, sir – begging your pardon, of course.'

'Orders of the Day?' Dacres asked.

'Stand to, sir. You know, the usual.'

Dacres' eyes levelled at the waiting line, 'Mr Neville's plane ready?' he asked.

'*Camberwell Beauty*? Champing at the bit sir. Did Mr Neville . . .?'

'I saw him earlier,' Dacres cut in, 'We had an early breakfast. I'm a bit rusty.' He walked through the grass. 'Thought I'd take a look at the Jerry lines. Reacquaint myself as it were.'

The flight-sergeant ferreted under his layers of greatcoat for the flight sheet. 'There's nothing here about . . .' he began.

'You cut along, sergeant,' Dacres said. 'This is off the record. All right?'

He saw the flight-sergeant hesitate. The eyes flickered, the tongue flicked over the balaclava'd lips. 'Well . . .'

'Oh,' Dacres said, 'I cantered over from Bapaume this morning. Look after these for me, will you?' He dug into the pocket of his flying coat, the long brown leather with the fur collar, and produced his spurs. 'Regulation 3416,' he smiled. 'Officers of the cavalry shall not wear spurs in the cockpit of their aircraft.'

'Quite right, sir,' the flight-sergeant grinned, taking the cold steel in his mittens. 'How long will you be, sir?'

'Well,' Dacres looked up at the propellers and struts of the Pup, 'If I'm not back in half an hour, start the war without me.'

He clambered up on to the *Beauty*'s aileron and, ducking to avoid the wing, swung himself into the cockpit. Mechanically, he checked the switchgear, momentarily resting his gloved hands on the twin butts of the Lewis gun. In the event of trouble, he prayed that the new Kauper gear would work. It was cold enough on the ground. It would be freezing up there. But the visibility was getting better. He'd be able to pick up the painted ladies of von Richtofen's Circus before they saw him and the sun, like God, was on his side.

He raised his thumb to the men of the ground, who swung on the propeller. Nothing. He glanced at the officers' horses champing away the frozen, silver tufts. Then he remembered something. He unbuttoned his tunic with a clumsy, gloved hand. He felt the butt of his Webley, nestling near his armpit

8

and pulled something from his inside pocket. A shaft of sunlight caught the locket as he held it, and illuminated her face for a second. His Emma, laughing with that merry tinkle of hers, the golden hair swept up for the studio portrait, away from the soft neck, the warm cheeks.

Then the engine spluttered to life in front of his knees. He stuffed the locket back, pulling the goggles down over his eyes. The propeller was an invisible blur before him, the Pup vibrating and pulsing as he eased the throttle. The men on the ground scrambled away, holding on to headgear and coats.

He taxied forward, the *Beauty* lurching to the right a little as she left the lines, eighty horsepower thumping under his feet. The wind took his breath away as it always did and the dials rocked and swivelled in his view. One glance at the flight-sergeant, still holding his spurs, and he turned the Pup into the runway for the take-off. The tents flashed white as he passed them, easing the stick, bracing his legs. He saw the horses, startled, pull on the ropes and shy, his own grey among them. His stomach dropped, as it always did and the rattling of the struts and the roar of exhausts suddenly died and he was up.

In the sky in the morning, he climbed above the wisps of cloud, turning in the sun like a great insect, gilded, armoured. In five minutes, he would be six thousand feet with the world before him. He saw the patchwork of fields, criss-crossed with barriers, scarred with trenches and gouged with craters. He saw the sun tumbling on the frosty steel of his own lines and the dark, dead woods around Bapaume where trees still stood in the morning, frozen upright in death.

The *Beauty* screamed as she turned in air, hurtling flat over France and he heard the distant thud-thud as enemy anti-aircraft guns spotted him and opened up. Would von Richtofen waken his gentlemen of Jasta II in pursuit of one Pup? In his heart, Dacres knew he would, for von Richtofen was a *junker* of the old school, all sabre-scars and saddle-sores – a man born to the hunt. He wouldn't – couldn't – leave it alone. A Pup in the air was to von Richtofen like a slap in the face. Dacres looked at the fuselage below the leather trim of his seat at Lieutenant Neville's six kills. It gave him some comfort that at least the *Beauty* knew what she was doing. Was it Neville who had scored those hits?

9

Or his machine? And what was von Richtofen's total? Sixty? Seventy? Odds enough, he thought.

The flight-sergeant stamped his feet, the butt of the Whiff damp and soggy in his mouth. He squinted, shading his eyes from the glare. The ground crew had scurried back indoors for breakfast, leaving him alone. Even so, the sound of his own voice startled him, 'Careful now, Mr Dacres, you're flying too close to the sun.'

Another cold January. Another young man in a fur-collared coat. Tom Hutchings, cub-reporter on the *Mirror*, wedged into the lift at Scotland Yard. He'd gone the wrong way twice today already and found himself up to the eyebrows in the shoe-boxes that called themselves proudly the Criminal Record Office. After that he'd backed out and found himself following a labyrinth of cream-painted pipes back to the river.

'Wapping's that way!' a Bluebottle had called to him from the bobbing deck of a police launch. 'Want a lift?'

Hutchings shook his head and doubled back. Stern and silent assistant commissioners stared at him from sepia photographs: the Honourable F. T. Bigham, who wore his CB like a halo; Sir Basil Thomson, outshining Bigham with his KCB; F. S. Bullock, whose name said it all; Major Sir E. F. Wodehouse, sporting a KCVO and still it seemed, from the vexed look on his face, denying knowledge of anyone called Jeeves or Wooster. But it was not these luminaries that Hutchings sought. He was after slightly less eminence. After all, he worked for the *Mirror*.

'Yes?' a senior detective with gold-rimmed glasses passed him in the upper corridors.

'Mr Wensley, isn't it?' Hutchings said.

The detective stopped, folding his briefcase to his chest for a moment. 'Mr Hutchings, *Daily Mirror*,' he said in the soft Dorset brogue that years in the East End had failed to destroy.

The reporter stood open-mouthed. 'I'm amazed,' he said.

'I never forget a face, laddie.' Wensley resumed his long stride along the passageway, the sharp light of the new year dappling his suit as he went. 'You covered the Voisin trial three years ago.'

'"Blodie Belgiam", eh?' Hutchings scuttled at the man's heels.

'Bloody, indeed,' murmured Wensley, '"And the wind blow-ing over London from Flanders has a bitter taste".'

'Er . . . I'm sorry?' The detective had lost him.

'Nothing,' Wensley said. 'Just something somebody wrote in a trench one day.'

'Ah, yes, I was a little young for that show. Unfortunately.'

Wensley stopped. 'How old are you, boy?' he asked.

'Twenty-one, sir.'

Wensley shook his head, 'No, you weren't,' he said. 'You were too bloody old. Well, what do you want at the Yard?'

'Ah,' Hutchings fought to regain his equilibrium. 'The paper is running a story on Nearly Famous Policemen. I was looking for . . .' he checked his notes, 'Superintendent Lestrade.'

Wensley stopped again. 'Who?' he said.

'Sup . . .'

'He's gone, boy,' Wensley said softly. 'We shall not see his like again. But if you seek his monument, look around you.'

'But I . . .'

There were no buts with Fred Wensley. 'Mr Venzel' to the Chosen People of his beloved East End knew how to end a conversation with the Gentlemen of the Press. He just walked through a door, careful, as Superintendent Lestrade had not always been, to open it first.

Hutchings walked on. Through the grimy post-war windows of Norman Shaw's Opera House he saw the black lighters on the gravy-brown sludge of the river, nodding in time as they had done for a century or more. He tapped on the next door he came to.

'Mr Kane?' The *Mirror* employed men who could read door signs in those days.

The harassed detective-sergeant at the desk pointed to the next office.

'Mr Kane?' Hutchings asked anew.

'That's me.' The youngish inspector put down the magnifying glass.

'Gosh,' Hutchings grinned inanely, 'do you chaps really use those things?'

Kane frowned, 'When I have a particularly small splinter in

11

my thumb, yes. Who are you and what do you want? I'm a busy man.'

'Oh, sorry, yes of course. Hutchings. *Daily Mirror*. I was looking for Superintendent Lestrade.'

'Lestrade?' John Kane resumed the search, leaving no loop or whorl unturned in his quest for inner peace. 'You're too late, I'm afraid. This time last year . . . His office was up on the next floor.'

'Could I have a look, do you think?'

'I don't see why not. What's all this about?'

'Well, it's an article. Er . . . an obituary, I suppose.'

'An obituary?' Kane looked up.

'On Nearly Famous Policemen. We'll be doing Brigadier Horwood next month.'

'Not before time,' Kane nodded slowly. 'Close the door on your way out.'

Hutchings did. He took the sharply twisting spiral to his left, along that dingy passageway that Shaw had planned as the Opera House's lavatories until they found another use for it. In letters of gilt on the only obvious door, slightly scraped and subtly peeling, he read the legend 'Inspector Blevvins'. Not much of a legend, really.

A cherubic young constable opened the door to his knock and Hutchings announced himself. He followed the lad, of his own age, through a tight corridor, floor to ceiling with yellowed paper.

'A gentleman to see you, Mr Blevvins,' the constable said.

'Right, Green.'

'Er . . . that's Greeno, sir,' the young detective coughed.

Blevvins scowled up at him. 'Is it?' he grunted disapprovingly. 'That's a bloody dago name, isn't it?'

'Er . . .'

'Never mind. You can't help being born the wrong side of the Channel. Who are you?' He focused his dark, dead eyes on the newspaperman.

'Hutchings. *Daily Mirror*.' He extended a hand.

'Oh, the gutter press. If it's the "Violin Case" I can't comment.'

'No, Inspector. It's not that.'

'Ah,' the detective's face fell several degrees, 'then let me assure you I don't know anyone by the name of Miss Tawse of 33 Abednego Street, East Thirteen and if she says I do, she's a bloody liar.'

'It's about Superintendent Lestrade,' Hutchings told him.

'Lestrade?' Blevvins frowned. 'Never heard of him.'

'Inspector Kane said this used to be his office.'

'Did he now?' Blevvins growled. 'What name again?'

'Lestrade.'

'Can you spell that?'

'Of course,' Hutchings assured him. 'I'm a journalist.'

Blevvins narrowed his eyes and cracked his knuckles as he leaned forward. 'Have you got a dog, Mr . . . er . . . Hitchin?'

'Er . . . yes,' Hutchings confided, though a little bewildered by the question.

'Is it muzzled?'

'Muzzled?' Hutchings repeated. 'Why, no. No, it isn't.'

'Green!' Blevvins roared. The young constable nearly of that name returned at the double.

'Yessir!'

'This gentleman is the proprietor of an unmuzzled dog. As such he constitutes a rabies threat. You look as though you could do with a few decent collars, lad. I want you to accompany Mr Hutchings here to wherever he hangs out, arrest him and impound his dog. You can kick it too, if you like.'

'Wait a minute . . .' Hutchings protested, 'the rabies scare is over.'

'Over?' Blevvins loomed to his full five feet nine. 'Over? It will never be over for us, newspaperman. This is Scotland Yard. We never sleep. The bloody government might want to build a tunnel under the bloody Channel, but that doesn't mean some of us haven't got our heads screwed on. And as for giving women the vote, well . . .'

'I'm not sure you can do this, Mr Blevvins,' Hutchings wriggled as much as he could in Greeno's armlock.

'Watch me, son,' the inspector grinned. 'Just you bloody watch me.'

'I suppose this means no story on Lestrade,' Hutchings shouted as he hurtled through the door.

'Lestrade's dead,' Blevvins told him, 'I shouldn't wonder. If you ask me, the old bastard's been dead for years, only nobody noticed.'

'Well, thank you for all your help and co-operation, Inspector,' Hutchings yelled.

'Not at all,' Blevvins bawled back, 'glad to be of service.' He spun back to another constable, sitting open-mouthed by the door.

'You didn't see that visitor then, did you, Cherrill?'

'What visitor was that, sir?'

Blevvins sneered, 'You'll go far. Now, get me Miss Tawse of Abednego Street on the blower and be quick about it. Or else you'll end up in fingerprints for the rest of your natural.'

'Yessir. Very good, sir.'

All that was left of Sholto Joseph Lestrade lay among the dried flowers. His face, that old yellowed one with the scars, was serene and composed, the eyes closed in peace. His arms were crossed over his chest and he looked far younger than his six and a half decades. Peace. Peace at last.

'Sholto!'

The voice burst on him like a dream.

'Get up. You look as though you're dead!'

He sat bolt upright. 'What time is it?'

'Nearly half past four.'

His eyes became acclimatized to the drawing-room. Then he was convulsed by sneezing and fell back into the innermost recesses of the armchair.

Fanny Lestrade put her sewing down on her lap. Their eyes met across a crowded, still-Edwardian room full of photographs and Clarice Cliff. He saw her eyebrows rise. 'That's the fourth time today,' she said softly. 'I'll take the flowers away.'

'It's not the flowers,' he said. 'I haven't been right since I was sprayed by that idiot on the 36 bus on the way to Peckham.'

'Darling, that was six months ago,' she told him, 'and it *did* save you from catching the flu.'

'That's only what the disinfectant people said. We only have their word for that.'

'Sholto Lestrade,' she scolded him, 'you old cynic! I was reading only the other day how the death rate has exceeded the birth rate for the first time since records began. That's the flu for you – the plague of the Spanish lady.'

'I've never forgiven them for the Armada.' He straightened in his chair again, 'Where's Gideon?'

'Sleeping, dearest. His afternoon nap.'

'Fanny, I don't want to be an old stick-in-the-mud, but when exactly is he leaving? He popped in for tea and toast in November and he's still here. It's a new decade, for God's sake.'

'We've plenty of room, Sholto,' she said. 'You don't begrudge him surely? He's a harmless old man with nowhere to go. We're all he's got. As soon as I saw his teeth chattering as he stood on the doorstep that afternoon, I couldn't turn him away.'

'But they were in his hand at the time, Fanny.'

'That's not the point,' she said. 'He's family, Sholto.'

'Just as well,' Lestrade muttered.

She looked at him. 'You miss it, don't you?' she said.

'What?'

She snorted, ' "What?" he says. Scotland Yard, of course. The cut-and-thrust. The cases. The chases.'

'The piles. The paperwork. No, I don't . . . Well, perhaps a bit.'

'Why, Sholto?' She crossed to him and perched on the arm of his chair.

'Fanny, my hand,' he hissed and she stood up sharply while he retrieved the crushed limb and nursed his tarsals.

'Sorry, darling. Why did you resign?'

'You know perfectly well. The strike.'

'Mutiny, you called it. You had no sympathy with striking policemen. Load of Bolshevists you called them. At least I think that's what you said.'

'It wasn't them.' He held her hand. 'It was Edward Henry.'

'The policeman's policeman.'

He nodded. 'He went like a lamb to the slaughter. The great British public don't pay their policemen a living wage and when they complain about it, that same public wants heads. Anybody's will do.'

'But why yours?'

'When they sacked Henry, I couldn't believe it. I went straight to the Home Secretary and offered my resignation . . . Just my luck the old bastard accepted it. Tom would have understood.'

She put her arm around his neck and kissed him. 'You and my father,' she said, shaking her head and clicking her tongue. 'What a pair.'

'Besides,' he held her at arm's length, 'I'm sixty-five going on four hundred. Old policemen never die. They just resign. I'd have gone in '14 if it hadn't been for the War.'

'Didn't you say that when the Boer War broke out?'

'Probably,' he chuckled.

'And don't let me hear you going on about how old you are. You don't look a day over sixty-eight!'

He threw a cushion at her and wandered to the cabinet to help himself to a brandy. 'What's this?' He took a letter from the mantelpiece.

She looked up from the sewing to which she had returned. 'Oh, it came in the afternoon post. Since Emma's coming home tomorrow, I didn't think it worth sending it on. Sholto, what are you doing?'

He had ripped the envelope. 'Needs must when the devil drives,' he said.

'What? Sholto, have a heart. Emma may be your daughter, but you can't go round opening her mail. It may be private.'

Fanny Lestrade would not have thought of doing such a thing. She had never known Emma's mother, Lestrade's first wife, and she would never presume to take her place. She watched as his face darkened. 'It is,' he said.

'What is it?' She crossed to the fireplace where he stood.

'You didn't recognize the handwriting?'

'No, I . . .'

'It's from Paul,' he said, 'Paul Dacres.'

Instinctively, her hand went to her mouth. Then she rationalized it. 'Oh, backdated, you mean? From the War Office?'

He shook his head, 'No,' he said, 'It's not backdated. It was written . . . two days ago. No address. He wants her to meet him.'

'My God.' Fanny Lestrade sat down abruptly. And rose just as suddenly. 'Sholto, this is wonderful! Wonderful! Oh, what

16

shall we do? Shall I ring her? At the Bandicoots'?' She scuttled round in a circle, sewing flying everywhere.

'No,' his voice was firm, then lighter, 'no, don't do that.'

'Oh, silly,' she slapped his shoulder, 'Emma won't mind that you opened her letter. She'll understand. Oh, heavens, I can't believe it.'

'Neither can I,' said Lestrade. 'That's why I don't want you to ring her. There's something fishy about this.'

'Sholto Lestrade,' she said, 'let it go. You're not a policeman now. I'm an ex-policeman's wife and a policeman's daughter. *I* have a nose for these things too. It's just a miracle, that's all. But it's not unique. Old Mrs Hill's boy, Cheviot, was listed missing and he turned up.'

'He was a vegetable, wasn't he?'

'Well, yes . . . but he wasn't very bright when he got his call-up, dear. There are miracles and miracles.'

Lestrade kept shaking his head. 'There's nothing miraculous about this,' he told her.

'What does it say?'

He showed her the letter. She slipped the spectacles from their chain around her neck and read.

'He wants to meet her. Tomorrow. Good Lord, that doesn't give her much time. Where is this?'

'Just off the Edgware Road.'

'We'll have to tell her, Sholto. She can catch an earlier train and be at Paddington by lunchtime . . .'

'No,' said Lestrade, 'I'll go.'

'You?' She let the glasses slip from her nose.

'Me.' He took the letter from her and popped it back into the envelope.

'Darling,' she coaxed, 'I know Emma is all the world to you, but they were engaged to be married. If this is anybody's business, it's hers.' She looked at the sad eyes, the knotted brow. She knew that look. It never failed to frighten her. And she never failed to take it seriously.

'There's something you don't know,' he said.

She sat down, the safest place when one of her husband's revelations was due; and she waited.

He paced the tiger skin, tripping over the bulging glass eyes as he always did. 'When I heard the news about Paul, I made some inquiries.'

'Oh?'

'I couldn't bear Emma's face,' he said by way of explanation. 'You remember how brave she was. It was after that that she worked in munitions and drove that tram.'

'And the poor dear still hasn't got the vote.'

'There's no justice,' he tutted. 'I learned that a long time ago.'

'What do you mean?' Fanny asked. 'Made some inquiries?'

'Winston Churchill was at the War Office, if you remember.'

'Ah.'

'Well, I thought; no sense in keeping a cabinet minister and barking yourself.'

'What did you find out?'

'A hell of a lot about Lord Kitchener, but that's another story.'

'Sholto!' she roared, infuriated when he hedged.

'What did the official telegram say?'

She shut her eyes tight. 'I can remember it clearly,' she said. '"Dear Madam, We regret to inform you that Captain Paul Dacres, gazetted Royal Flying Corps, has gone missing, believed killed in action. Bapaume. January 1917. Captain Dacres was a gallant officer and will be missed. We share with you your loss." It was signed by Churchill himself, wasn't it?'

Lestrade nodded. 'So I went to the War Office. Churchill and I go back a long way. He was a cadet at Sandhurst when I first knew him. I used to wear a bowler and Donegal in those days.'

'Sholto,' she pointed out, 'you still do. What did you find out?'

'Fanny,' he placed his hands on her shoulders, 'I want you to promise me this will go no further. It would break Emma's heart.'

She pursed her lips at him, hurt that he had not confided already. It was a look he knew. A look he trusted.

'After he spent that Christmas with us, he went back to Bapaume, to the aerodrome there.'

'That's right. We had that letter from his Squadron Leader, didn't we? Or rather Emma did.'

'Which said he'd gone up in a formation and they ran into some Hun at seven thousand feet.'

'Yes. And in the mêlée, Paul's plane was lost. Disappeared into some woods.'

'That's where the official line and my inquiries part company,' Lestrade told her, staring into the leaping flames. 'You see, there was no action the morning Paul disappeared.'

'No?'

He shook his head. 'He just took up a plane – it wasn't even his apparently – and flew towards the German lines.'

'Why?'

Lestrade shrugged. 'You're better at men than I am,' he said. 'You tell me.'

'Thank you,' she said disapprovingly.

'No, I mean, moods, behaviour. When Paul was with us that Christmas, did you notice anything odd about him? His manner, I mean?'

She frowned for a moment. 'Ah, you mean shell-shock?'

He nodded.

'Sholto,' she suddenly froze, 'you're not telling me that Paul intended to commit suicide?'

'Men did in the trenches,' Lestrade said.

'But Paul wasn't in the trenches. He told us what fun it all was . . .' She caught the look in his eyes. 'He didn't mean that, did he?'

Lestrade shook his head. 'I don't know whose benefit that was for,' he said. 'I wasn't fooled. I know now you weren't. And certainly not Emma. She least of all.'

'Perhaps he was trying to delude himself,' Fanny said.

He smiled, 'Perhaps.'

'But they never found his plane. Or his body. Did they?'

'His plane, yes. Days later, there was an attack by the Flying Corps. They spotted Paul's plane in a field. One of them went down to have a look.'

'And?'

Lestrade shrugged again. 'Nothing,' he said. 'No damage. No fuel. No pilot.'

'So . . .?'

'So Paul flew as far as he could on the petrol he had and landed. Then he just walked away.'

'Why?'

Lestrade knelt down on one knee, the slightly better one. 'Isn't it obvious, Fanny? He deserted. God alone knows what pressure he was under.'

'Sholto. This is 1920. We're all a bit past the white feather era, you know.'

'We may be, Fanny,' he struggled to his feet, 'but the great British public aren't. In an odd sort of way, I'm not sure Emma is. Everything is black and white when you're young. When you're old . . . older . . . there are just shades of grey. I can just imagine it – it's like that poster really. "What did my fiancé do in the War, Daddy?" He ran away, dear. While thousands of other poor bastards stood up to their waists in water and took it, your fiancé just got up and left. Like an aviator's excuse-me.'

'Sholto,' she held his hand, 'you're not that bitter.'

'I'm not,' he agreed. 'But this country's grown up in the past few years. It's not the cosy world we once knew, Fanny. I don't want Emma to have to live with that. Better she shouldn't know.'

There was a silence.

'But she'll have to, now,' she said.

Lestrade crossed to the window. 'Perhaps,' he said, looking out to where the long winter night came rolling in beyond the cedars, 'but not yet. Not just yet.'

'Sholto,' she rested her head on his shoulder, 'she's a woman grown now. Not your little girl any more. You can't always be a buffer for her.'

'Can't I?' he said, turning with a smile. 'I thought that was what fathers were for.'

She smiled back at the eyes, twinkling in the firelight and the oil-lamp's glow. 'I expect you'll be gone for a while. I'll get Madison to pack you a bag.'

He kissed her forehead. 'Thanks,' he said. 'Oh, and Fanny.'

She turned at the drawing-room door.

'Tell Madison to put the brass knuckles in my Donegal, would you?'

For the briefest of moments, a frown flew across her face. Then she was smiling again. She hadn't had that feeling for months, not since Sir George Cave had accepted her husband's resignation. Now she had it again. That old, silly feeling. The

20

one she'd had every time he had gone out of the door. The one that told her that this time, he might not come back.

He slipped the letter into his pocket and quaffed the last of the brandy.

2

Lestrade caught a tram for the last leg of his journey and then found the dingy Cedar Hotel in Connaught Street. Here the glamour and opulence of the ragtime West End fell away and in the tiny cul-de-sac before the Victorian villas of Maida Vale came into view, he pushed open the door.

A jaunty young man lolled at the counter, ignoring Lestrade entirely.

Lestrade brought the flat of his hand down sharply on the bell.

'All right, grandad,' the clerk said. 'Keep yer 'air on. Rooms are three and six a night. Without breakfast. If yer want a bath, the nearest ones are in Castle Street. Bring yer own towel. Oh, and I wouldn't bend over if I was you. Even at your age.'

'The gentleman in room 34,' Lestrade said.

'Who? Mr Smith?'

'Er . . . yes, that's right. Is he in?'

The clerk looked him up and down. 'Well now, maybe he is and maybe he isn't. We don't have no regular visitin' times here.'

Lestrade plucked a newish pound note from his wallet, the one his former colleagues at the Yard had never seen open, and flourished it under the young man's nose. He moved it away again sharpish as itchy fingers snatched for it.

'Yeah, he's in,' the clerk told him. 'At any rate, his key's still here. Quite a popular bloke, your Mr Smith.'

'Oh?' Lestrade still clutched the pound note.

The clerk hesitated. Lestrade tore the paper carefully down the middle, keeping the king's head in his fist. The rest he passed to the helpful young man. 'Some bloke,' the clerk shrugged, 'come to see him . . . ooh . . . couple of hours ago.'

'Did he give a name?'

'Nah.'

'Has he left?'

'Nah.'

'What did he look like?'

The clerk coughed and whistled, busying himself with a polish cloth.

Lestrade passed over the other half of the torn pound.

'Can't remember,' grinned the clerk. With an agility that surprised Lestrade and astonished the younger man, the ex-superintendent grabbed the clerk's tie and bounced his forehead on to the counter.

'Let's try that again, shall we?' Lestrade said.

'About six foot, square-looking gent,' the clerk gurgled, his face pressed against the mahogany. 'Natty dresser. Astrakhan collar. Fedora.'

'What?'

"Is titfer . . . It was a fedora.'

Lestrade released his man, 'Thank you so much for your time and trouble,' he smiled, 'A knob of butter on that head will do wonders.' And he made for the stairs.

So 'Mr Smith' had had a visitor already. Had he written to the man in the Theodora as well as to Emma Bandicoot-Lestrade? And why was a man in his position – reputedly dead – hiding in a hotel even the cockroaches appeared to have vacated? Lestrade padded up the indescribably-coloured stair carpet, past the peeling wallpaper and the scraped dado of extinct pattern. He paused on the second floor to regain his breath, then found the door.

He knocked lightly. No response. He checked the corridor, to right and to left. He knocked again. Then he placed his weight gently against the door and twisted the knob. He let the thing creak open to its fullest extent. A chill light seeped into the room under a half-closed blind. He waited until his eyes were fully accustomed to the gloom. He nestled his hand in his pocket, feeling the cold brass of the knuckles. Then he jabbed his left elbow against the door, in case there was someone behind it.

Nothing. Except excruciating pain to his capitellum. He slipped in and clicked the lock behind him.

It was the feet he saw first. A pair of expensive brogues pointing upwards from behind the third-rate sofa through which the horsehair was visible in places. He knelt down beside the body. One arm was outstretched and inches from the fingers, the butt of a revolver. Paul Dacres, late of the Royal Flying Corps, lay with his face towards Lestrade, as though chastising him for his lateness. The skin was pale, the eyes half open and the teeth shone dully through the parted lips. There was a large, nearly round hole in his left temple and a pillow of dark blood had seeped across the threadbare carpet, soaking into the planks beneath.

Lestrade sighed, closed his eyes. It was, as he had feared, business as usual. Thank God he had opened that letter. Thank God he hadn't let Emma stumble into this. He put the bowler on the sofa arm and peered closer at the wound. There were specks of powder across the hair and down the cheek. The bullet had been fired at point-blank range. Lestrade pulled a handkerchief from his other pocket and carefully picked up the pistol. A Webley revolver, Mark V, stamped and dated 1915. He felt the weight in his hand and smelt the short muzzle. Cordite. He rocked back on his haunches until his old trouble caught him and he had to change position.

'Why?' he found himself saying softly. 'Why did you do it, Paul?'

He stood up, careful to place the revolver back where it had been. The room yielded no clues. There was no letter of explanation. Lestrade swiftly rummaged through drawers and wardrobes. An RFC greatcoat, spare shirts, collars, studs. Nothing incriminating. Nothing helpful. Just another wreck of a life after the War to End All Wars.

The ex-superintendent went back down the stairs to the counter. The clerk instinctively jerked backwards.

'Is there another way out?' Lestrade asked.

'Through the fire-escape.' the younger man said, raising his hands, ''s all right – there's no charge.'

'Do you have a telephone in the hotel?'

'No, guv.'

'Right. Go outside. The nearest bloke in a pointed hat you see with the letter "D" on his collar is a policeman. Fetch him here. Today!' Lestrade slapped the counter so hard his hand stung.

The clerk leapt to it. It was no more than ten minutes later that he came back together with a caped bobby.

'Name?' Lestrade asked.

'Now, then; now, then,' the bobby was all of twenty-one, 'what seems to be the trouble?'

'I stopped worrying a long time ago about policemen looking younger than me. Do you know where Scotland Yard is, Constable 341D?'

'That's for me to know and you to find out, Mr . . .?'

'Lestrade,' said Lestrade. 'Ex-Superintendent Lestrade. Would you like me to show you my significant features?'

'No, sir,' The constable stood to attention.

Just as well, Lestrade mused; they'd probably be invisible in this light anyway.

'Right. You get to the Yard. Or faster still, find a telephone. This gentleman will give you the pennies.'

Lestrade clicked his fingers and the clerk coughed up, jamming his finger momentarily in the till as he did so.

'You are to speak to either Inspector John Kane or Inspector Elias Bower of the CID. Do you understand? Nobody else. Tell them I've got a body; room 34, the Cedar Hotel.'

'Yessir, Mr Lestrade. Very good sir.'

And he was gone.

But it was not John Kane or Eli Bower who crashed through the front door of the Cedar. It was the squat, obnoxious figure of Edward Blevvins.

'Good God, Lestrade,' he muttered. 'I've just cuffed this young constable round the ear for telling lies. He said it was you, but I didn't believe him.'

Lestrade looked at the crimson lobe of the victim. 'You'll be pressing charges, of course, Constable?' he said.

'Well, I . . . er . . .' The boy was clearly flummoxed.

'Of course he will,' grinned Blevvins. 'There'll be a full internal inquiry, won't there, Constable?'

'Er . . . yessir.'

'Right, Lestrade, where's the body?'

'When I was at the Yard, Blevvins, I outranked you in everything except nauseousness. Now that I am a member of the public, I still do. Remember that and we'll do all right. I asked this young man to contact Kane or Bower.'

'I know you did,' said Blevvins. 'That's why his other ear's red. I needed to stretch my legs a bit, so here I am.'

'On second thoughts,' said Lestrade, 'we can probably leave this to the CID of "D" Division.'

'"No-Collar" Pearson?' Blevvins raised an eyebrow.

'Is he in "D" Division?' Lestrade was appalled.

'Transferred from the Public Carriage Office last month. You might as well trust your detection to Jack the Bloody Ripper.'

'All right,' sighed Lestrade. 'But this is temporary, Blevvins. I'll have you off the case by tomorrow. And it's personal. I knew the deceased. You so much as fart off-key and I'll set Fred Wensley on you.'

'Oh dear and oh dear,' said Blevvins, 'I am undone.'

'The carelessness of your attire is no concern of mine, Inspector. Shall we?'

And Lestrade took to the stairs again, Blevvins dragging the clerk along with him by the ear.

The ex-superintendent stood back while Blevvins went through his paces.

'I'll send for you when I need you,' the Inspector said.

'That'll be any minute now,' Lestrade assured him. 'I'll wait,' and he winced as Blevvins picked up the Webley by the butt and broke it open.

'One shot,' he said, secretly hoping for Lestrade's confirmation.

Lestrade remained impassive.

Blevvins noted the carpet. Unrucked. Untrampled – until now. He knelt on his heels, taking in the dingy order of the room. 'No signs of a struggle.'

He stood up, checked the window, the door. 'Right,' he said. 'Suicide.'

Lestrade didn't blink.

'Yes,' he kicked the corpse gently with his boot, 'his balance

26

of mind looks decidedly disturbed. We get a lot of it these days. Blokes whose nerves have gone because of the War. Bleedin' shame, really. I'd have volunteered of course, but I was too indispensable where I was.'

Lestrade's mouth opened a little. Was this a glimmer of compassion in his erstwhile subordinate? Perhaps there was hope for mankind after all.

'Yes,' Blevvins lumbered on, 'embarrassing, isn't it? I don't see what all the fuss was about, meself. These bloody Tommies were better paid than our boys. And as for all this bloody poetry they wrote! When did you last read a poem written by a copper, eh? I'll tell you when – never. And why? Because we haven't got the bleedin' time. And we're not a load of Mary Annes, that's why.'

Lestrade clicked his fingers. 'I thought the *Police Gazette* was rather low on original literary contributions recently. Will you send your constable for Photographs and Fingerprints?'

'Ah, the two Fs,' Blevvins, ever the professional, smiled. 'In the fullness of time. But first, what is your connection with all this? Who is this?' He nudged the corpse again.

'He was Paul Methuen Dacres,' Lestrade said. 'And if you kick him again, Blevvins, I will sever your windpipe.'

The inspector shrugged. Over the years he had learned to take Lestrade's threats seriously. 'How did you know him?' he asked.

'He was my daughter's fiancé,' Lestrade said.

'Ah. So you didn't happen upon the body by chance.'

'No, Blevvins,' sighed Lestrade, astonished anew by the intellectual thrust of one of Scotland Yard's finest. 'May I ask you something?'

'*I'll* ask the questions,' Blevvins assured him.

'How *did* you get promotion?'

'Pure skill,' the inspector assured him. 'That and the fact that I know something about the Commissioner that you don't. Was there anything in this bloke's mental make-up to indicate suicide? Was I right about the War?'

'He was an officer in the RFC.'

Blevvins was thrown. 'The Royal Fife Constabulary?'

'Close,' Lestrade nodded. 'The Royal Flying Corps.'

'Ah, well, there you are. Stands to reason. Unless . . .'

'Unless?' asked Lestrade.

'Unless there was something else in his past. Straight, was he?'

'Straight?'

'Well, you know. "As Other Men"?'

'I think so.'

'I'll have to talk to your daughter.'

'No.'

Blevvins grinned. 'I don't think you understand, *Mr* Lestrade. That is not a request. That is an order from an Inspector of the Metropolitan Police.'

'Hmm,' murmured Lestrade. 'I'm quaking already. Take my word for it, Blevvins, my daughter can be of no help to you.'

'Well, we'll see about that. Now then, I'm finished here, I think.'

'I wouldn't be at all surprised.'

Blevvins caught something in Lestrade's tone he wasn't sure about. 'I *am* right though, aren't I? It *was* suicide?'

'It certainly looks like it,' Lestrade agreed.

Blevvins grinned. Beneath the rough, contemptible exterior lay a rough, contemptible interior. But the presence of his old guv'nor unnerved him – just a little.

They walked out and Blevvins posted his man on the door.

'You,' he said to the clerk waiting in the corridor, 'get a message to Dr White.' He flipped a piece of paper at him. 'This is his address. Catch a 21 bus and look sharp.'

'What about the fare?' the clerk asked.

Blevvins rounded on him. 'You pay it to the clippie,' he said. 'And don't get too agitated if it's a bleedin' woman. That's the way the country's going these days – to the dogs. Lestrade . . .'

The ex-superintendent paused in the corridor.

'. . . You'll be at home if I need you?'

Lestrade nodded. 'You've got my address in a shoe-box somewhere,' he said and padded downstairs with the clerk. At the doorway, he gripped the man's shoulder. 'How long have you been on duty?' he asked.

'Since eight. Why?'

'You heard nothing?'

'Like what?'

'Like a gun being fired.'

'A gun? Is that it then? Did Smith top himself?'

'Did you hear a shot?'

'Nah.'

'You're sure?'

'Course I am. Look, mate, this is Paddington, not the bloody Somme. I didn't hear nuffink.'

'Right,' said Lestrade. It hadn't helped.

''Ere,' the clerk stopped him as he tottered off down the steps into the raw morning, 'should I tell that detective about Smith's visitor?'

Without turning, Lestrade called, 'I should tell him the moon's made of green cheese if I were you. He'll find that more useful to his inquiries.'

Lestrade put off the inevitable all day. Early in the afternoon, his Emma had come back from the New Year spent at Bandicoot Hall and had brought Ivo Bandicoot with her. It had been some time since the Lestrades had seen the young man. He had served on the Western Front and before that at Gallipoli and had seen his share of dying. Now he was 'Something in the City', trying, like many other young men, to put the past behind him.

He took tea with them, laughing over the old times at Bandicoot Hall when Emma, Ivo and his dead brother had raced each other through the Somerset woods where they had hand-cuffed Lestrade to a tree. Then he had to go, to the world of hard-faced men and the merry-go-round of money.

In a quiet corner of the library, as the frost settled on the rhododendron leaves beyond the lattice of the window, Sholto Lestrade told his daughter all about Paul Dacres and he held her until the crying had stopped and she was calm again.

'Oh, Daddy, you don't think he killed himself, do you?'

'No.' He patted the golden curls. 'No, I don't.'

She smiled through the tears. Then she sat upright, suddenly changed. No longer the grieving widow-who-never-was. Now, the policeman's daughter. 'Why not?' she asked.

He smiled. 'Because', he held both her hands in the firelight, 'a man does not write to his fiancée, asking her to meet him and then shoot himself. Paul Dacres wasn't that kind of man.'

'No,' she sniffed, 'he wasn't.'

'Emma,' he moved the curls away from her wet cheeks, 'Fanny says I shouldn't have opened the letter. Shouldn't have interfered . . .'

She put a finger to his lips. 'No,' she said, 'you were right. If I had gone to that hotel and found . . . what you did, I couldn't have borne it. It would have been like losing him twice. As it is, it's only confirmed my worst fears.'

He nodded, grateful that she felt that way.

'Except . . .' he saw the frown darkening her lovely face, 'except that if it wasn't suicide, then it must be . . .'

He nodded again. 'Murder.' He said it for her.

'But who . . .?'

'Would want to kill him?' Lestrade was way ahead of her. 'To answer that I'll need to know where he's been for the last three years.'

'Right,' she sniffed defiantly for one last time. 'Where do we start?'

'We?' Lestrade echoed.

'Daddy,' she squeezed his hands, 'Paul Dacres was engaged to me. He wrote to me before he died. That gives me the right to be involved in this. He'd want me to be.'

'Would he?' Lestrade wasn't so sure.

'Yes.' Emma was. 'Besides, you haven't got the Yard at your disposal any more and you're four hundred years old. You need all the help you can get.'

He tapped her playfully on the chin with his fist. 'All right,' he chuckled. 'We.'

'For a start,' she pulled the crumpled, tear-stained letter from her pocket, 'what's this?'

'It's Paul's letter, dear. You've already read it,' he explained. Obviously, the shock of the news had hit her harder than he feared.

'Yes, Daddy, but hold it up to the firelight.'

Lestrade did. There was something he hadn't seen before. A watermark in an unusual language.

'It's a watermark in an unusual language,' he said.

'It was the first thing I noticed,' she said, dabbing her eyes, 'before I read the letter itself. I was holding it at that angle and I saw it. What do you make of it?'

Lestrade twisted the paper first this way and then that.

'It's all Greek to me,' he admitted.

'I think it's Russian, Daddy.'

'Russian?' The ex-Superintendent scrutinized more closely. It could have been a fancy Churston Deckle for all he knew.

'So we start . . . where? Petrograd?'

'Isn't there a war going on over there?'

'Mmm,' she nodded, 'I suppose it is a bit impractical.'

'I know where we start,' Lestrade said. 'You've still got Paul's letters?'

'Until he disappeared, yes.'

He held her hand again. 'Can you bear to go through them?'

'I often do,' she smiled. 'But what am I looking for?'

'Names, dates, places. Anything. Anything that will give us a clue as to why a man should want to disappear.'

'Why?' she was musing to herself. 'Why?'

She didn't sleep that night. Instead, she sat by the moonlit window, wrapped in a shawl that was the only tangible reminder of the mother she'd never known. She read his letters, smiled at his jokes, cried when she read the plans he'd had for them both. She remembered that day at the Fitzwilliam, when Paul was still at Cambridge, and how he'd amazed her with his astonishing knowledge of art. And she remembered the day they had first made love, among the buttercups of a golden summer before the Great War had separated them for ever. She didn't sleep that night.

The wind whipped around the corner of Lestrade's Donegal and he held the battered bowler firmly on his head. They were both made by the redoubtable old firm of Timothy White's, Tailors to the Nouveau Riche. At Biggin Hill, nothing stood between the aerodrome and Siberia and the winds that blew between those worlds were like no other Lestrade had known. Even the Scottish Highlands had been less raw than this, he fancied, although a dram or two of single malt inside might have brought its own insulation and he had been several centuries younger when he had visited them.

And the whole journey was pointless. Lestrade's quarry, it transpired, was to be found to the south, in the curious jumble of flat-roofed buildings of the Royal Aircraft Establishment at Farnborough.

It was later than he thought, therefore, as he stood in a draughty tunnel where some Leading Aircraftsman had left him. He looked up at the great arched roof. Not a patch on St Paul's. Not even as good as St Pancras. Only a model plane with a single wingspan. It appeared to be made of wood. Quite big for a model, though.

He was not prepared for what happened next. There was a roar that surged through his ear-drums and his hat vanished. He felt his lungs near to bursting as a torrent of wind hit him full in the chest and at the far end of the gloomy tunnel, he saw a huge propeller turning. He only saw it for an instant before hurtling back in a tangle of clothing, crashing painfully against the end wall. He lay on the floor as the hurricane whistled around him, his mouth opening and closing dumbly as he tried to speak. Above the bellow of the wind, an alarm was clanging madly. And the wind died down and droned and ceased.

'Good God, man!' He heard what he hoped was a human voice, but intermittently as his ears came and went. He forced the tears from his eyes and realized he was being helped up by a man in the fetching powder blue of this week's Air Force uniform, the face above the walrus 'tache a mask of concern. 'Are you all right?'

'Just a bit windy,' Lestrade confessed.

'I shouldn't wonder,' said the officer. 'Look, I'm deuced sorry about all this; your first day and all. I must confess, I thought you'd be younger.'

'Really?' Lestrade staggered uneasily out of a side-door of the wind-tunnel and collapsed gratefully into a chair. 'Before I arrived here, I was.'

'What do you think of the Hawker-Horseley, then?' The moustachioed officer grinned proudly, jerking his head back towards the door that had just closed.

'Very nice,' said Lestrade.

'Of course, we're in the early stages, what?'

'What?'

'Quite. Now, then, won't beat about the bush. Any ideas?'

'Well . . .' Lestrade wondered where his hat had gone. He was having similar ideas about his lungs. 'I was hoping to hear from you.'

'Me? Oh, I see. Well . . . er . . . cigarette?'

'Thank you. I only smoke cigars.'

'Very wise. I'll get Bader to make you some tea.'

'Bader?'

'The chappie who showed you into the wind-tunnel. Look, hang it all, I'm damnably sorry about that. He probably misheard what you said. Had a bad war. Too much of the Avro-Whitworths have taken their toll on his ears, I'm afraid.'

'Not at all. Now, about this problem . . .'

'Ah, yes.' The officer had clearly forgotten the tea already. 'Well, we've all tried shouting of course, but that's hopeless. Then there are the flags. Well, that's all very well, but when you're going into action, you just haven't time to run up "England Expects" and so on.'

He took off his cap and smoothed the Macassared hair into place, adjusting his cravat as he went on. 'Now, the wireless gadget last March was obviously a breakthrough, but it's this damned static. What does Mr Marconi think?'

'Marconi?' Lestrade blinked. 'Didn't he sell ice-cream in Notting Hill?'

The flying officer blinked back. 'No, he is the founder of the Wireless Telegraph Company. In the War he was in charge of all radio operations . . . Look here, are you Horatio Tirade or not?'

'Who?'

The flying officer leaned back in his chair, trying to look casual. Then he leaned forward, whipping a pistol from a desk drawer. 'All right, chummy,' he said. 'Put your hands on your head. Sprechen Sie Deutsch?'

'No, I'm not Dutch,' Lestrade assured him, plaiting his fingers together over his hair, still standing to attention after the shock waves of the tunnel. 'Neither am I Horatio Tirade.'

'I see,' said the flying officer. 'Condemned by your own mouth. Well don't you move a cat's whisker. I'm going to call an MP.'

'They're still on holiday, aren't they? It's the Christmas recess,' Lestrade reasoned with him. 'Look, could you point that thing somewhere else? I have reason to believe they sometimes go off.'

'Who are you?' The flying officer stood his ground, the Webley cocked firmly in his hand.

'Superintendent Lestrade,' Lestrade was a little economical with the truth, 'Scotland Yard.'

'Scotland Yard?'

'Your man Bader *obviously* misheard me.'

'So you're not Mr Marconi's assistant?'

'Absolutely not,' Lestrade said. 'I've never knowingly sold a cornet in my life. May I put my hands down now?'

The flying officer hesitated, then uncocked the revolver. 'Very well, but just remember I am considerably younger than you. I shall place this gun on the desk. One false move from you and it's the Last Post, understand?'

Lestrade nodded grimly. He'd read only the other day that a postcard sent in 1888 had only just reached Leeds. He knew the Royal Mail wasn't what it had been.

'I was looking for Squadron Leader Boumphrey.'

'I'm Humphrey Boumphrey. What is it you want?'

'Information,' said Lestrade. 'About a fellow officer of yours.'

'Now, look,' Boumphrey demurred, 'if it's about old Bodger . . .'

'It isn't,' Lestrade assured him.

'Ah, well, anyway, it wasn't his fault. His kite wasn't up to it, you see. And those old-age pensioners shouldn't have all stood in a line like that. It's deuced difficult to tell them apart from dummies in the air. It really is. And once you've locked your Brownings on to 'em, well . . .'

'It's not the old-age pensioners,' Lestrade reassured him.

'Oh, dear, it's not Wazzer's funny letters, is it? He's not really an extortionist, you know. He's never been the same since Bapaume.'

'Bapaume?'

'He caught a bit of flak from a Fokker.'

'Yes,' Lestrade nodded grimly, 'those German bastards.'

'Well, live and let live, Superintendent. We were all young chaps doing an absolutely spiffing job and enjoying it like hell. Er . . . if it's not Wazzer, then who . . .?'

'Paul Dacres.'

'Ah, old Cobbler.'

'If you say so,' said Lestrade. 'He was in your outfit, wasn't he? At Bapaume?'

'That's right. But I'm afraid you're three years too late, old chap. Cobbler's dead.'

'I know,' said Lestrade. 'I'm trying to find out who killed him.'

'Are you?' Boumphrey was a little perplexed. 'Well, I realize there's War Guilt and so on, but we can't really go around insisting on an eye for an eye, you know. It isn't cricket.'

'No, it's murder,' said Lestrade. 'Not in some dogfight over France in 1917, but in a Paddington hotel – two days ago.'

'Good Lord, but I thought . . .'

'That was what we were supposed to think, Squadron Leader. I'm interested in the truth. Tell me about Bapaume.'

'Look, I'm not one to be picky, but you seem a trifle . . . er . . . elderly for a policeman.'

'Yes, they usually look younger than one, don't they? I confess I was to have retired in 1914, then somebody shot that Austrian bloke at Sarajevo and I was asked to stay on.'

'I see. Well . . . er . . . do you have any means of identification?'

'Of course.' Lestrade ferreted first in one inside pocket, then another. 'I seem to have mislaid my warrant card,' he said. 'It must have been the wind in that tunnel of yours.'

'Very well,' Boumphrey said quickly, 'we'll say no more about it.'

'Good,' smiled Lestrade. 'Now, about Paul Dacres.'

'Ah, yes,' the squadron leader settled back into the leather swivel, 'if I remember rightly, he joined us from the Lancers.'

'The Twelfth,' agreed Lestrade.

'Well, most of us were cavalry in those days. Just exchanging one sort of charger for another, really. I must confess there were some hairy moments. I, for instance, didn't know an aileron from my elbow.'

It was a bit like that for Lestrade, too. 'You flew with Dacres?'

'Never. We had one-man jobs. And then of course he got a Blighty . . .'

'A Blighty?'

'A slight wound. Enough to send him home for a while.'

'Where?'

'Ah, now you've asked me. Baudricourt, I think. Or it may have been Wadicourt.'

'No, I mean, where on his body?'

'Oh, I see. The foot. Left one. Or was it right? Well, one or the other.'

'Quite. How did that happen?'

'It was back in '15. We were constantly being strafed by Boelke's Circus throughout the autumn. We had a little pub near the base, what the Bosch call an *auberge*. I remember it was called the *Nid de Coucou*.'

'The Knee . . .'

'The Cuckoo's Nest. Well, we were in there one lunch-time. We'd been up since before first light, expecting a dawn raid. That was their usual pattern. When nothing happened, we were stood down. Then the cunning boundahs hit us shortly after twelve.'

'Tut, tut,' Lestrade shook his head. 'Unsporting.'

'Well, that's what comes of eating cabbage as a national pastime. They gave us a helluva pasting.'

'What about Dacres?'

'Well, he managed to get his kite up. The only one of us who did. He saw the whole Jasta off.'

'Really?'

'I saw him shoot three down. One exploded in mid-air; another flew over the Cuckoo's Nest. Pretty spectacular stuff, I can tell you.'

'But Dacres was hurt?'

'Yes. Bought it in the foot. But the curious thing was, his plane wasn't touched.'

'That was curious?'

'Yes, of course. Look,' Boumphrey slid his chair back and

placed his hands on ethereal controls in front of him, 'imagine I'm in the cockpit of a Camel.'

Lestrade tried hard, but the hump kept getting in the way.

'Notice where my feet are.'

Lestrade did. At no time did they leave Boumphrey's legs.

'Now for a bullet to hit him in either limb, it would have had to have passed through the fuselage.'

'The . . . er?'

'The body of the plane.'

'And it hadn't?'

'No. The ground crew who overhauled it sent in a clean report. No damage at all.'

'Did you see Dacres' wound?' Lestrade asked.

'Well, no, not precisely. I remember him limping as he got out of the cockpit.'

'What was he wearing on his feet?'

'Well, flying boots, I suppose.'

'How are they different from ordinary boots?'

'Well, they're bigger. Fleece-lined. Ruddy great fluffy things.'

'You didn't see any blood?'

'Look here, Lestrade, what's all this about Cobbler's wound? I thought you said he'd just been murdered.'

'Bear with me, Squadron Leader, please. Why were you so surprised that Dacres' plane was undamaged?'

'Well, I mean, how could he have been shot, otherwise? Unless tracer bullets do some funny things – a ricochet shot, perhaps.'

'Or?'

'Or? I don't think I understand.'

'What did a Blighty imply?'

Boumphrey straightened in his cockpit. 'Oh, no, Lestrade. Not in the RFC. You'll take that back.'

'In the RFC, as in every other unit, isn't it true that some men deliberately shot themselves, just to be sent home to Blighty?'

'It may have been true in some other units, Superintendent, but not in ours. That's an outrageous slur.'

'Yes, it is,' Lestrade agreed. 'I can't speak for the Royal Flying Corps, but for a man like Paul Dacres, certainly.'

'You knew him?'

37

Lestrade nodded. 'If things had turned out differently, he would have been my son-in-law, the father of my grandchildren.'

'Well, then,' Boumphrey said, 'you ought to know better than to imply . . .'

'What's your motto, Mr Boumphrey?'

'Eh? *Per Ardua Ad Astra*. Why do you ask?'

'That means "Through Hardship To The Stars" doesn't it?'

'Yes.'

'Well, we'll get to the stars later. At the moment, I'm still suffering some hardship. I'm only just finding out about the man my daughter chose to love. And some of it doesn't add up.'

'At least the wound had to be real,' Boumphrey told him.

'Why?'

'Because the Medical chappies would never have shipped him out, otherwise.'

'When did you see him next?'

'Ooh, now,' Boumphrey twirled his cravat and adjusted his moustache, 'it must have been six months later. Not to speak to. He was in a motor car with some top brass, going up to the Somme.'

'Was he in that show?'

Boumphrey shrugged. 'I lost track of him then. Never saw him again.'

'But when he reappeared and disappeared . . .'

'I know. But I'd flown three missions in as many days. I was sleeping it orff. He came out of nowhere, borrowed somebody else's kite and just took orff. Had no right to, of course. Pulled rank on some flight-sergeant.'

'Whose plane was it he borrowed?'

'Er . . . "Tiddler" Neville's, I think. Poor bugger bought it later that month. Richtofen got him.'

'Did you find Neville's plane?'

'Yes. We were out raiding when I caught sight of the *Beauty* in a clump of trees.'

'You landed?'

'Rather. Damnedest thing I ever saw. It was perfectly intact.

No trace of blood and no sign of Cobbler. Now of course we know why, don't we?'

'Do we, Squadron Leader?' Lestrade sighed. 'Do we?'

They buried Paul Dacres the following Wednesday in the little churchyard of St Anselm's. In view of the oddity surrounding his death – officially, thanks to Inspector Blevvins and a particularly dim coroner, by his own hand – the Royal Flying Corps did not send a detachment. Squadron Leader Boumphrey turned up, however, and he unhooked his sword and laid it on the coffin before saluting Emma Bandicoot-Lestrade and making his excuses. Lestrade stood, black-coated like the rooks that circled and cawed in the elms above, feeling slightly ashamed of the fact that, unbeknownst to his wife and daughter, he had gingerly prised up the coffin lid while it lay in the Chapel of Ease and examined both the feet of the dear departed. There was no trace of a tracer-bullet track; no sign of a wound at all. The dead man's past began to echo like a hollow sham. The little cluster of Lestrades, with the Bandicoots and the vicar, wandered back to the Georgian manor-house which had been Fanny's father's and was now, in his retirement, Lestrade's.

At the lych-gate with its lichened stones, a man with a gammy leg hailed them.

'Am I too late?' he asked.

'For what?' Lestrade enquired.

'This is St Anselm's?'

'Yes.'

'The funeral of Captain Dacres.'

'You knew him?' Lestrade asked.

'Yes. In the same corps.'

'At Bapaume?'

'No. I copped some shrapnel a couple of months earlier. Squadron Leader Leonard.' He saluted with the finger position pinched from the Navy.

'Ex-Superintendent Lestrade,' said Lestrade. 'This is my wife, my daughter and Mr and Mrs Bandicoot and their son.'

There were nods all round.

'Poor Paul,' muttered Leonard. 'I read about the service in the local paper. What happened? I thought he'd been shot down in '17.'

'So did we,' said Lestrade. 'Curious business, isn't it.'

'Damned curious,' nodded Leonard.

'You've just missed Squadron Leader Boumphrey,' Lestrade told him.

'Old Bum?' smiled Leonard. 'I haven't seen him for years. How is he?'

'Very well, I believe,' Lestrade said.

'Would you join us, Squadron Leader?' Fanny asked. 'Our house is just up the road.'

'Thank you, no,' the Squadron Leader demurred. 'I'll just pay my respects if you'll excuse me. Been to one too many of these, if you know what I mean.' He blew his nose viciously, tipped his hat and hobbled off.

'Poor bugger,' muttered Bandicoot. 'Rotten business all round. Good of him to come, though.'

'Yes,' said Emma, 'it was.'

It had been a long time since Harry Bandicoot and Sholto Lestrade had stood before a blazing fire, sipping brandy. Lestrade moved away as he felt his trousers singe.

'I can't believe it, Sholto,' Bandicoot was saying. 'Paul Dacres. It doesn't make any sense.'

'Do you speak Russian, Harry?' Lestrade asked him.

'No.'

It was a forlorn hope, really. There were days when the tall, blond Etonian had trouble with English.

'Do you still have that contact at the Foreign Office?'

'Stanley Accrington? Yes, he's still there. At least, his Christmas card had a picture of the place on it. Good God, you don't think he killed Paul Dacres, do you?'

'No, Harry, I don't. But our friend Mr Dacres wrote what may have been his last letter on Russian stationery.'

'You can't get that in W. H. Smith's, can you?'

'I wouldn't have thought so.'

'Still,' Harry had to be frank with his old guv'nor, 'if this chappie Trotsky has his way, we'll all be eating potatoes soon and singing the Blue Standard.'

'That's the Red Flag, Harry,' Lestrade corrected him.

'It certainly is, Sholto,' Bandicoot agreed, 'the red flag to a bull. I know they've had it a bit rough in Russia all these years, but I'm not sure Karl Marx has the answer.'

'If he has, he's keeping it to himself,' Lestrade agreed.

Madison, Lestrade's man, interrupted the cut and thrust of this intellectual debate and current affairs had to take a back seat. 'There's a telephone call for you, sir. A Mr Kane, from Scotland Yard.'

'John Kane? Excuse me, Harry.'

Lestrade went into the hall and spoke into the Machine That Speaks. 'John? How are you? Yes. Yes, very well. That's all right. Who? Ha, don't I know it. Yes. Really? When? Where? I see. Well, I'm not really sure. Yes. Of course. Oh, absolutely. Not a soul. No. You have my word. I shan't tell a living soul. See you there.'

He returned to the library, running his fingers round the rim of his brandy glass.

'We'd better join the ladies, Sholto.'

'Hmm? No, Harry. Not just now. Can I borrow your Silver Ghost?'

'Now, Sholto . . .' Bandicoot was embarrassed.

'You know I couldn't see very well that night because of the snow.'

'Even so, Sholto, the hedge was twenty-three feet high.'

'Well, will you drive me then?'

'Where to?'

'A building in Hertfordshire. They've found a body. Shot through the head at point-blank range. I mustn't tell a living soul about it.'

'Well, that's all right, then. But why . . .?'

'Save the questions until we arrive, Harry. Let's make our excuses.'

Lestrade had been this way before – crotchety, cold, lost. But he also knew this part of Hertfordshire. Eternity ago, in a bright

Victorian summer, he had pedalled at the heel of Dr John Watson, no less, in the 'Case of the Guardian Angel'. That cycling party had rested at the little village of Lemsford and it was here, or somewhere near here, that Lestrade and Bandicoot were now.

Unfortunately, the fog had closed in with the night and familiar old Surrey had given way to the treeless lanes of less familiar old Hertfordshire.

'But it's not on the map, Sholto,' Harry Bandicoot had insisted.

'Of course not,' Lestrade explained, 'they've only just started building the damned thing. There isn't even a name for it yet. Kane said they were near Lemsford. I've heard it described as Second Garden City, Digswell, South Welwyn. It's only a bloody field.'

'With a body in it.'

'Sshh,' Lestrade held a finger to his lips, 'the utmost secrecy, mind.'

He was walking ahead of the dim silver work of Bandicoot's immense car, like a man of old with his red flag, tapping his way with a walking-stick that Bandicoot's chauffeur always kept in the boot. The hedge occasionally leapt out and caught him a nasty one around the face, but he kept moving.

'Will you be careful with that bumper?' he screamed at Bandicoot. 'I've only got one pair of legs and you're not prolonging their active life by fetching me one behind the knees every few yards.'

'Sorry, Sholto. Where do you think we are?'

Lestrade stopped. 'There's an old mill by the stream to our left. There ought to be a pub to our right.'

He crunched on through the cold, damp air. 'Little cottages to our left,' he saw them twinkling in the evening. 'And just here . . .' There was a crunch and a tinkle of glass as the Silver Ghost hit an obstacle with its headlight, 'there's a wall. Sorry, Harry.'

'Marvellous,' he heard the Etonian mutter.

'At least it's only a little one,' Lestrade consoled him. 'Not twenty-three feet high.'

'Oh, good. So where are we now?'

'Definitely Lemsford.' Lestrade hopped in beside Bandicoot.

'Now, follow the road round and we'll come to the Great North Road.'

'Ah, yes. I can see car headlights.'

'Right. Go beyond that. Then turn left and we're on our own. Some place called Stanborough.'

A wagon bound for market narrowly missed them as they crossed the giant artery that linked London and York. Ever one steeped in folklore, Bandicoot was heard to comment he didn't know how Dick Turpin had done it in the time. Lestrade confessed he didn't have a clue either. The car took the slight incline and perched itself on the natural scarp overlooking the valley, thick with mist.

A feeble light flickered from a hastily erected tent.

'See?' said Lestrade. 'What did I tell you. A field.'

A torch shone in his face and he recoiled from the glare.

'Ex-Superintendent Lestrade to see Inspector Kane,' he said, large white circles filling his vision as he tumbled out of the Ghost. 'Harry, would you mind waiting here?'

Bandicoot shrugged. It was not the first time he had driven Lestrade to a murder scene. But the old man was knocking on. It might be the last.

Helmeted constables, torchlight catching their Hertfordshire plates, ushered Lestrade into the cold damp of the tent.

'Guv'nor.' John Kane shot out a hand. 'Inspector Mulloch, Hertfordshire CID. This is Superintendent Lestrade.'

The two men shook hands. 'Retired, I understand?' Mulloch said. He had the growl of an off-duty bear and a beard to match, curiously out of joint with the clean-shaven 'Twenties.

'On and off,' Lestrade smiled. He knew open resentment when he saw it. The Yard was not always welcome in the Styx anyway, but ex-Yard was probably as popular as the plague.

'I want it understood', said Mulloch, 'that you're only here on Mr Kane's say-so, because he says you can help with our inquiries. There'll be no privileges. And no expenses.'

'Thank you, Mr Mulloch,' said Lestrade, 'it'll be just like old times. What have we got, John?'

Kane knelt on one knee. Lestrade joined him on two and the inspector lowered his storm-lantern past his gleaming black locks to the earth floor. The partially decomposed body of a woman lay in the clay. What had once been blonde hair was matted and woven into the skull and sightless eyes gaped up at them. Ribs protruded through the breast cavity and mould and worms lay half frozen beyond the tent flap.

'Workmen found her yesterday. They were carrying out diggings for the new town. This will be the south-western extent of it.'

'I want you to know', Mulloch said, 'that my boys and I could easily have handled this. It was my Chief Constable that insisted I should call in the Yard.'

'Yes,' Lestrade smiled up at him, 'Chief Constables will be Chief Constables, won't they? Cause of death, John?'

'As I said on the phone, guv, gunshot. One bullet. Or at least that's all we've found so far. In the back of the head. Blew away most of the lower jaw, as you can see.'

Lestrade did. 'A word outside, John?' He had no wish to stay in the tent of death for longer than was strictly necessary. He led Kane towards Bandicoot's waiting car, away from Inspector Mulloch's earshot. 'I don't want to be an old stick-in-the-mud, John,' he whispered. 'You can handle this with one hand tied behind your back. You don't need me.'

'Nice of you to say so, guv'nor,' Kane watched his breath snake out on the night air, 'but it's not exactly "Flatter Lestrade Week". We found a cigarette lighter on the dead woman.' He fished it out of his pocket.

'I'm sorry,' said Lestrade, 'I can't see in this light.'

'It occasionally becomes necessary for me to talk to Ned Blevvins,' Kane said.

Lestrade patted the younger man's shoulder understandingly. 'Life's a bitch, isn't it?' he commiserated.

'He told me you had called him in on the suicide of one Paul Dacres.'

'Not exactly,' Lestrade frowned, 'but he came anyway.'

'Well, here's a nice little coincidence for you. Inscribed on this lighter it says "To F.S., keeper of the secrets, from Paul Dacres". It's dated 1916.'

'That was a good year, John,' said Lestrade. 'Where are you staying?'

'The White Hart in Welwyn.'

44

'Good?'

'Excellent.'

'They must be getting more generous at the Yard than in my day. Do they do a late supper?'

'The best.'

'Good. This is my driver, Mr Bandicoot.'

Kane shook the driver's hand. 'Harry, it's been a while . . .' he began.

'Yes,' Lestrade said loudly for Inspector Mulloch's benefit, 'my driver,' and then to Kane in a whisper, 'I don't know how many civilians this man will tolerate on his patch.' Then louder, 'I expect there are some servants' quarters available for him at the White Hart.' Then the return to the hush-hush. 'Tell Mulloch not to so much as breathe in there. You and I have some talking to do.'

3

There was a sharp knock on his hotel-room door a little after dawn. He threw a pillow over his head and pretended it wasn't happening. But it was. For the knock persisted. He staggered to the door.

'Good Lord!' a deep, female voice bellowed from the gloom.

Lestrade's hands instinctively clutched at his shirt-tails. He found himself thrown backwards into the room and collapsed on the bed. His assailant was a stately woman in her late forties, not unlike his good lady wife, except that this one was more nearly a man. Her stout, lace-up brogues kicked his coverlet into position and her huge, calloused hands threw him his trousers and hauled open curtains and window in one fluid movement.

'Why do men always sleep in their combinations?' she wanted to know.

'I forgot to pack my pyjamas, madam,' he told her, as patiently as he knew how. 'How may I help you at . . .' he fumbled for his old half hunter, '. . . a little after six thirty on an extremely cold January morning?' He closed the window again.

'I was told you were in charge of this case.'

'What case?'

'The body on Stanborough Hill.'

So much for close secrets, Lestrade thought. 'I see,' he said, rummaging in his Gladstone for a collar. 'And who told you that?'

'Some whipper-snapper in room 16. Said he was an Inspector of Scotland Yard. Well, I ask you . . .'

'Mr Kane *is* an Inspector of Scotland Yard, madam. Who, may I ask, put you on to him?'

'My brother, of course; Inspector Mulloch.'

'Ah, so you are . . .?'

'Romilly Mulloch, sister of the aforesaid.'

'Ah. Professional to the core, then, your brother?' He turned to the mirror to tie his tie.

'As a matter of fact, he is.' She scowled at him over his shoulder until the very proximity of her made him move away. Horse liniment was never his favourite essence of perfume. 'But when it comes to archaeology, we must leave no stone unturned.'

Now, Lestrade had met archaeologists before. One of them had tried to seduce him. Another had tried to kill him. He would be naturally wary of this one.

'I don't follow,' he said.

'Well,' she straddled a stool so that her fol-de-rols were on display, 'what does the name Stanborough mean to you?'

'Not a lot,' Lestrade confessed.

'I thought not. A rummage through *Heneage's Hertfordshire* will explain the etymology of the place. "Stan", a stone or rock. "Borough", an ancient fortress.'

'I see,' Lestrade lied.

'Which means there was once a stone fortress on the very site my philistine brother has seen fit to pitch his tent.'

'I don't believe, in all fairness to him, that *he* selected the spot the body was found. Unless, of course, Miss Mulloch, you know something I don't.'

'I know a great deal that you don't,' she observed and proceeded to light a pipe from a tin of the darkest shag balanced on her knee. 'That, for instance, where there is an ancient stronghold, there will be ancient human remains. You have stumbled on to a Saxon warrier, perhaps older.'

'The body was that of a woman.'

'Ah,' Miss Mulloch puffed away while Lestrade found his waistcoat, 'the wider pelvic girdle. Very well, then. A warrior queen, perhaps. It could even be Belgic, you see. There again, the frontier of the Danelaw was only a mile or so away.'

'At the moment, madam, I am interested only in British Law.'

'Oh, please,' said the mannish lady. 'Merely because I intend to stop you destroying vital archaeological evidence does not mean that we cannot be friends.' Her grin terrified him. 'Call me Romilly.'

'No, thanks,' said Lestrade. 'Tell me, what do you know about Saxon or Belgic smoking habits?'

Miss Mulloch let the pipe stem slip from her lips. 'Clod,' she said. 'Tobacco was unknown in these islands before the sixteenth century.'

'I see,' said Lestrade. 'So it's not likely that this', he fished the lighter out of his jacket pocket, 'dates from before the Conquest?'

'Where did you get that?' she snapped, standing up sharply.

'From your Saxon Belgic warrior queen.'

'It looks familiar,' she said, 'may I see?'

He withheld it for a moment, then threw it at her. She caught it with the dexterity of a member of the First Eleven and shuddered so that her pipe went out.

'I thought so,' she said. 'It's Fallabella's.'

'Whose?' Lestrade's mood changed altogether.

'Fallabella Shaw's. That's the "F.S." of the inscription. She . . . We were told she was killed in an air raid on London three years ago.'

'Were you now? Miss Mulloch . . . er . . . Romilly, would you do me the honour of joining me for breakfast?'

After breakfast, while Lestrade pumped the inspector's sister for all he was worth at the table nearest the fire and Kane and Bandicoot kept a respectful distance allowing the Master to perform his wonders, a deputation arrived at the White Hart in the form of a trio of anxious gentlemen.

'Are you Inspector Kane?' asked their leader. He was a man of about Lestrade's age with a white moustache and spectacles. In a poor light he would have passed for Lloyd George.

'I am.'

'Ah, may I join you?'

'Please, Mr . . . er . . .'

'Howard, Ebenezer Howard. This is Mr Purdom and Mr Osborn.'

'Gentlemen.'

They all squeezed round Kane's overcrowded table.

'This is Mr Bandicoot.'

They all got up again and shook hands.

'And', Kane motioned to Lestrade in the wake of Miss Mulloch, polishing off his Welwyn Weeties, 'Mr Lestrade.'

They shook hands again.

'How may we help you, gentlemen?'

Howard looked furtively round the room. 'We happened to see a lady leaving as we came in,' he said, wiping his glasses nervously.

'We were careful', said Purdom, in ringing, theatrical tones, 'that she should not see us.'

'Ah,' said Kane.

'Are you referring to Miss Mulloch?' Lestrade cut the Gordian knot of dither at a stroke.

'The same,' Osborn leaned forward conspiratorially. He was a man in his early thirties with a shock of upright hair and the pebble glasses of a demonic town planner.

'Er . . . might we inquire as to her business?'

'I think that's rather our business,' Kane told them.

'You'll have to help us a little, gentlemen,' Lestrade said.

'Very well. We'll put our cards on the table,' said Howard.

Bandicoot sat back to allow them to do so.

'We are members of the Provisional Board of the Second Garden City, Limited.'

'The second . . .' Lestrade wanted to check his facts.

'Yes. The first was Letchworth, where our watchwords were "Low Rents and High Wages", "A Field for Enterprise" and "Flow of Capital".'

'"Freedom and Co-operation",' chipped in Purdom. 'Don't forget that, Eb.'

'No, indeed. "Freedom and Co-operation".'

'Unfortunately,' said Osborn, 'we made a mistake in allowing a non-alcoholic public house to open.'

There was a sharp intake of breath from Lestrade, Kane and Bandicoot.

'I know,' moaned Osborn. 'The general public associated the place with sandal-wearing and vegetarianism. Damned if I understand why.'

'Quite,' said Howard, attempting to cover one of his sandals

49

with the other. 'But we have such dreams for Welwyn Garden City, gentlemen. Who needs lime-juice champagne when we can have houses, laundries, baths, reading rooms, writing rooms . . .'

'A shop,' said Purdom.

'Only one,' Howard reminded him. 'We aren't in this for a profit, Charles.'

'Which brings us to our problem,' said Osborn.

'Time is of the essence,' said Howard.

'We have our shareholders to consider,' said Purdom.

'We plan to build our first houses along Handside Lane as soon as the weather breaks. I was saying to Lord Desborough only the other day . . .'

'Mr Howard,' Lestrade interrupted, 'I fail to see how your dream has any relevance to us.'

'It's that woman,' said Osborn. 'I've nothing against archaeology, *per se*.'

Lestrade wondered which one of them Howard believed to be Percy.

'I'm a town planner myself,' Osborn went on. 'I like to think that some Belgic town planner was not a million miles removed from myself.'

'But young Fred had thought to put a school there,' said Howard.

'Where?' said Kane.

'Where the water-borers found that Iron-Age body.'

'Iron-Age body?' Lestrade repeated.

'Yes, of course,' said Purdom, increasingly exasperated. 'That's why we're here. I know you police chappies have to investigate any body that's found, but hang it all. A burial site on the edge of the Garden City will bugger up all Fred's plans. Not to mention the delay. People are expecting a return on their money.'

'Not that that's our reason for building, Charles,' Howard reminded him again.

'No, no, quite. But if we are going to have theatres and cinematographs in the town, we must make a start. It's a new decade. I can hear the 'Twenties roaring already.'

'Would you give us a day, gentlemen?'

The three Bashaws of Letchworth looked at each other.

'A day?' Osborn found his voice first. 'Is that all?'

'Am I being too sanguinary, John, do you think?' Lestrade asked.

'I don't know, guv'nor,' Kane confessed, 'but a day should do it.'

'So you won't give in to her outrageous demands, then?' Purdom clapped his hands.

'Miss Mulloch? No. Have no fear.'

'Ah,' the three Board Members sighed in unison.

'Mr Osborn,' said Lestrade, 'do I understand that the area was surveyed by you?'

'Myself and Captain James, yes.'

'James?'

'He's our chief engineer. We appointed him earlier this month.'

'And why did you decide to drill for water at that particular spot?'

'Well, it's rather complicated,' hedged Osborn.

'Don't you remember?' Howard reminded him. 'We built this city on rock and . . .'

'Yes, thank you, Eb. It's just that a layman like Mr Lestrade wouldn't understand.'

'It's the sedimentary rock and the water-table,' said Bandicoot. Everybody looked at him.

'"Artesian Wells and their Importance in Forensic Science",' beamed Kane. 'I think you missed that lecture, guv'nor, though I don't remember you there, either, Harry.'

'So it was chance?' Lestrade asked.

'More or less,' admitted Osborn. 'Why?'

'No reason,' said Lestrade. 'I was wondering what we'd do without our two most vital colleagues.'

'Who are they?' Kane found it hard to come up with *two* names.

'Inspector Luck and Sergeant Chance,' said Lestrade. 'Good morning, gentlemen,' and he rose to go.

'Er . . . before you rush off,' Purdom produced some papers from an inside pocket, 'would you gentlemen be interested in some ordinary £1 shares in the Second Garden City Company?'

There was a resounding silence from the policemen, but Harry Bandicoot reached for his wallet. 'Well, actually . . .' he began.

'Harry,' said Lestrade sharply, 'we've got to release a field for these gentlemen. Shall we go?'

'Where is it again?'

'Ayot St Lawrence.'

'Ayot St Peter?'

'No, Harry,' Lestrade had clearly had enough of rural Hertfordshire, 'Ayot St Lawrence.'

'We passed Ayot St Peter back there.'

'Thank you, John,' Lestrade snapped. 'Rather than artesian wells, I wish you'd both gone to that lecture on "Map-Reading For Policemen".'

'At least it's marked,' said Bandicoot, turning the Ghost down another identical leafless lane, 'unlike the Second Garden City. This place has been here since Domesday, hasn't it?'

'Haven't we all?' muttered Lestrade pulling the motor-rug tighter round him.

'Sholto, are you sure you won't catch cold in all this?' Bandicoot asked. 'I don't know what Fanny would say.'

'Yes, you do,' Lestrade told him. 'She'd first berate you for bringing a motor with an open top and the rest of it isn't repeatable in front of young John here. Fanny Berkeley was a policeman's daughter, remember.'

'There!' Kane shouted.

Bandicoot jumped on the brakes, so that Lestrade slid forward and buried his front teeth in the upholstery.

Kane turned with a grin. 'That's why I sat up here in front,' he said.

'There what?' Lestrade asked, seeing nothing but frosty hedgerows beyond the frost of his own breath.

'Stanborough. Where we started.'

'Good God, Bandicoot. We've done a complete circle, man. Are you practising for Brooklands or something? Ayot St Lawrence. Look.' Lestrade wrestled with the Ordnance Survey again. 'There. There.'

'Oh. *Left*.' Bandicoot hit the wheel in disgust. 'Right.'

'Whatever you say, Harry,' Lestrade buried his head in the map. 'Whatever you say.'

It was a little after lunch that the tall chimneys of the house appeared over the hedgerows. Bandicoot parked where he could and the three men crunched on the gravel drive up to the front door. They saw an immensely thin old man with a wild white beard and outrageous plus-fours pottering in the garden.

'Is that him?' said Kane. 'He looks like Mr MacGregor.'

'Who?' asked Lestrade.

'Mr MacGregor,' the Inspector explained, 'You know, that vicious old gardener in *Peter Rabbit*, the one who . . .' He sensed Lestrade and Bandicoot looking at him. 'It's a book my kiddies are fond of, guv'nor.'

'Yes, well, let's get to business, shall we? That vicious old gardener is one of the most outstanding literary figures in the country today. He's also a sociologist . . .'

'Really?' interrupted Bandicoot. 'You'd never think it to look at him.'

'. . . and critic.' Lestrade finished his sentence.

'Oh, yes,' grunted Kane. 'Everybody's a critic. It's your case for the moment, guv'nor.'

'Thanks, John. Very equilateral of you. Mr Bernard Shaw?'

The vicious old gardener rose with effort from a rose-bed.

'The same.' He peered at the three under his rambling old eyebrows. 'Look,' he said in an intelligent brogue, 'I've already told you, I'm not buying any more shares in the damned Garden City Company. Good morning.'

'We are police officers,' said Lestrade.

Bernard Shaw paused in mid-trowel. 'Ah, the underpaid lackeys of a reactionary government.'

'The same,' bowed Lestrade. 'I am Superintendent Lestrade, this is Inspector Kane and . . . er . . . Constable Bandicoot.'

Bandicoot had not been a constable for twenty-nine years. Even so, he thought Lestrade might have given him a little promotion by now.

'You're not the Hertfordshire force,' Bernard Shaw said.

'Scotland Yard,' Kane told him.

'Well, you'd better come in.'

He showed them into a large, comfortable drawing-room with French windows which opened on to a wide-frosty lawn.

'Celery?' He offered them a jar of the stuff.

53

'Thank you, no,' Lestrade bridled. 'Do you mind if I smoke?'

'Yes. Have a seat, gentlemen. I'll pop the kettle on.'

'Fallabella Shaw,' Lestrade stopped him.

'Cousin Fal?' The literary giant paused in the doorway. 'She's dead, I'm afraid.'

'We know,' said Lestrade. 'Haven't we met, Mr Shaw?'

'Yes,' the Irishman gave a broguish twinkle, 'not a moment ago.'

'No, I mean before.'

Bernard Shaw stood his man up and pointed him in the direction of the light. He took in the lightly Macassared grey hair, the tipless nose, the scarred cheeks, the sad eyes. He began to chuckle. 'You had all of your nose then,' he said.

'You have the advantage of me,' Lestrade said. Most people did.

'Wait here.' Bernard Shaw giggled and disappeared.

Kane browsed the bookshelves. 'Lots of subversion here, guv'nor,' he mumbled. 'Special Branch would have a field-day. Marx, Hyndman, Lenin. This man's a Bolshevist.'

'Ssh,' said Lestrade. 'Better not let Sir Patrick Quinn find out. I wonder why the only policeman ever to receive a knighthood is a homicidal maniac?'

'Now!' Bernard Shaw leapt into the room with a hat on his head and a muffler across his face, wielding a placard in both hands. Kane and Bandicoot went for him, but Lestrade held them back.

'Bloody Sunday,' Lestrade roared with laughter. 'Trafalgar Square, 1887. I was in hospital for three days after you clouted me.'

'Hah!' bellowed Bernard Shaw. 'I was in hospital for eight days after you clobbered me. What did you hit me with?'

'A detective constable.'

'How is he?'

'A cabbage, I fear.'

'Oh, I'm sorry,' frowned Bernard Shaw.

'Don't be,' said Lestrade, 'he was a cabbage before.'

'What did the placard say?' Lestrade craned to see it. 'I didn't get a chance to read it before the lights went out.'

Bernard Shaw turned it a little sheepishly into Lestrade's vista.

'"Hang Henry Matthews",' Lestrade read aloud.

'Who's he?' Bandicoot asked.

'He was Home Secretary at the time. Most of us on the Force felt the same way.'

'I'm hideously embarrassed about all that, Mr Lestrade.' Bernard Shaw unwrapped his scarf. 'There I was, pledged with Sidney Webb to make socialism respectable and on that particular Sunday, I took to the barricades. Disgraceful. There are better ways. I lost my temper for a moment.'

'You've some interesting literature here, Mr Bernard Shaw,' Kane said, wandering back to the bookshelves.

'Oh, feel free to browse,' said the playwright, 'though please, not the novels. They're all awful and I sincerely wish they'd not been published.'

'I rather liked *Cashel Byron's Profession*,' Bandicoot chirped. They all stood and gawped at him. 'Er . . . I found the Southpaw action brilliantly described.' He shadow-boxed the air for a moment.

'Constable Bandicoot used to box for "H" Division,' Lestrade smiled, uneasily. He had no idea Harry had ever read a book.

'Ah, fascinating sport,' beamed Bernard Shaw. 'I hope you all like rose-hip tea,' and he vanished to make it.

Kane shook his head as he read the leather bindings.' *The Perfect Wagnerite*,' he muttered, '*The Quintessence of Ibsenism*. Ned Blevvins would have this man's kneecaps hanging off by now.'

'You don't look happy, John,' Lestrade couldn't help noticing. 'The Fabians are a pretty harmless lot, you know. Some of your colleagues even espouse the cause . . .'

'A Fabian at the Yard.' Kane blanched. 'Surely not! But it's not that. I've just remembered his views on the War. He was pretty outspoken against the government.'

'I've heard you moan now and again.'

'But I don't have an Irish connection . . .' Kane winked at him.

'Now, gentlemen,' Bernard Shaw returned with a perfumed brew with bits swimming in it, 'cousin Fal.'

Lestrade nodded to Kane, who sat near the fire. 'It is my duty to inform you, as Mr Lestrade has already, sir, that your cousin is dead.'

'When a stupid man is doing something he is ashamed of, he always declares that it is his duty,' Bernard Shaw smiled.

'I beg your pardon?' Kane was hurt.

'Sorry, Inspector. It is a line from my *Caesar and Cleopatra*.'

Lestrade thought Shakespeare had written that, but it wasn't his place to say so.

'My cousin died in an air raid three years ago, gentlemen. We weren't close, for all she lived nearby.'

'Really?' Lestrade was grateful for an excuse to leave the tea alone.

'Yes. Over at Tittenhanger. As a matter of fact she left her place to me. I sold it, cleared out all her things.'

'Where are those things now?' Lestrade asked.

'Her books are in reading rooms various. Her clothes are on the backs of poor people the length and breadth of the East End. Her soul is with the saints, I trust.'

'Something else you wrote, Mr Bernard Shaw?' John Kane could be a taciturn bugger when he liked.

'No,' the dramatist chuckled, 'that was Coleridge. "Oh where is the grave of Sir Arthur O'Kellyn".'

'Her body is on a slab in Hatfield Mortuary,' Lestrade said. 'Until this morning it lay in the clay of a hillside near Handside.'

'What?' Bernard Shaw clutched his cup convulsively.

'Mr Lestrade said . . .' Kane began.

'I'm not deaf, young man,' the critic snapped, 'merely confused.'

'Do you recognize this?' Lestrade showed him the lighter.

Bernard Shaw nodded solemnly. 'We had a row about it,' he said. 'Since 1881 I have abhorred tobacco. Fallabella was a woman of the twentieth century however and smoked – before, during and after sex, I understand. She lit up here, in this very room, in my corner of old England. I didn't approve. We had words. You will agree, Mr Lestrade, that all living creatures are experiments in the production of instruments of a creative purpose, which is the attainment of power over matter and circumstance with the necessary accompanying knowledge and comprehension?'

Lestrade nodded and shook his head at the same time.

Clearly, Mr Bernard Shaw had asked the wrong man the wrong question.

'When did you argue with your cousin, sir?' the ex-Superintendent asked.

'Oh, let me see. It was . . . April 1917.'

'You said you were not close,' Kane broke in.

'Indeed not,' Bernard Shaw adjusted the amplitude of his plus-fours. 'I often feel rather guilty about the fact that on the last occasion I saw her we quarrelled.'

'The last occasion you saw her . . . alive?' Kane was jotting in his notebook.

The literary giant looked at him, a look that would have devastated a civilian. 'Those who can, do,' said Shaw. 'Those who cannot, teach, And those who cannot teach, become policemen.'

'Sir, I . . .'

'Sir,' Bernard Shaw interrupted him, 'your inference was plain. You believe I killed my cousin during that silly quarrel of yesterday and that I buried her on Stanborough Hill. I am quite familiar with the phrase "I'd kill for a cigarette" but I just told you; I gave all that up in 1881.'

'You said you were not close,' Lestrade took up Kane's attack, 'and yet Miss Shaw moved near you.'

'She moved here before I did. Some chap she worked for suggested it as a lovely spot. You could have knocked me over with a policeman when we bumped into each other in Welwyn High Street.'

'Who told you that your cousin was dead?' Lestrade said.

'You and he did,' Bernard Shaw was a stickler for the literal.

'I meant before today,' Lestrade was patience itself.

'As her nearest blood relative – her parents were butchered by the Masai some years ago – I was informed by the War Office. I'm afraid I threw the telegram away.'

'The War Office?' Lestrade repeated. 'Why the War Office?'

'She worked for them. Typist, or something.'

'I see. Where did you say she lived?'

'At Tittenhanger. A little cottage called Owls' Roost.'

Lestrade rose to go. 'Mr Bernard Shaw, you've been very kind. Please accept our condolences.'

Bernard Shaw shrugged. 'It's odd,' he said. 'Like hearing the same news twice. By the way, who's Paul Dacres – the name on the lighter?'

'Someone else who died twice,' Lestrade told him.

In the car, John Kane reached for the map. 'Tittenhanger?' he asked.

'Tittenhanger,' nodded Lestrade. 'Harry,' he looked at the silent chauffeur, 'you look a little preoccupied.'

'That Bernard Shaw chap knows more than he's letting on, Sholto,' he said.

'Oh?'

'Well,' Bandicoot turned to them both, 'who's this Arthur O'Kellyn and where the hell is his grave?'

It was true that Inspector Mulloch didn't relish the prospect of the late Fallabella Shaw littering up his police station, but there was really nowhere else to put her. The canteen wasn't used much anyway and they could always swab the place down before Mrs Miniver prepared her delicious Hertfordshire Hotties.

The late Miss Shaw wasn't talking. Lestrade thawed his fingers out around a steaming mug of cocoa before he went to work. The Chief Constable had left his rattan cane behind when he had called the other day to wish the station all the best for 1920 and it was a perfect probe for Lestrade to assess the bullet's trajectory; or failing that, the angle of the shot. John Kane had been right – like Ned Blevvins, he had learned at Lestrade's knee, rude nurse that it was; unlike Ned Blevvins, Kane had a brain – the lady had been shot from behind at close quarters. The bullet had snapped her spine and travelled on, separating her lower jaw from her skull. Lestrade now placed the joints together again and carefully closed her mouth. But someone had done that already. What was left of the body was partly wrapped in thick material made brown by the clay – once a natty herring-bone, he fancied. He could not tell from the corpse how old she had been when someone killed her, but it was certain she'd grow no older.

That night, at the White Hart, as the fire spat in the grate and the locals spat in the spitoons, three less-than-jovial Englishmen sat huddled in the ingle-nook, cogitating.

'Well, John,' Lestrade spoke first, 'what have we got?'

There were no shoe-boxes as yet and no blackboard in front of him, but Inspector Kane needed no such aids. 'Miss Fallabella Shaw, deceased spinster of this parish or near enough, cousin to the celebrated George Bernard.'

'Cause of death?'

'Gunshot wound to the back of the head.'

'From which we infer?'

'The killer is a coward.' No one had excluded Bandicoot from this conversation.

'Or a professional,' said Kane. 'Typical, no-nonsense shot. Close range, from a position where he couldn't miss.'

'Or she,' said Bandicoot.

'She, Harry?' Lestrade quaffed his brandy. 'Do you know something we don't?'

'Er . . . just a shot in the dark, Sholto,' the big Etonian shrugged.

'It may well have been. John, what do you make of Mr Bernard Shaw?'

Kane sucked on the stem of his briar. 'Too clever by half,' he said. 'On his own admission, he didn't like the woman.'

'Didn't like her enough to kill her?'

'That's the three-guinea question, isn't it?'

'No.' Lestrade stared into the crumbling log towers, perishing in the flames. 'The question is: what was her link with Paul Dacres and what are the secrets he referred to on the lighter?'

'Did he have any family, Dacres?' Kane asked.

Lestrade shook his head. 'Parents killed in that train crash at Croydon before the War. Emma was his nearest and dearest.'

'Where did he live?'

'He had rooms, I believe, in Curzon Street.'

'Re-let by now, I suppose?'

Lestrade nodded.

'Did you find anything in his room at the Cedar Hotel?'

'Nothing relevant,' Lestrade said, 'just the sparse bits and pieces of a man on the run.'

'On the run? From what?'

'*That's* the three-guinea question, John. And I don't think we'll answer it tonight, not by staring into the fire. Gentlemen, it's past my bedtime. You young things may be able to frolic the night away – I need my beauty sleep. Tittenhanger tomorrow.'

'I couldn't agree more, Sholto,' beamed Bandicoot. 'Sleep well.'

The raw, biting frosts of January gave way the next day to the raw, biting frosts of February. They crossed the Mimram where stiff and broken reeds stood sentinel by the sedge and found Owls' Roost soon after breakfast.

A woman of indeterminate age with eyes as grey as a Dreadnought and a temperament to match the day answered the door.

'Ah, at last,' she said, 'I expected you people last Thursday.'

'Really?' John Kane was in charge of investigations today.

'Well, never mind. Make a start in the hall, will you? Good Heavens!'

She was staring past the giant shoulders of Harry Bandicoot to where the Ghost stood sleek and silver in the morning.

'The decorating business must be exceptionally lucrative,' she said archly, 'or are you people teachers on the side?'

'We are police officers, madam,' Kane informed her.

'Oh, I see,' she bridled. 'And does your Chief Constable know you decorate on the side?'

'We don't, madam,' Kane assured her. 'We don't decorate at all.'

'Oh,' she said, 'well, now you're here, you couldn't look at my woodworm, could you?'

'Of course,' Lestrade edged his way forward. 'Mr Bandicoot here happens to be the Yard's official woodworm treater. Isn't that so, Constable?' he arched his brow at Bandicoot.

'Er . . . yes, sir,' the Old Etonian replied.

'We were wondering', Lestrade led the lady into the drawing-room, 'if you could help us with our inquiries.' He cleared his throat in the direction of John Kane.

'Ah, yes,' said the inspector, flashing his warrant card. 'I am Inspector John Kane of Scotland Yard. This is . . . Sergeant Lestrade and the gentleman feeling your panelling is Constable Bandicoot.'

Bandicoot popped his head around the door-frame and waved.

'You are . . .?'

The lady had not taken her eyes off Lestrade, '. . . Amazed that promotion comes so slowly in your trade. That man must be a hundred.'

'And three, madam,' Lestrade beamed.

'May we know your name?' Kane asked.

'Oh, yes, forgive me . . .' she gushed. 'Davinia Troop, Mrs.'

'Mrs Troop,' Kane accepted her offer of a chair, 'er . . . is your husband in?'

'Mr Troop is "Something in the City",' she explained. 'Consequently, he is out.'

'When do you expect him back?'

'September. The City in question is Ulan Bator.'

'Oh, I am sorry,' Kane commiserated. 'May I ask you how long you have lived here?'

'A little over three weeks.'

'I see. And the people who lived here before; do you remember their name?'

'No. The place was empty for a while. I was led to believe that a lady lived here but she was killed in an air raid. Quite beastly, the Great War, wasn't it?'

'Quite,' said Kane. 'So how did you come to buy Owls' Roost?'

'Ridiculous name for a house,' Mrs Troop informed them. 'Owls don't roost; they perch, I believe, and swoop a little, but roost – never. We are going to re-name it Dunroving. Picturesque, don't you think?'

'Lovely, madam,' grimaced Kane.

'Shol . . . Mr Lestrade,' Bandicoot called.

'Excuse me,' Lestrade stood up. 'This had better be important, Constable.'

He joined Bandicoot in the hall. The Old Etonian whispered in his ear, 'Mrs Troop has some bally big woodworm.'

61

'Good God, man,' Lestrade hissed, 'I didn't *really* intend you to do that. It was just a subterfuge to get us in here . . . what?'

He followed Bandicoot's finger to what at first sight appeared to be a knot-hole some way above the third stair that rose from the hall. He flicked out the brass knuckles and probed the switch-blade point into it. The click of metal on metal. He dug deeper and squeezed his fingers into the cavity.

'Damn!' he exploded.

'Is everything all right?' Mrs Troop emerged from the adjacent room.

'Madam,' Lestrade pocketed the knife quickly, 'would you do me the honour of standing here?'

'Why?'

'I am not at liberty to divulge that,' he said.

'Very well.' She did as she was told.

'No.' Lestrade stopped her. 'Cross, would you, from the front door as though you were going up the stairs.'

She paused, frowned, hauled up her Edwardian skirts and did so.

'Thank you,' said Lestrade when she had reached the third stair. 'Stand there, could you?'

She did.

'Now, turn your face to the wall.'

'Look,' Mrs Troop's limited patience was clearly at an end, 'what *is* all this about?'

Bandicoot joined her on the stair. On the wall, two feet or so above the wooden panel with its knot-hole, a short nail projected from the rather awful wallpaper.

'I'm very sorry, Mrs Troop, that you have been bothered,' Lestrade said. 'Inspector? We have that other call to make?'

'Er . . . yes, of course. Thank you, Mrs Troop, for your kindness. We'll see ourselves out.'

Lestrade tipped his bowler.

'I'd get someone to have a look at that woodworm, if I were you, madam,' Bandicoot smiled and they made for the car.

'What other call?' Kane asked when they were out of earshot.

'Just my quaint little way of getting us out of there,' Lestrade explained.

'Why?'

62

He held up a twisted pellet of lead.

'What's that?'

'It's a bullet, John,' Lestrade smiled triumphantly. 'Found in a panel on the staircase by one Harry Peregrine Bandicoot who I want you to promote to Commissioner immediately.'

'Eagle-eyed, eh?' Kane slapped Bandicoot's shoulder. 'No wonder you're called Peregrine.'

'Actually, I'm not,' Bandicoot replied, 'I am the only Bandicoot not to have a middle name. Papa took one look at me and after Harry was lost for words.'

'So what are you saying, guv'nor?' Kane asked.

'You saw Miss Shaw's cadaver. What was she? Five foot three? Five foot four?'

'The same height as Mrs Troop,' Kane nodded.

'You know, you should have been a detective, John,' Lestrade told him.

'So Miss Shaw died there, at Dunroving?'

'It's my guess she did. As she was climbing the stairs, but . . .'

'But?' Kane and Bandicoot chorused.

'But she stopped on the third stair. And her head was turned towards the wall.'

'How do you know?'

'The woodworm hole Harry found angled to the right. The hole in Miss Shaw's skull was almost dead centre of the vertebrata.'

'So?'

'So our murderer shot her from the floor of the hall while she had her back to him.'

'Or her.'

'Yes, thank you, Harry.' Lestrade wrapped his muffler tighter round him. 'Or her. And that limits our field quite considerably. Because the angle, both in the skull and the wall, is virtually straight. Our murderer must have been well over six feet. Harry's height.'

The policemen turned to look at their driver.

'Good God,' he shouted, suddenly aware, 'you don't think it was me do you?'

'Do you know what sort of gun fired this bullet, guv'nor?' Kane held it in his gloved fingers.

'No,' said Lestrade, 'but I know a man who does.'

Lestrade took a cab, one of the last horsed ones in London, to the building at the corner of Orange Street. Unannounced, he climbed to the second floor to where a squat, balding man with a toothbrush moustache, of the type favoured by Bavarian corporals, was hunched over a microscope.

'Mr Churchill,' the ex-Superintendent said quietly.

Churchill shrieked, scattering shells and papers in all directions.

'Dammit, Lestrade, don't you knock?'

'Only when I haven't got the right cards,' smiled Lestrade.

'I thought you'd retired.'

'I thought you had. How's business?'

'Forensic or otherwise?'

'Both.' Lestrade lifted a green bicycle off a swivel chair and sat down.

'Quite quiet on the trial front since Colonel Rutherford. He's mad as a hatter, of course.'

'Rutherford?'

'No, that Blevvins fellow of the Yard. I'm beginning to have my doubts about Marshall Hall too.'

Lestrade nodded, 'I've *always* had doubts about Marshall Hall,' he confessed. 'I forgot to stop by to congratulate you on that Chinaman killed while catching bullets in his teeth.'

'Chung Ling Robinson? Yes, bizarre, wasn't it? Most excitement the Wood Green Empire's seen in many a long year, I shouldn't wonder. But you didn't come here to saunter down Memory Lane, Lestrade. What is it?'

'Business, I fear.' Lestrade fished out the mangled piece of lead from his pocket. 'What do you make of this?'

Churchill strapped to his head a weird appliance with a magnifying lens which he lowered down over his right eye. 'It's not crapshot,' he proffered.

'No, indeed,' Lestrade agreed. 'Whoever fired that is a professional, have no fear.'

Churchill looked oddly at Lestrade. With that huge, all-seeing eye, it was difficult to do otherwise.

'Nothing as high-powered here as in the "Leviathan" case,' the expert witness murmured. 'Look at the lands, the striations.'

'Hmm,' Lestrade nodded, able only to see a squidge of lead.

Churchill sniffed the bullet. 'This has been buried in plaster and mahogany,' he said. 'Rather inferior mahogany, though.'

'Ah,' smiled Lestrade, as always with Churchill, secretly impressed, 'but what did it pass through first?'

Churchill produced a tool from a drawer at his desk, tapped the bullet's end with it, threw it into the air once or twice and caught it, not, like Chung Ling Robinson, in his teeth, but in his hand. 'Hair, skin, flesh, bone, more flesh and skin,' he said.

Lestrade was dumbfounded. 'You wouldn't care to tell me who pulled the trigger, I suppose?' he asked.

Churchill sniggered. 'Ever heard of a comparison microscope, Lestrade?'

The ex-Superintendent shook his head.

'Neither have I,' muttered Churchill, clamping the bullet in his teeth after all, 'but I wish someone would invent one. *Then* I might just be able to tell you the answer to that question. As it is, will you settle for the make of gun?'

'I will,' said Lestrade.

'Revolver. Point 455 calibre. Pull four to five pounds. It could only be a Webley, probably Mark V, and almost certainly a four-inch barrel.'

'A service revolver?'

'There's a misnomer if ever there was one,' said Churchill, but Lestrade couldn't see what he was looking at so he let it pass. 'There are probably as many civilians as Forces people with one of those, especially after the War. But there's something else . . .'

'Yes?'

Churchill tilted the lens and sat back in his swivel, chewing the ends of his moustache. 'I don't know,' he said at length. 'Don't tell Bernard Spilsbury, but it's got me stumped. There's a mark here I've never seen before.'

'Could the mahogany or plaster have caused it?'

Churchill shook his head, 'No,' he said, 'can you leave this with me?'

'It *is* evidence,' Lestrade said, 'but I couldn't think of it in safer hands. How much do I owe you?'

'I'll send you the bill,' said Churchill, 'but not until I've got the answer to this – whatever it is. To where shall I send it?'

'Scotland Yard – care of Inspector Kane. Good morning.'

'And to you. And mind my bike.'

'Well, Blevvins?' Superintendent Fred Wensley turned his beady Dorsetshire eyes on the lump sitting furthest from him.

'Not bad, thanks, sir.'

'The case, Blevvins,' Wensley reminded him. 'The body in the Cedar Hotel.'

'Ah, yes, sir. Suicide.'

'Mr Lestrade thinks otherwise.'

A number of eyes swivelled towards Wensley. It was well known that the superintendents had been as close as peas in a pod or testicles in a scrotum, but no one had breathed Lestrade's name on this floor of the Yard for over six months. His locker had been emptied, his office filled by Blevvins. Even his old sparring partner, Chief Inspector Walter Dew, had sensed the way the political wind was blowing and had clammed up. He had taken the photograph of Lestrade down from his wall where it had stood alongside that of Mrs Dew and the now-not-so-little Dews. He was a thoroughgoing family man, give him his due.

'I was under the impression', Blevvins jerked his bull neck forward, 'that Mr Lestrade didn't work here any more.'

There was a silence, painful to all but Blevvins.

'You're not catching my drift, Blevvins,' Wensley told him. 'Sholto Lestrade has dealt with more murders than you've had cautions. I am well aware that Mr Lestrade has no jurisdiction, but he does have experience. And I'd weigh that against brawn any day. Now, go back to that hotel and start again.'

'But I've got no body,' Blevvins complained.

'Nor any brain,' Wensley observed. 'That will certainly make life more difficult for you, Inspector, but you should have thought of that before you had Captain Dacres' body committed to the deep. We needn't keep you.'

Blevvins looked at the scarcely contained glee on the faces of his fellow-inspectors. He scraped back his chair and crashed through the doors, cuffing a passing constable around the head as he went and kicking his dog.

'Now,' said Wensley, 'the Bishop of Chichester's daughter. Bower?'

'I'm afraid, sir,' said the inspector, 'the lavatory door was a bit of a sticker and nobody knew she was there.'

The smoke hung like a pall of death over the city ahead. The sounds of that city coming to life hummed through the fog and the frost: the hoot of barges on the river and the shouts of draymen and the rattle of milkbottles. One by one the electric lamps went out, as they had done recently over Europe, and the February day promised early snow.

The man on the tall bay straightened in the saddle. It reminded him again of the packet he'd already bought on the Ypres salient and he cursed the metal bits that held his knee together. Surely, though, he wasn't mistaken? Either that was a bloody big mallard on the frozen surface of the lake or . . . He spurred the animal forward, ducking under the trees with their dead, grey branches, and reined in at the water's edge. Stiffly, he dismounted and looped the reins over the horse's neck.

That was no mallard. It was the body of a man lying face down in the water of the Serpentine, the frost still hoary across his black frock-coat. His top hat lay some yards away on the ice. The watcher looked at the dead man's feet. No skates. Perhaps he had been a foolhardy bather, braving the elements as a certain kind of idiot did on New Year's Day. There again, the dead man was hardly dressed for a swim.

The watcher looked about him. He had merely been a horse-man riding by. What could he do? Why was there never a policeman around when you needed one? He climbed to the saddle again. He'd seen plenty of corpses in No Man's Land out there, where the rusty cans clattered and clashed on the barbed wire and brains lay matted in mud. But not here, not in Hyde Park. There was sure to be a row about this. And quite a rotten one, he shouldn't wonder.

4

Inspector John Kane took Sergeant Norroy Macclesfield with him to the Belgian Embassy. Like the country it represented, the building was small, grey and nasty. Lestrade had gone home to Surrey to prompt Emma as gently as he could on the late Paul Dacres; whether there was anything in his letters that could shed some light on his double death. He had bought King Albert's book in 1914 along with everyone else, but secretly hadn't thought His Majesty was much of a writer. He'd give the Embassy a miss.

Their man in Britain was M. Hercules Lapotaire, a prissy little diplomat who occasionally reached Kane's shoulder, but not on a regular basis.

'Ah,' he said in the gloom of his winter office, 'you are 'ere about ze body in ze lake, *n'est ce pas*?'

'Indeed,' said Kane, once he had effected introductions, 'I believe the late M. Euperry was one of your staff.'

The ambassador shrugged. 'In a manner of speaking. He was a translator.'

'Had he been in this country long?'

Lapotaire tapped the desk top with an ornate paper-knife. 'What is 'e writing zere?' he demanded of Macclesfield.

Kane glanced at the sergeant's notepad. 'It's his shopping list, sir. Mrs Macclesfield is something of a trial. Isn't that so, Norroy?'

'She avulsed her first husband, sir,' Macclesfield told them solemnly. 'Quarter of cashews, half a pound of best . . .'

'How long had M. Euperry been in England, sir?' Kane asked again.

'Er . . . about three weeks, I believe.'

'Where did he live?'

'Right 'ere. In ze Embassy. I was led to believe zat Special Branch would be asking ze questions,' Lapotaire said.

'Oh, I'm sure they will,' smiled Kane. 'Macclesfield and I are the Advance Guard.'

'Ze . . . Advance Guard?'

'Yes. It's official policy. An inspector and a sergeant always make preliminary inquiries. It saves time in the long run and makes sure no stone is unturned. Tell me, can you think of any reason why anyone should want to see him dead?'

Lapotaire twitched his silly little moustache and shook his head, ''E was a mild man. Very popular in Bruxelles. Fond of painting and sketching.'

'When did you see him last?'

'Ah, let me zee. We 'ad lunched with Monsieur Bishop.'

'Bishop?'

'Sir Eustace Bishop. Ze Keeper of ze King's paintings. At ze Palace of Buckingham.'

'Was he married?'

'Monsieur Bishop? I 'ave no idea.'

'No. Monsieur Euperry.'

'Ah, no. 'E was, 'ow you say, "not as other translators."'

Kane and Macclesfield looked at each other. 'Was there anyone . . . special . . . in this country?'

'Ah,' nodded Lapotaire, 'I see. I see. No, not zat I am aware. Such things in Belge are not frowned upon as over 'ere. Vive and let vive, *n'est ce pas*?'

There was a knock at the door and a tall footman entered, muttering something incomprehensible to His Excellency.

'Ah, ze rest of your mob 'ave arrived. Special Branch. Please, Alain, show Sir Patrick in.'

'Oui, Patron.'

'Well,' Kane was on his feet in an instant, 'we really must be on our way, sir. You have been extremely helpful. We'll see ourselves out. Norroy, the sash.'

The giant sergeant put away his shopping list and hauled up the window-frame.

'But messieurs,' said Lapotaire, somewhat taken aback, 'zat is ze window.'

'We know,' called Kane, 'we know.'

'But it is four floors up.'

Kane took the man by the arm. 'You probably find British police methods a little bewildering, but believe me, we have our reasons. I'd be most grateful if you did not mention our little visit to Superintendent Quinn.'

'Not?' The Ambassador was more than a little confused.

'Someone put a bullet into the head of your translator, Monsieur,' Kane hissed out of the corner of his mouth. 'How can any of us be sure who?' He nodded in the direction of the door.

'Er? You mean . . .?'

Kane tapped the side of his nose. 'A nod's as good as a wink to a blind horse, as I expect you say in Brussels. Don't worry, Monsieur, we'll see ourselves out.'

And the work of balancing gingerly along a ledge sixty feet up was that of a moment.

'Euperry?' said Lestrade. 'Jean-Cocteau Euperry. Anything previous?'

'Yes, well, thank you, Superintendent,' the voice crackled on the far end of the line. 'We'll certainly check our records here, but frankly it's all rather needle and haystack. Good morning.'

And he hung up.

'What did he say, Daddy?' Emma Lestrade looked up from *The Times* crossword.

'Something about a needle and haystack,' said Lestrade, still holding the bakelite in his hand.

'Is that a pub?'

'No,' Lestrade's eyes gimletted more than usual. 'No, I suspect it's John Kane's way of telling me that someone had come into his office.'

'So what did he want?'

'To tell me a bloke had reported a murder. A body in a lake . . .'

'Clothed in white samite?' Emma asked, wrestling at the same time with fourteen across.

'I didn't ask what he was wearing,' said Lestrade. 'Apparently he was Belgian.'

'Really? Shouldn't that be . . .'

'Special Branch? Yes. Patrick Quinn will have his balls . . . oh, begging your pardon, my dear.'

'You forget, Daddy,' she clucked, 'I was brought up with the Bandicoot brothers. What I didn't know about boys' anatomy by the time I was twelve wasn't worth knowing.'

'Emma!' Lestrade found himself frowning.

'Now, now,' she laughed, 'keep your helmet on. Why should John Kane involve you in this?'

'Because', he said, suddenly seeing his radiant little girl in rather a new light, 'Monsieur Euperry was shot in the head with a revolver.'

Emma put the paper down, the smile gone, the eyes hard and cold. 'Made to look like suicide?' she asked.

'I didn't have the time to find out,' he said, 'but I'd give a year's pension to have a peep at the wound.'

'Where would they have put him?'

'Let's see. The Serpentine. St George's would be my guess.'

She glanced at the time. 'Come on, I'll drive you to the station. We can be there by three o'clock.'

'We?' He raised an eyebrow.

'Yes,' she said, 'we. You do realize what you've become, don't you, Daddy?'

'Er . . . let me see. Cantankerous? Opinionated? Irritating? Not yet incontinent, thank God.'

'All these things, yes.' She threw him his Donegal unceremoniously, then wrapped the muffler lovingly around his neck. 'But you've become a sort of consulting detective. You are Sherlock Holmes and I am your Doctor Watson!'

He took a swipe at her, but she had gone laughing down the hallway, out of reach.

'Wash your mouth with soap and water, Emma Bandicoot-Lestrade!' he bellowed.

71

It had not been Lestrade's idea. He had been against it from the start. But Emma had insisted. She had her mother's steel and fire and all the charm of generations of Bandicoots. Against that, Lestrade was powerless. He stood outside St George's Hospital, flapping his arms like some demented penguin, while she hailed a cab and was gone.

'This way,' said a passing nurse very loudly in his ear. 'Have you come for your weekly? How are your movements today? Have you opened your bowels?'

Passers by looked a little oddly at the pair, but Lestrade stood his ground, clawing free of the harpy. 'My movements, madam, are as precise as a Swiss watch and let me assure you I open my bowels to no man. Which way to the morgue?'

'Ooh, no ducks,' the nurse gripped his arm, 'you don't wanna be so down. There's a good few years in you yet. Let's see if I can't find the almoner and get you a nice cuppa tea.'

It was just Emma Lestrade's luck that the desk man that afternoon was 'Twenty-Twenty' Johnson, who could read the advice on a packet of Swan Vestas at fifty paces.

'Can I help you, madam?' He looked at her over the desk.

'Er . . . yes,' she smiled, 'I've come to join.'

"Ave you, now?' His eyes widened. 'Well, I'm not sure . . .'

'Sir Nevil suggested I drop round,' she said, dewy-eyed, dropping the name of the Commissioner with immaculate timing.

'Oh, I see,' Twenty-Twenty stood to attention. 'Well, in that case. Constable Greeno!'

The lad of that name appeared from nowhere, clutching an aspidistra. 'Sarge?' he gasped.

'Second floor. On the double. Take this lady to Mr de la Rue. I believe he's in charge of women.'

'Women?' repeated Greeno.

'Yes,' said Twenty-Twenty, crossing his elbows on the counter, 'the reason we're all 'ere lad. Now move along before I find somewhere painful to plant that flower.'

'Very good, Sarge.' And Greeno stood back while Emma swept to the stairs.

'After you,' she said.

'No, no, miss,' he tried to nod over the blades of the leaves.

'I don't want you staring at my legs, Constable,' she said softly. 'Skirts are shorter this year.'

Greeno turned crimson, 'I . . . I . . .' and was lost for words.

'Never mind,' she reached through the foliage and pinched his cheek, 'we might be working together soon.'

'Why, miss?' Greeno asked, staggering upwards as he went. 'Why do you want to join the Metropolitan Police? The pay's lousy. The hours stink . . . begging your pardon, miss. And now that Mr Dew is a Chief Inspector and doesn't belittle himself, the tea's horrible as well.'

'Yes,' said Emma, 'his tea was legendary, wasn't it?'

Greeno stopped. 'Do you know him, miss? The Chief Inspector?'

'No,' she said, wide-eyed, 'I have second sight.' And she flashed one of those smiles that would have buckled the knees of anyone but a Metropolitan policeman. 'Is it through here?'

Clearly, the lady's second sight didn't extend to directions inside a building, and the Yard was one of those where you needed a ball of twine to find your way out again, rather like that bull and that Greek bloke.

'No. Next left,' grunted Greeno, the weight of the plant beginning to take its toll.

'How long have you been on the Force, Constable?' Emma asked him.

'Ooh, nearly three months, now, miss. Come August.'

It was the typical Yard *non-sequitur* she had heard all her life.

'And how are you enjoying it?'

'Well, it could be worse. The blokes are all right, you know. And Sir Nevil, well, he's a real toff, he is. But some of the buggers – er – the officers who are my superiors – well, they give you the runaround, you know. That Mr Wensley, he's all right. But he sent me out to find a long, felt want the other day. I stood on the Strand for three hours before I got it. Then Mr Kane, he sent me for a bucket of elbow grease. Then Mr Blevvins boxed my ears. I want to be a detective really, like . . .'

But Emma wasn't listening. She had long since doubled back, kicking off her shoes and had tiptoed along John Kane's carpeted

73

corridor to the office of the great inspector. At the door, an ox-like figure of a man burst out, nearly flattening her against the wall.

'Who are you?' he growled.

Emma swallowed hard, praying that Inspector Blevvins's memory was as short as his temper.

'I'm collecting for the Distressed Gentlefolks' Society. Did you know it was Save a Gentlefolk Week? The cost of silk hats has gone up this month by thirty per cent.'

'Bugger off!' Blevvins told her and swept on in his valiant pursuit of anything smaller than he was.

'Madam?' A rather good-looking detective appeared above a steaming mug of tea.

'I must see Inspector Kane.' She closed the outer door that separated her from the world. 'It's a matter of life and death.'

'Is it now?' he smiled. 'Well, perhaps, I can help, Miss . . . er . . .?'

'Macintosh,' she lied.

'Macintosh,' the detective repeated. 'Yes,' he twinkled, 'you've got your father's nose.'

'Emma!' John Kane emerged with his hat in his hand from the inner sanctum. 'What a pleasant surprise. It must be, oh, two years. You've met Detective-Sergeant Macclesfield?'

'No,' she raised an eyebrow, 'but he has clearly mistaken me for someone else.'

'Have you Norroy?' Kane asked.

'Not a bit of it, sir,' Macclesfield's face was poker straight. 'I knew Miss Macintosh as soon as I saw her.'

'Yes. Well. Norroy – a cup of that bevvy you persist in calling tea. Emma, let me hold various parts of you to warm you up.'

She tapped him with her umbrella so that tears welled in his eyes. 'How is Mrs Kane?' she asked.

'Ah,' Kane clicked his fingers in mock anguish, 'you know how to hurt a man. Did your dad tell you I was on to something?'

'He told me you'd rung off. That's why I'm here. He'd have come himself, only . . .'

'Only Commissioner Macready would hang him, yes, I know. Where is he now?'

74

'St George's. That *is* where the body is?'

'You know,' Kane smiled, 'Sholto Lestrade would have made a fine detective some day.'

'Did you get into trouble?' she asked. 'Special Branch?'

'Ah,' Kane swivelled so that his feet were on the desk. 'I was on my way to the top floor when you called. Still, no hurry. I've been on the carpet before. Though never, of course,' he leered at her, 'with you.'

'Sorry,' said Macclesfield, arriving with a steaming mug, 'didn't mean to obtrude.'

'Is he always like this?' Emma asked him.

'Never with me, Miss,' Macclesfield said. 'Never with me.'

'Hmm,' she sipped, 'not a bad brew, Sergeant. Worthy of Walter Dew at his best. How is he?'

'Not the same since your dad left,' Kane told her. 'We none of us are. When Sholto Lestrade went, they broke the mould.'

'They did,' said Macclesfield.

'At least, I think it was Inspector Blevvins who actually broke it. Now, to cases.'

'The dead Belgian,' Emma huddled forward, cradling the cracked mug in both hands before the crackling fire. 'Has he anything to do with Paul?'

'It's too early to say,' Kane said, 'except that I think they both died by the same means. We don't get too many shootings in Hyde Park, not since Lord Cardigan hit Captain Tuckett.'

'When was that?'

'1840. And come to think of it, that wasn't Hyde Park at all; it was Wimbledon Common.'

'Do you think that this was a duel?' Emma asked.

'Well, Belgians are a touchy lot. All that Cadre Noir and Saumur and so on. But no, unless, of course, M. Euperry was running away when his opponent hit him.'

'You've been to the Embassy?'

'We have. What did you make of His Excellency, Macclesfield?' Kane lit a cigarette. 'Emma?'

'I thought you'd never ask,' she accepted gratefully. 'Daddy doesn't approve. Neither does Harry. Thanks.'

'I felt he wasn't sufficiently grateful for 1914, sir,' the sergeant said, perching on the corner of a desk.

'Yes, my sentiments entirely,' the inspector agreed. 'At any rate, he was no help, It's all by the by now, of course.'

'Why?' she asked.

'No sooner had we got there than Special Branch arrived. I thought we'd steal a march on them and nip the whole thing in the bud, so to speak. I'm afraid I've had my chance and muffed it. I'm for a wrist-smacking in a minute. Foreign national. Sensitive area. Utmost secrecy. Too foreign, too sensitive and too secret for an ordinary inspector of the Criminal Investigation Department. I'll have to bow out of this one.'

She looked at her watch. 'So will I. John, you've been very kind,' and she kissed his cheek.

'Tell your dad,' he rose and took up his hat again, 'a man to talk to is Sir Eustace Bishop, Keeper of the King's Paintings. His best bet is Buckingham Palace. Euperry had lunch with him recently. The dead man was something of an art lover. There may be something in it.'

'Thank you, John. And thank you, sergeant, for your excellent tea.'

'Miss . . . Macintosh,' he bowed stiffly and her hand lingered for a second longer than was strictly necessary on his, 'please give my regards to your father. I think his coats are lovely.'

There was a furious knocking at Kane's outer door and a flustered Constable Greeno tumbled in.

'Sir, there's a woman loose in . . .'

'Ah, there you are, Constable.' Emma extinguished her cigarette in the aspidistra pot the lad was still carrying. 'I'm afraid I got rather lost. These nice gentlemen have persuaded me that the Women's Police Service is not, after all, for me. The hats, you see, are so utterly repugnant. Good morning.'

It was the top floor. The top floor that Lestrade had always dreaded. Near the green door. The door through which Lestrade had never gone. The view from the windows was the same, if a little higher; the carpet the same sludge colour; the walls the same institution-green and-cream. But there was an atmosphere here, tense, tangible. It hit John Kane like a brick privvy.

Before him, as he stood in what had been Lestrade's customary place, on the carpet but two floors higher, sat two men, both titled, both inscrutable, both policemen – of sorts.

'You know Sir Basil, of course,' said the shorter of the two.

'Indeed,' Kane said, looking for somewhere to put his hat.

'Kane,' said Sir Basil, 'we have reason to believe you've been straying from your patch.'

'Really, sir?' John Kane could look as vacant as Ned Blevvins when it suited him.

Sir Basil sat like a bloodhound with a moustache, his Homberg squarely on his head.

'Don't come the innocent with me, Inspector,' the shorter of the two thundered. 'You know full well that in cases involving foreign nationals, Special Branch investigate. This is a sensitive area.' He leaned forward, his eyebrows curling cryptically. But then, Kane knew that. 'A matter involving the utmost secrecy.'

'May I ask why, Sir Patrick?' Kane said.

Sir Patrick looked at Sir Basil and Sir Basil looked at Sir Patrick.

'I thought we'd got beyond the stage of recruiting baboons into the service,' said Sir Patrick. 'Or at least we will have when Inspector Blevvins retires. Take my word for it, Kane. This little affair is none of your business.'

'In short,' Sir Basil twisted in his chair and took off the Homberg so that the lamplight flashed on his slicked-down Macassar, 'keep your nose out or Superintendent Quinn here will have you back filling shoe-boxes. And that sergeant of yours – Buxton?'

'Macclesfield, sir.'

'Yes, well, I knew it was somewhere north of Berkshire. He'll be in Lost Property, trying to work out why the great British public leave eight hundred umbrellas a day on their various transport systems.'

Kane winced on Macclesfield's behalf. He knew his sergeant would much prefer to lose either of his testicles.

'It *was* my patch, sir.' Kane stood his ground with the grit he'd shown in the McAdam Case.

'In what sense "your patch"?' Quinn demanded.

'London,' Kane said.

'Balderdash!' bellowed Sir Basil, his obsolete moustachioes flying in his own breeze. 'Whose patch is it really?'

'Superintendent Pearson's, Sir Basil,' Quinn told him.

'"No-Collar" Pearson?' Sir Basil demanded.

Quinn nodded.

'Even so,' Sir Basil would not be brow-beaten, 'procedure is procedure, Kane. You may safely leave it in our hands now. And thank your service record that I'm prepared to overlook what I can only assume is a mental aberration. If it happens again, of course, I shall be forced to ask Dr Bettelheim to strap you to his couch and ask you pertinent questions about your early childhood. Clear?'

'As a bell, sir.' Kane stood to attention.

'Very well. Now get out.'

The inspector knew his place and left.

'How much do you think he knows, Paddy?' Sir Basil asked.

'I think he's bluffing, sir,' the Irishman told him.

'I didn't get to be Director of Intelligence by thinking,' Sir Basil said. Quinn had realized that. 'Have you got a man to watch him?'

'Oh, a tail, you mean?' Quinn caught the Director's drift.

'No, a man,' Sir Basil insisted.

'Burgess is good.'

'Hmm.' Sir Basil was not impressed.

'Maclean?'

'He's Cambridge, isn't he?'

'Afraid so.'

'That won't do. What about that Marks chappie?'

'Load of rubbish,' said Quinn. 'All that guff about the bourgeoisie and lumps of proletariat.'

'No, no,' snarled Sir Basil, 'not him. George Marks. Fellow from Chiddingfold.'

'Oh, him. Sorry, Sir Basil. Crossed wires there. He'll need a number two. Kane is no fool. If he spots Marks, we'll need a replacement.'

'Anyone in mind?'

'Spencer?'

'Why not. Nobody'd give him a second glance, would they?'

'That's the hallmark of the Branch, sir. To a man we're ordinary.'

'Yes,' sighed Sir Basil. He knew it to be true.

*

If M. Euperry had anything to tell Lestrade, he was doing it damned cryptically. Having shaken himself free of the ghastly, starched harridan who had waylaid him at the entrance to St George's Hospital, the ex-Superintendent had found his way through a maze of corridors dominated by Victorian plumbing to the Belgian's temporary resting place while the police conducted their inquiries. The mortuary attendant was one of the old school who would cheerfully have tagged and bagged his mother for five bob. Not that Lestrade gave him any such denomination. On the contrary, he had always been rather undenominational. The cause of death, Lestrade did not need Bernard Spilsbury to tell him, was a single bullet which had entered the spine an inch or two below the hairline on the neck and exited below the epil . . . epilg . . . Adam's apple. Other than that, there was nothing. It was all rather disappointing.

Emma's news had been better. For all Lestrade had not wanted her to go to the Yard, he was glad she had and realized again that his little girl could, in fact, take care of herself. All right, so John Kane had nothing beyond the cause of death to link the Belgian with Fallabella Shaw and Paul Dacres, but John Kane had grown at Lestrade's knee, been suckled on canteen food, cut his teeth on a truncheon (that time when he'd tripped on his way home from the Police Ball); his were the gut reactions of an original. It could have been Sholto Lestrade himself two hundred years ago. And if John Kane said 'See the King's Keeper of Paintings', then the King's Keeper of Paintings it was.

'I'll only be gone for the day,' he said to Fanny over breakfast.

'I'm coming with you,' Emma chirped over her coffee.

'Not this time,' smiled her father, shaking his head.

'You don't think the Keeper of the King's Paintings is a deranged maniac, do you Daddy?' his daughter asked.

'Well, there must be some reason why he got the job,' Lestrade winked at her.

'Redvers Buller,' said the reedy old man in the corner.

'Eat your toast, Uncle,' Fanny smiled at him.

'There was a first-class pego if ever I saw one.'

'Gideon,' Lestrade put down his coffee cup, 'not now . . .'

'And as for that Gatacre chappie. Absolute boundah. No pedigree,' the marmalade dribbled down his chin, 'no class.'

'Uncle, you'll upset yourself again,' Fanny warned, 'and that will be the third pair of trousers this week.'

'The mistake was dealing with that old bastard Kronje in the first place. I said to Roberts "Look, sonny," I said. But he wouldn't. All a bloody waste of time.'

'It's all over, Uncle,' Lestrade said. 'The Boer War. That was twenty years ago. We won.'

'One?' Gideon snapped. 'Don't talk such piss, you whipper-snapper. When're you going to get a decent job? Sitting round here all day. One, indeed. There were thousands of them at Spion Kop alone. They're only bloody farmers. Why is it taking so long to beat them? What's this?' he suddenly screwed up his parchment face to stare at the cup in his trembling hand.

'Coffee, Uncle,' Fanny said. 'It's your favourite.'

'Favourite, be buggered,' and he threw it at the wall.

'Oh, God,' moaned Lestrade, 'one of his better days.'

'Oh, Sholto,' Fanny dabbed at the flock with a napkin, 'don't mind him. It's just Gideon's way.'

'What about these armoured trains?' Uncle Gideon demanded to know.

Emma was on her feet, taking the old wreck gently by the hand. 'Come on, Uncle,' she smiled, 'let's go to your room and you can tell me how you relieved Ladysmith.'

'Oooh,' the old man's shriek ended in a hacking cough and a spasm that nearly pole-axed him, 'you're a wicked girl, little Emmeline, and no mistake.'

'Emma, Uncle. Little Emma.'

He solemnly shook her hand, 'Pleased to meet you, m'dear,' he said, standing as erect as his eighty-six years would let him. 'Major-General Halifax,' he nudged her in the ribs with a razor-sharp elbow, 'but you can call me Giddy.'

'As a gander,' sighed Lestrade.

Gideon stopped on his way to the door. 'Since you're a visitor,' he said to Emma, 'I'll show you my collection of Dervish teeth, shall I? Always been an interest of mine, dentistry. After soldiering, of course. Got some exquisite molars, the Fuzzy-Wuzzies.'

'Lead on, Uncle,' Emma smiled, 'I'll get Madison to bring us some cocoa, shall I?'

'Emma,' Fanny called, 'keep him away from the brandy, for God's sake. We've only just redecorated the conservatory.'

'Shame about old Wauchope, buying it at Magersfontein like that. He'll be sorely missed,' muttered the old man as they made for the stairs.

'She's got the patience of a saint, that girl,' Lestrade toyed with the last of the kedgeree.

'Yes,' Fanny sipped her coffee, throwing a sideways glance at her husband, 'I wonder where she gets it from?'

'You can't needle me, Mrs Lestrade,' he said, 'I am immunized.'

'I'm very glad to hear it. Where to today, dearest?'

'Buckingham Palace.'

'The Palace? Have you been asked to return your OM?'

'I can't put my hand on it at the moment,' he said. 'No, that's the only address I've got for this bloke Bishop who's the royal art-expert.'

'Is he any good?'

Lestrade shrugged, 'I suppose he knows what he likes.'

The ageing detective walked resolutely down Constitution Hill, careful to avoid the blip in the ground where Sir Robert Peel's horse had stumbled seventy years earlier, when that ageing detective hadn't even been a gleam in his father's eye; more a dull reflection off the buttons of his police coatee.

He flashed his wallet to a less-than-stringent sentry at the side-gate and waded through the goose- and swan-droppings until he passed the new, gleaming frontage design by Sir Arthur Webb, the Portland stone dazzling in the sunshine. Here, the King's guards were rather more alert and he found himself staring down the bayonetted muzzle of a short Lee-Enfield with thirteen stone of overdressed Coldstreamer behind it.

'Halt!' the guardsman barked. 'Who goes?'

Who indeed? wondered Lestrade. Another of life's little imponderables.

'I'm Mr Lister,' he tried the old alias, 'Sir Eustace Bishop's new assistant as Keeper of the Royal Art. Is Sir Eustace in?'

'Where's your pass?' the sentry demanded.

Lestrade fumbled in various pockets. He wasn't sure his four-inch switchblade would be much of a match for the seventeen-inch bayonet facing him. And he could give the Coldstreamer forty years. Anyway, what about the hundred or so nosey admirers whose faces pressed to the wrought iron to his left? No doubt Inspector Blevvins would have demolished a wall to get in, but Lestrade had to have recourse to subtler methods.

'Damn,' he tutted, 'it's in my other suit. If you'll point me in the direction of Sir Eustace, I'm sure I can find him.'

'This is the Royal Residence of the King-Emperor,' said the sentry, affronted by Lestrade's impudence, but lowering his rifle nonetheless. 'I can't have you wanderin' about. How do I know you aren't workin' for the Indian National Congress?'

'Do I look like a fakir?' Lestrade pointed to the Donegal, the bowler hat.

'Look, mate, what you do in your spare time is up to you. And at your age, they should give you a bleedin' medal.'

'I've got one,' said Lestrade and showed the guard the gold-and-enamelled cross with the crown above it, the one he'd told Fanny he couldn't find. He hoped it would give him *some* kind of credence. 'Given to me personally by His late Majesty Edward VII, who was also a King-Emperor, I believe.'

'Blimey!' The guard brought his rifle butt sharply down on the gravel and saluted. 'Sorry, sir. I had no idea. I can take you as far as the door. A hequerrry will show you to the Picture Gallery.'

Lestrade nodded, grateful that the fringe of the bearskin or a lack of intellect had prevented the Coldstreamer from reading his real name on the back of the Order of Merit, and trudged through the weak February sunshine where a gaunt fellow in tails took him through endless corridors of power until they came to a vast, panelled room. Here, somewhat tiny in the one hundred and eighty foot chamber, he waited, while heavy, rheumy-eyed ladies of the eighteenth century looked down at him. A good painting, he knew from Mr Alma-Tadema, was one where the subject's eyes followed you around the room. All these dutifully did, obviously suspicious lest someone as obviously disreputable as Lestrade should nick something.

'Watteau!' a voice called from the far end of the gallery.

'Good afternoon,' Lestrade replied.

'Mr . . . Lister?'

'The same,' lied Lestrade. 'Sir Eustace Bishop?'

'Even so. Look, my dear chap, there seems to be some mistake. I already have four assistants. There's really no space for any more. If it's a post you're after, how about public hangman? The pay's not marvellous, I believe, but there must be lashings of job satisfaction.'

Lestrade took in his man at a glance. The wrong side of sixty, like himself, with a shock of white hair and an aquiline nose. His suit was sober enough, but his waistcoat, of twisted silk, shrieked loudly of the art deco movement – the last lecture Lestrade had attended at the Yard before he had resigned.

'Oh, I already have a job,' said Lestrade.

'Then . . .'

'Sir Eustace. This room is rather . . . large. If there is anywhere a little more private?'

'Who are you, sir?' Bishop's eyes narrowed a little and his long, elegant fingers strayed to the bell-pull on his left. 'I fear I must call security.'

'I'd rather you didn't, sir,' said Lestrade a little too loudly. His wife's Uncle Gideon was prone to shouting out meaningless words. It jarred rather. 'I apologize for the rather weak subterfuge, but a man is dead.'

Bishop straightened. 'You're not a Jehovah's Witness, are you?' he said. 'Because I warn you, I am a Church of England Sixth Dan. You argue theology with me at your peril.'

'No, no,' said Lestrade, whispering. 'I am from Scotland Yard.'

'Ah,' Bishop's voice dropped a semi-cope as well, 'your Mr Quinn has already been.'

'I know, sir,' Lestrade bluffed, 'but it's a little policy of ours in the Branch. Tell me, did you find Sir Patrick a little rude? Brusque, even? Perhaps bordering on the offensive?'

'Well, I . . .'

'Deliberate policy. Look, do you mind if we sit down? It's a long walk down the hill.'

'Yes, not the mention wading through the goose-shit, eh? My dear fellow, be my guest. You were saying . . .?'

Lestrade sank gratefully on to the cold mahogany. The Dutch master above him clearly disapproved. 'I was?'

'Deliberate policy.'

'Ah, yes. The human mind is a wonderful thing, isn't it?'

'Indeed,' nodded Bishop. 'Can I offer you a drink?'

In this huge, marbled hall, Lestrade could see no sign of refreshment at all. 'Well, thank you, yes . . .'

Bishop clicked a switch on the circular table at which they sat and a door swung open, catching Lestrade's shins a nasty one. 'Oh, sorry,' said the Keeper of Paintings. 'Scotch?'

'Just a tincture.'

'. . . Or are you on duty?'

'Ah, we're exempt in Special Branch.'

He poured for them both. 'So,' he slipped the decanter away again, 'deliberate policy. Human mind.' Bishop was a little terrier when it came to conversation.

'The human mind,' said Lestrade, warming to his theme as the Scotch hit his rocks. 'In that something you'd forgotten yesterday, you might remember today.'

'Shrewd,' nodded Bishop.

'And deliberate policy in that Paddy . . . Sir Patrick . . . always plays the nasty policeman. And I always play the nice policeman.'

'Yes,' Bishop patted Lestrade's knee, a little too appreciatively perhaps, 'yes, I can see you do.'

Lestrade's smile faded. Was Sir Eustace just being friendly or was he 'not as other Keepers of the King's Paintings'? A stone perhaps best left unturned.

'So,' Bishop refilled Lestrade's glass, the ex-Superintendent being careful to move his shins this time, 'it's probably not Mr Lister?' he beamed.

'Ahah!' Lestrade tried to make his titter as manly as possible. 'you don't miss much, Sir Eustace. Actually, it's Blevvins. Inspector Blevvins.'

'No relation to the animal who broke the nose of the journalist William Stead a few years ago?'

Lestrade remembered that. 'No,' he said. 'Now, about Monsieur Euperry . . .'

'Ah, yes.' Sir Eustace produced a huge monogrammed handkerchief and blew into it so that the dust rose in clouds from the Vermeers. '*Pauvre* Jean-Cocteau. How tragic.'

'You knew him well?'

Bishop's eyelids flickered once or twice. 'Let's just say we had mutual interests. I hadn't seen him for some time. Not since the early months of the War.'

'He was a translator, I believe.'

'Yes, that's right. Except . . .'

'Except?'

The eyelids flickered again. 'Except that I knew him in his capacity as a lover . . . er . . . of art.'

'Quite. When did you see him last?'

'Last Tuesday. The eighth. We had lunch with Lapotaire, the Belgian Ambassador.'

'Was there anything in the conversation that you found odd?'

'I found nothing odd about Jean-Cocteau, Mr Blevvins.'

'No, no, indeed,' said Lestrade quickly. 'I meant anything which may have a bearing on his death only, what . . . four days later?'

Bishop frowned, sucking the whisky in his teeth. 'No, I don't . . . oh, wait a minute. There was something odd. He asked about the *Gioconda*.'

'He knew him?' Lestrade double checked.

'Who?'

'Monsieur Euperry.'

'Yes. Knew who?'

'The *Gioconda*.'

'Mr Blevvins,' Sir Eustace knew a philistine when he saw one, 'the *Gioconda* is the *Mona Lisa*. It's a famous painting.'

'Ah, *the Gioconda*,' Lestrade clicked his tongue, 'I thought you meant . . . the other thing. Why was that odd? Do you have it here?'

'Er . . . no,' Bishop had already decided not to offer any more whisky. 'It's in the Louvre. That's a museum in Paris. But Jean-Cocteau seemed more interested in how it was stolen.'

'It was stolen?'

'Lord, yes. Back in 1913. They got it back intact. And the chappie who did it.'

'Was Monsieur Euperry interested in art theft?'

85

'No. He was interested in art.'

'For art's sake, of course.'

'Of course.'

Lestrade shifted in his chair so that he was out of reach of the Keeper of the King's Paintings. 'Can you think of anyone who disliked Monsieur Euperry?'

'Enough to kill him, no. Oh, he was petulant sometimes, pouting, silly. His nervous giggle could empty entire salons, but what kind of monster would put a bullet in his back?'

'The same kind of monster who was probably aiming for his head.' Lestrade remembered the other victims.

'Appalling,' shuddered Bishop, 'simply appalling. Is there anything else?'

'I think not, sir,' Lestrade rose, only to be held too close for his liking in an artistic grip.

'Come round to my house in Arlington Mews at eight this evening. I have some little-known Beardsleys which I think will amuse you.'

Lestrade was about to explain that he had planned to wash his hair when a telephone rang from nowhere. Bishop flicked a switch and another door flung wide, cracking Lestrade's knee with unerring accuracy.

'Yes,' said Bishop into the receiver. 'Oh, very well,' he cupped his hand over the speaker. 'Mr Blevvins, I fear the von Herkomer has arrived.'

'It had to come,' nodded Lestrade solemnly.

'I wonder, could you see yourself out? Third corridor on your left, past the bust of Lord Salisbury and you can't miss it. *A bientôt.*'

And Lestrade backed out of the room.

What happened next wasn't really his fault. He had known Lord Salisbury, not well, it is true, but they were on mutually ignoring terms. It was Lestrade's misfortune that the noble Earl had not translated too well into bronze or alternatively, that Mr W. E. Forster, the Liberal who had gone to his grave with the shame of knowing that he had given the world Elementary Education, looked so much like him. So it was that Lestrade got the wrong party, in both senses of the word, and the wrong bust and found himself ascending some dark stairs. The twist to the left didn't suit him. Not since the altercation with Lord Combermere's boa constrictor in the 'Snakeskin Case' some years ago. The beast had certainly constricted his bowler, and, had there not been a God in Heaven, would have done much more.

So he gripped the handrope manfully and followed the corridor. Surely, this couldn't be right? He was going up. Logic and the prevailing draughts told him he should be going down. There was a door on his right. Perhaps this led to some more stairs or at least to a clear window from where he could get his bearings. Alas, he chose badly. He found himself facing, in the fog of a darkened room, a woman sitting upright with a mask over her face and her hands clasped across her breasts. She whipped off the mask and stared at the ominous silhouette in the doorway. Her scream made Lestrade bounce backwards and as he stretched out his hand to calm the terrified soul, a whole kingdom of lackeys fell on him and he remembered no more.

When he awoke, there was a sickening pain in his head and his vision swam. He took in the room. It was vaguely familiar, except for the blur. The hard, iron bedstead, the solid door with the tiny grille in the centre, towards the top, the brickwork painted an off-white. Slowly he became aware that his arms were folded around his body and his elongated sleeves stretched further to buckles and straps he could not reach. An iron shackle secured each leg to a corner of the bed so that movement, except a little roll to the left or right, was impossible. What perturbed him most was the balding little man with the suspicious moustache sitting in a chair nearby. And because of his vision, there appeared to be two of him.

'Paddy, me boy,' Lestrade said and his head reverberated like an empty basket.

'That's Sir Patrick to you, Lestrade,' Quinn said.

'Yes, of course. May I be among the last to congratulate you. Where are we, the Tower?'

'Sadly, no. If that place still doubled as a jail, believe me, I'd throw you in the darkest dungeon and lose the key.'

'Well, better that than your sense of humour. Isn't it in this sort of situation that I'm supposed to ask what happened?'

Quinn looked at him with undisguised venom. 'I always had my doubts about you, Lestrade. The lucky breaks, the rapid promotion and as for that ludicrous gesture over the mutineers . . .'

'Strikers,' Lestrade corrected him.

'If a Bradford boiler-maker downs tools, that's a strike. If a Metropolitan policeman hangs up his helmet, that's mutiny.'

'I could argue semitics with you all night, Paddy. The fact is they made a scapegoat out of Edward Henry. I thought someone should go with him, that's all.'

'And who's "they", Lestrade? Hmm? I'll tell you. "They" are our political masters. The very government of the very country that you and I swore to protect and defend – remember? "I, being appointed . . . blah, blah, blah . . . do solemnly, sincerely and truly declare and affirm that I will well and truly secure our Sovereign Lord the King in the Office of Constable . . . blah, blah."'

'Forgive me, Paddy, I'm not feeling very patriotic at the moment.'

'I should damn well think not. It's not many sixty-nine-year old men who find themselves in the bedroom of the Queen of England.'

'The . . . oh, God.'

'I wouldn't appeal to Him, Lestrade. The only one to have His ear is my boss, Sir Basil Thomson. When we heard about this he told me to come down here and shoot you. The Press will have a field-day. "Maniac at Palace", "Embittered Ex-Policeman Exposes Self to Queen Mary". God, I *ought* to shoot you; Thomson's right.'

'Exposes himself? How dare you! Oh, in the past, I'll grant you, there were some unfortunate incidents. That business with the killer corset at Miss Thingummy's, but (a) I had no idea whose bedroom it was, or indeed that it was a bedroom and (b) I remained fully clothed, at least while I was conscious, that is. What fell on me?'

'Three equerries of the Royal Household fell on you. I understand the bruise on your left temple was caused by a mis-timed kick from one of my boys on duty in the Palace.'

Lestrade was suddenly aware of it, throbbing above his eyebrow ridge. 'Mis-timed?' he winced.

'Yes. He had orders to kick your head off.'

'Wait a minute,' said Lestrade, 'it was the middle of the day.'

'So?'

'So what was Queen Mary doing in bed in the middle of the day?'

'She had one of her heads,' Quinn told him. 'She was resting. The last thing the old duck expected was a pervert . . .'

'Paddy, I believe I have the right to call my lawyer.'

'You haven't got a lawyer . . . have you?'

'It'll cost you tuppence to find out,' Lestrade said. 'In the meantime, this is not the most comfortable of positions.'

'I'll unbuckle you, Lestrade, when you tell me what the bloody hell you were doing wandering around Buckingham Palace in the first place. And if you tell me you'd come to read the meter, I'll have you hanged.'

'All right, Paddy. It's a fair cop. I'm working on a case.'

'Lestrade,' Quinn was exasperated, 'you resigned from the Force six months ago.'

'Nearly eight,' Lestrade corrected him.

'Right. And I heard the Commissioner himself tell all ranks that your name was never to be spoken of again in his hearing and that if you so much as put your sawn-off nose around the door at the Yard, he'd throw the book at you.'

'I believe that's the gist of what he said, yes.'

'Then how can you have the brass neck to tell me that you're on a case?' Quinn screamed.

'In my capacity as a private detective,' Lestrade said.

'As a . . .' Quinn looked pole-axed. Then he let his head drop into his hands. 'God, tell me this isn't so.'

'I'm afraid it is, Paddy. I have a client.'

'Who?'

'Haha,' Lestrade shook his head, clicking his tongue. 'Secret of the confessional, that. As a good broth of an Irish boy, you ought to understand.'

'No client and no detective, private or public, has the right to wander through a Royal Residence without the *express* permission of Special Branch. And then only under close and armed scrutiny.'

'Sorry, Paddy,' Lestrade beamed, 'I'll remember to ask next time.'

'Next time!' Quinn roared, springing to his feet. 'If your story had been remotely plausible, Lestrade, I might have unbuckled you, at least a notch. As it is, you can damn well stay there like that until morning.'

'Wait a minute,' said Lestrade as the Superintendent of Special Branch made for the door. 'I'm bursting for a pee. I need a Policeman's Friend.'

Quinn turned back to him. 'You should know by now,' he said darkly, 'policemen don't have any friends.'

And he slammed the door.

Lestrade waited in the near darkness with only the light from the grille for company. Then that too was slammed shut.

'By the way,' he shouted, 'I'm only sixty-five. You've got that wrong as well, Paddy!'

5

The two men sat in the Greasy Chip Café a little after breakfast time. One had the look of a man whose police expenses, frugal though they were, could extend much further if he really tried. The other bore all the hallmarks of having spent the night in a strait-jacket.

'So how did you get out?' John Kane asked.

'Well, I'd like to tell you my middle name is Houdini,' said Lestrade, tucking into his saveloy with relish (well, it was all included in the price), 'but I'd be being economical with the truth. In fact, good old Fred Wensley pulled some strings.'

'I thought being found in the Queen's bedroom was a treasonable offence, guv'nor.' Kane adeptly crushed the third cockroach of the morning under his size nines.

'So it is. So it is. But the old girl's husband and I go back a long way. And I had done a few favours for his dad over the years, so I was bound over.'

'Friendly magistrate?'

'No. I mean I was bound over the bed and thrashed black and blue. I'll have to see the magistrate tomorrow.'

'Any bail?'

'Why do you think I'm eating here? If I'd gone within a hundred yards of the Grand, they'd have lifted me and my wallet. Anyway, there's too much damned cutlery at the Grand. I get confused. What happened at the War Office?'

'Ah,' Kane emptied his hip flask into Lestrade's tea, 'I had hoped to spare you this, Sholto.'

Lestrade groaned. Not many people spared a copper these days, ex- or otherwise.

91

'Well if I was to tell you that the investigating officer was one Edward Absinthe Blevvins . . .'

Lestrade groaned again. 'Absinthe doesn't make the heart grow fonder, it's true. Tell me.'

'Well, needless to say, I couldn't get a word out of him. Luckily he attends truncheon practice with Norroy Macclesfield.'

'Good man, Norroy?'

'Shaping up nicely,' Kane nodded. 'For some reason, Blevvins takes to Norroy.'

'Perhaps it's the way both their knuckles drag on the ground?'

'Yes, that might be it. But Norroy has had to cultivate that. He wasn't taught it at Manchester Grammar, you know.'

'Whereas with Blevvins it just comes naturally?'

'Yes. Anyway, while they're marching up and down the assault course, thumping seven bells out of the tailors' dummies with "Striker" written on them, old Blevvins becomes quite loquacious.'

'But does he say anything?' Lestrade asked in all seriousness.

Kane looked at the older man oddly – an expression he had often used. 'If Norroy got it right, the thing went something like this. Fred Wensley told Blevvins he'd got the Paul Dacres' suicide wrong . . .'

'That was his first mistake,' grunted Lestrade.

'So Blevvins goes back to the Cedar Hotel and causes forty-three pounds worth of damage tearing up the room for clues.'

'What did he find?'

'A rather embarrassed young couple in bed together.'

'Married?'

'Yes, they both were. But to two different women.'

Lestrade could see it all. He buried his face in his hands. 'So Blevvins . . .'

'. . . Had a field day. One broken jaw and suspected spinal damage.'

'Caused by falling downstairs?'

'Exactly.'

'And then?'

'Then, working on your assumption that Dacres was murdered, Blevvins leaves no stone unturned by going to his former employers.'

'The Royal Air Force?'

'The same.'

'I don't want to hear this.'

'A Warrant Officer, Second Class, confined to a wheelchair for three weeks. One wind-tunnel out of commission for the foreseeable future.'

'And after lunch?'

'Well, by this time, the trail of havoc was a little obvious, even for Blevvins. Wensley got to hear of it – wrongful arrest, overzealous questioning, the usual thing – and slapped dear old Ned's wrists.'

'So at the War Office. . .?'

'. . . He was sweetness and light. He demanded to see the Permanent Under-Secretary who was unavailable. So he had a go at the Financial Secretary, who needless to say had never heard of Captain Paul Dacres. So in exasperation he tried the Quartermaster General.'

'And?'

'There was a slight misunderstanding. Blevvins told him where he could stuff his bloody tents.'

'Somewhere physically impossible, no doubt.'

Kane thought for a moment. 'If I remember my "Rectal Possibilities for Policemen", yes, you're right.'

'So in short?'

'In short, no officer from Scotland Yard is allowed over the War Office's threshold unless there's a Z in the day and the Chief of the Imperial General Staff is going to sue Blevvins personally.'

'Oh, shame,' tutted Lestrade.

'Probably makes no difference,' said Kane. 'They couldn't tell us any more than we know, could they?'

'I don't know, John,' Lestrade cleared his plate and leaned back. 'All I know is that Paul Dacres didn't have quite the War he said he did.'

'Really?'

'For instance, his foot wound.'

'A Blighty?'

'Yes, but not so much as a scratch.'

'Oh?'

'Now you tell me how that was possible. I know the military were stretched to breaking-point and army doctors have never been quite the ticket, but even they can tell a bullet wound from a piece of skin presumably.'

'What are you saying, guv?' Kane was craning forward.

'I am saying that Captain Paul Dacres volunteered in September 1914 – the Twelfth Lancers. He was gazetted to the Royal Flying Corps the following year. And then he left the Front for several months. He wasn't really wounded and there was no talk of a nervous breakdown. Then he went back, back to the RFC in January 1917, and simply vanished. He just flew into the sun one day.' Lestrade put down his cup. 'And I want the answer to two questions, John. First, I want to know where Paul was for those months when he was recuperating from the wound he never received. I think the War Office can tell us that.'

Kane nodded. 'And the second question?' he asked.

'I want to know who that bloke is out there.' He glanced at the shabby figure with the pet dog and the stall saying "Please give generously, ex-serviceman with wife and four children" standing across the road from the café in the freezing drizzle of that mid-February.

'That copper?' asked Kane.

'Yes, that's him.'

'Name of Marks. Special Branch.'

'All right. I've got a third question. Who's he following? You or me?'

'No, Sholto,' Fanny put down her sewing, 'it's just not safe.'

'It's the War Office for God's sake,' he told her. 'They were on our side in the last War – at least for most of it.'

'I just don't like the sound of it. That's all.'

'Let me go,' a voice said from the corner. Lestrade spun round, expecting to see Uncle Gideon in one of his frisky moods, but he'd already gone to bed with his packet of Peek Frean's, the ones he dunked into the glass of water on the bedside cabinet, the glass with his teeth. It was just Emma. His Emma. The one he'd carried all those years ago to Bandicoot Hall. He'd stood under the spreading elms in the rain, looking at Harry and Letitia. His Sarah was barely cold. He had a daughter, three weeks old and he was an Inspector of the Metropolitan Police. What could he do? Where could he turn? Numb with the pain of death, he had bundled the helpless thing into his Gladstone and caught a train.

Letitia was heavy with child herself, carrying the Bandicoot boys. She took one look at the bedraggled bundle and clutched it to her. And all four of them stood crying in the rain – Letitia and Harry Bandicoot, the Inspector and little Emma Lestrade.

'Out of the question,' he said, 'Fanny's right.'

She crossed the room to him, reading his mind as she always did. 'I'm not a baby any more, Daddy,' she said. 'I shall be twenty-eight next birthday. If Paul . . . were alive today, I'd have babies of my own. Someone killed him. I want to know who. And I want to know why.' She looked at him hard. He did the same. The steady grey eyes, fierce, flashing. Just like her mother.

'Besides,' she said, 'I don't wish to be personal, but do you really think they'd take you on at the War Office? How's your typing speed?'

'Emma's right, Sholto,' Fanny said.

'You were just telling me how dangerous it was,' he rounded on her, sensing conspiracy.

'Since when has that stopped the Lestrades?' Emma demanded. 'They're crying out for staff at the moment. I'll offer my services.'

'How's *your* typing speed?' Lestrade countered.

Emma sat on the edge of an armchair and crossed one leg languidly over the other so that her skirt fell away. 'I don't think we're going to worry about a little thing like that, do you?'

'Emma!' Fanny and her husband chorused.

'This is 1920,' she laughed. 'If Oxford University can give us women degrees, I'm damned sure the War Office can give us a job.'

It was the first day of March when they found the next one. He was floating with the ebb-tide off Limehouse Pier and as such became the responsibility of the River Police, based at Wapping. It was a bobby who found him. PC 453R Wallace, taken short on his early-morning beat, had crept down Fanmet Street to the water's edge to add his three-quarters of a pint to the volume of Father Thames. A drop in the ocean really. It was the hand he saw first, the left arm held upright and rigid, the fingers clawing the leaden sky. In the dawn's light, the constable had seen the dull, dead eyes staring at him and he saw the body roll and bob with the swell. He found a grappling hook minding its own business and hauled him in. There was a mist creeping over the river as the crane lights winked and nodded in the distance. The constable lashed the swollen swimmer to an iron ring embedded in the wall and blew loudly on his whistle.

So it was that the cadaver lay by lunchtime in the Rotherhithe Street Morgue, the arm still upright. And on it rested the bowler hat of Sholto Lestrade.

'I want it understood, Lestrade,' the large, uniformed man was saying, 'that you have not seen this body. Neither have you seen me. Neither have I clapped eyes on you since you left the Yard.'

'Nod's as good as a wink to a blind horse, Mungo,' Lestrade said. 'What do you make of this?'

'Gorgonzola, I think,' he said, peering carefully.

'Not your sandwiches, Superintendent. Could we stay on an even keel?'

'Ah, the corpse. Well, he's a real swell, isn't he?'

Lestrade could see that. The dark hair was plastered with the river mud across his face. The features were the colour of old leather, swollen with the effects of the water into a hideous balloon. It looked as though the dead man were trying to whistle, only his pea had long since fallen out.

'You're the expert,' Lestrade said through clenched teeth, and such comments cost him dear. 'How long has he been in the water?'

Mungo Hyde squatted to the best of his ability so that he was level with the cadaver's hip. He appeared to be sniffing, but it was doubtful whether he could pick up much over the gorgonzola. 'A couple of days. Perhaps three.'

'Let's say three, shall we?'

Hyde didn't really see why he should. After all, he and Lestrade had never exactly seen eye to eye when the ferrety old bastard had been on the Force. Now he was doing him a favour just talking to him.

'That would make it Monday.' Lestrade was talking to himself. 'I have to concede, my dear Mungo, that you are more familiar with river deaths than I am, but shouldn't he be rather more bashed about?'

'Yes,' Hyde pontificated, straightening with some difficulty, 'there seems to be some bruising about the shoulders. Oh, and he's got a finger missing.'

'Not recently.' Lestrade peered at the stub. 'That's an old injury. Come on, Mungo, give me the benefit of your years of service.'

Hyde's lips twisted into a scowl. He had no reason to be helpful, but, like royalty, he liked trowelsful of flattery and he fell for it. 'Well. Try this scenario,' he said, concentrating hard.

'Er . . . that's Sholto,' Lestrade corrected him.

'Judging by the state of the body, he went in somewhere around Tower Wharf. Most of this bruising would have been caused by hitting the buttresses at Cheny Gardens Pier or possibly Shadwell Entrance.'

'From upstream?'

'Yes. But the tide does peculiar things this far down. The Isle of Dogs is a grey area. He could have been carried up.'

'So he went in downstream?'

'Possibly. And if so, somewhere around Bugsby's Reach or Angerstein Wharf. And yet . . .'

'Yet?' Lestrade had crossed to the wall-map of the river in Superintendent Hyde's morgue. The perimeters of the possible falling-in place gave Lestrade a vast acreage of London to contend with. And the thing about rivers is that they usually have two banks.

'Yet for both of those, he looks too damned good.' Hyde produced a pipe from his pocket and tapped its contents out on the elbow of the dead man. 'What about this arm, Lestrade?' he asked. 'The rest of him's as soft as a jellyfish. Why is this arm rigid?'

'We'd have to ask Bernard Spilsbury that,' the ex-Superintendent told him, 'but I've got a rough idea.'

'What?' .

'Uh-huh,' Lestrade shook his head and collected his bowler. 'You're not happy,' he observed. 'You tell me, if he didn't float up or down, where did he come from?'

Mungo Hyde waddled across to the map. 'From the nearest large body of water,' he said, tapping the wall-map. 'From the basin of the West India Docks.'

'Wouldn't he have been spotted earlier there?' Lestrade asked.

'Not necessarily,' the Head Bluebottle told him. 'It depends how many ships are in. If it's crowded, he could have bobbed around the anchor chains for weeks. Out of sight, out of mind.'

'And how would he have reached the river?'

'Through the sluices under Bridge Street. Or . . .'

'You're very cryptic this morning, Mungo.' Lestrade's patience, never an asset, was shortening in his old age. 'Or what?'

'Or he could have been carried.'

'Carried?'

'Look at the map. He could have been carried from almost any point at the Dock and through any of these Limehouse streets. Then – splash – and he's in. Another anonymous piece of flotsam of Old Father Thames.'

Lestrade produced a cigar and lit up. With Hyde's smog and his own, the stench from Flotsam on the slab was a little less. 'That presupposes two things,' he said.

'Oh?'

'What would you say Chummy here weighs?'

'Difficult to tell with all that swelling. Thirteen, fourteen stone?'

'Right. Not an easy bundle to carry along a Limehouse street. Not for one person, anyway. That means there must have been two men involved.'

'Two men?'

'Yes,' said Lestrade. 'The secondary suppository is that Chummy was murdered.'

'Where's your evidence?' Hyde asked.

'Would you grab his hair?'

With reluctance the Superintendent did so and hauled the corpse into a sitting position, his left arm pointing ahead in an accusatory fashion at the door.

'There,' said Lestrade. 'A neat little hole at the nape of the neck.'

'Well, I'll be blowed.' Hyde let go so that the body flopped back, the arm now making accusations against the ceiling, Lestrade's bowler still bobbing there. 'Why wasn't I told about this?'

'I don't know,' said Lestrade. 'Charlie Cadbury of "R" Division was, by his man Wallace. The constable noticed it straight off,' he beamed, and slapped Hyde's blubbery shoulder. 'You're slipping, Mungo. If you have a little dig around in that hole, you'll find a little piece of lead which used to be a bullet fired from a Webley .45.'

'Get away! How do you know all this?'

'Just a lucky guess,' said Lestrade, puffing anew on his cheroot. 'Do you have a list of the ships in the Docks at the moment, or, at least, three days ago?'

'Are you mad?' Hyde suddenly asked him.

'No,' said Lestrade. 'At least, not the last time I looked. Is there a problem?'

'You don't know Gerald Hobhouse then?'

'Hobhouse? No. Who's he?'

'Superintendent of the Dockyard Police.'

'New?'

'Since your time, I think. There's a rumour the French kicked him out of the Foreign Legion for being too nasty. Makes Ned Blevvins look like Edith Cavell.'

'But the Dockyard boys are being phased out, aren't they?'

'Precisely. That's what makes Hobhouse all the meaner. When he heard they were closing him down at the end of the year, he issued a memo to all his Division. It said "No more Mister Nice Bloke". He hasn't spoken to me for five months.'

'So much for inter-divisional co-operation.'

'Sorry,' mumbled Hyde, 'but you're on your own on this one.'

Lestrade smiled. What was new?

*

Superintendent Sir Patrick Quinn was just trying out his new niblick when Detective Constable Spencer arrived. The frost had gone, but there was still an 'F' in the month and the merciless wind of Balham reached the parts no beer could.

'This had better be important,' he snapped. 'I'm on the course with the Commissioner in half an hour.'

'Message from Constable Marks, sir,' Spencer said.

'Well?' Quinn crouched from his shot, twisting his hips like a snake.

'Inspector Kane met a man at the Greasy Chip Café, Bermondsey, sir.'

'So?' Quinn was concentrating on his swing. 'Where, apart from confirming the inspector's appalling lack of taste, does that leave us?'

'The man was ex-Superintendent Lestrade, sir.'

Quinn's shot sliced badly and a clod hit him square in the moustache. 'Lestrade?' he snarled. 'Why wasn't I told?'

'You have been, sir,' Spencer explained.

Quinn rounded on him. 'If there's anything I hate more than defrocked policemen who ought to be in a Home, it's insubordinate damned rookies! One more crack like that, Spencer, and it's Lost Property for you *and* a transfer to the Lincolnshire Constabulary to look for King John's jewels. He lost them in the Wash, you know.'

'Yessir.' Spencer stood to attention in the bunker.

'Did Marks pick up any conversation?'

'No, sir. He was too far away, sir.'

'Damn. All right, Spencer, what are you doing here, man? Get back to the job, dammit. Tell Marks to stay with Kane. You get on to Lestrade. There's something afoot here I don't care for.'

'Where will I find him, sir?' Spencer asked.

Quinn held his iron horizontally under the young man's chin so that the steel caressed his Adam's apple. 'Are you or are you not a member of Special Branch?'

'Yessir,' Spencer assured him.

'Then behave like it! I realize that Lestrade's file has been expunged from the Yard, but he's in Surrey, somewhere.'

'Right, sir,' Spencer nodded. 'Er . . . any idea where?'

'Good God, man, there are only so many thousand people living in Surrey. Do I have to do everything?'

Spencer all but saluted and hurried away.

Quinn returned to his niblick, his knuckles white on the shaft. 'Lestrade,' he muttered, and bent the thing around a tree.

Lestrade remembered the headquarters of the Dockyard Police from the days when old Chief Inspector Biddle was the incumbent. It had changed now. The old horsehair sofa had been replaced by hideous government-surplus upright furniture and not so much as a whisker remained of the old man's eighteen cats. Little did Lestrade know that they were all floating in the river on the orders of Superintendent Gerald Hobhouse.

The officer of that name was on the telephone when Lestrade arrived that March afternoon, but the invention of Mr Bell was fairly superfluous. Whoever Hobhouse was talking to could have heard him without it.

'Rubbish!' the Superintendent was shouting. 'Search him again. A detailed, in-depth body search. We may have given the bastards the vote, but there is no such thing as a lady docker.' He slammed the receiver back. 'Who the hell are you?'

'Lister,' lied Lestrade. 'Port of London Authority.'

'Good God,' Hobhouse muttered. 'What age do you blokes retire?'

'Forty-five,' smiled Lestrade. 'I can't wait, I can tell you.'

Hobhouse looked at him oddly. 'Well,' he said, 'what do you want? I'm a busy man.'

Lestrade noticed the kepi of the French Foreign Legion on the wall above a lithograph of what appeared to be a bearded lady – obviously Mrs Hobhouse. 'Routine check,' he said. 'Ships in the West India Docks at the moment. As of . . . Monday, February 27th.'

Hobhouse clumped across to a filing cabinet, painted regulation green. 'Bloody red-tape,' he growled. 'Haven't you blokes got your own lists?'

'Yes, of course,' said Lestrade. 'New instructions, though. Check and double check, you know how it is.'

'Bloody right I do,' Hobhouse snarled. 'I hope you're going to check and double check with that old bastard Hyde.'

'Superintendent Hyde of the River Police?'

'That's the old bastard in question,' Hobhouse told him.

'Do I get the impression you don't care for Mungo, Gerry?' Lestrade asked.

The big man turned with the grace of a Zeppelin. 'That's Mr Hobhouse to you,' he growled. 'You're an astute little bugger and no mistake.'

'No,' said Lestrade. 'My instructions don't run to the river. May I?'

Hobhouse threw the sheet of paper at Lestrade. 'So there are six in at the moment?' he asked.

'That's what it says, isn't it?' Hobhouse sat back at his desk, his feet crossed on the scarred surface.

'But only one that's been in for the past three days?'

'That's right,' Hobhouse humoured him. He'd never seen senility in a man under forty-five before. 'All the others came in yesterday.'

'The SS *Motley*,' Lestrade read, 'from Archangel. This name here . . .' He pointed to the sheet.

'That's the Master, Captain Reynolds. Look here, are you sure you're from the Port Authority?'

'That's what it said on the door when I left the office this afternoon,' Lestrade smiled.

'Oh, I get it,' grinned Hobhouse. 'You're checking and double checking on *me*, aren't you?'

Lestrade smiled.

'Well, you can piss off out now, Lister. This is the Metropolitan Police. I'm not answerable to you. I've got another nine months in this bloody job and no faceless bloody civil servant is going to give *me* the runaround. Get out.'

Lestrade tipped his bowler. 'You've been very gracious, Gerry . . . er, Mr Hobhouse. Thank you for your time.'

'That's it there, sir,' the rating told Lestrade.

'That dirty British coaster?' Lestrade asked.

'Yes, that's the one; with the salt-caked smoke stack.'

'How did it get all that corrosion?'

The rating shrugged. 'Must be all that butting through the Channel,' he said. 'It's particularly bad in March. I'll take you up, sir. Captain Reynolds is expecting you.'

He followed the lad up a rickety gangplank that swayed under his feet. It was eight years since he had done this and then he was climbing aboard the White Star's *Titanic* on her ill-fated maiden voyage. He had unhappy memories of that trip. He had fallen off in Southampton Water and only the extraordinary biceps of Harry Bandicoot had saved him from the undertow. His knuckles tightened on the ropes now, just in case.

Captain Reynolds was everything Lestrade expected of a Master of a merchantman in what was still the biggest navy in the world – powerful, bearded, dark, drunk.

'Scotland Yard?' Reynolds tried to make his eyes focus in the gloom of his cabin.

'Routine inquiries,' said Lestrade. 'I'd like some details about your ship.'

'Vessel,' Reynolds correct him. 'Drink?'

'Occasionally,' Lestrade confessed.

'Ah, of course,' Reynolds poured from a flat-bottomed decanter for himself, 'you blokes don't on duty, do you?'

'On duty?' said Lestrade. 'Never,' and held out another of Reynolds's glasses.

His eyes steamed, then watered when he sampled the contents. 'What is this?' he managed to whisper.

'Vodka,' Reynolds told him. 'It looks like water. It smells like water. And it's got the kick of a donkey.'

Lestrade could only nod in agreement.

'Here's my manifest,' Reynolds said. Lestrade didn't really want to know the captain's personal problems until he realized it was only a list of his cargo.

'So you've come from Archangel?' Lestrade said. 'Let me see, that's . . .' and he hastily tried to summon up memories of the 'Geography for Policemen' lecture he had attended back in 1893.

'Damn near frozen over at this time of the year. I was lucky to get out.'

'Yes,' said Lestrade, 'but where . . .?'

'Russia,' Reynolds said, sensing the dilemma of a man who

103

had never been further east than Dungeness, 'or whatever the Bolshies are calling it now. What is it? Union of Socialist Sovereigns or something? Not my business, politics. Don't understand it.'

'The Russians still trade with us, then?' Lestrade felt his mouth shrivel as he took a second sip from the glass.

'Lord, yes. Desperate for roubles, you see. If they don't go on trading with us Capitalist, Imperialist bastards, who *are* they going to trade with?'

'The Americans?' suggested Lestrade, whose grasp of such things was hazier than Reynolds's. 'Tell me,' he tried to focus on the sheet in front of him, 'is this your crew?'

'That's right. Fourteen of 'em.'

'Thirteen,' said Lestrade.

'Eh?'

'I have reason to believe that one of them was fished out of the Thames early this morning.'

'Good God.'

'Are they on board now?'

'No. They're on leave. There's only me and Ibbotson, the First Mate.'

Lestrade perused the list again. 'How well do you know these men? Have they sailed with you before?'

'All of them,' said Reynolds, 'except Varushkin.'

'Varushkin?'

'He signed on in Archangel. Between you and me, he wasn't very good.'

'No?'

'Didn't seem to know the sharp end from the blunt end.'

'Tell me,' said Lestrade, 'do new crew members have to sign something, when they join?'

'All crew members do. New or not. For each voyage.'

'Did you witness Varushkin's signing?'

'Oh, yes,' Reynolds assured him, 'it's regulations.'

'Do you remember,' Lestrade edged forward, 'was he right- or left-handed?'

'Right,' said Reynolds.

Lestrade frowned. 'You seem very sure,' he said. 'Why is that?'

'Because the index finger of his right hand is missing,' Reynolds said, topping up their glasses.

Lestrade leaned back in his chair. 'Captain Reynolds, if I weren't the worse for drink, I'd kiss you.'

'So how did you get on with the *Motley*, Daddy?' Emma asked, helping Madison with the weeding.

Lestrade lolled in the sun that promised an early spring. 'I think we're a little further forward,' he told her.

'Go on,' she dabbed her cheek with soil in an attempt to keep the hair out of her eyes. 'I don't know, Madison,' she surveyed the little plot – rather like a de Vere Stacpoole novel, really – 'I think I'd rather have a square garden.'

'Well,' Lestrade tilted back his ancient boater and watched the daffodils nod in the breeze, 'all the *Motley* crew were British, except Sergei Varushkin. He was Russian.'

Emma raised her eyebrows. Not for all the world would she have said anything at that moment.

'Captain Reynolds was very accommodating. After the third vodka he gave me a guided tour of the ship. I've never seen so many rats in my life and they showed no signs of deserting. He brought his decanter with him and after the fourth drink, he told me his life story.'

'Interesting?'

'I don't know. After elementary school he passed out on the floor.'

'Good heavens,' Emma frowned, recalling her training when she had driven ambulances during the War, 'he could have choked on his own vomit.'

'No. His First Mate kicked him over on to his side. He just flopped naturally into the recovery position and we left him snoring.'

'Did you find anything out, about Varushkin, I mean?'

'This.' Lestrade fished in his pocket and showed the contents to his daughter.

'What is it?' she asked, feeling cold metal and watching the sun flash on it.

'It's an icon,' he said. 'I called in to one of those bookshops in

Charing Cross Road. There was a picture of almost exactly the same thing in *Any Old Icon* by J. R. Hartley. It was made by some Frenchman. There's a little clip at the side.'

So there was. Emma pressed it and two little silver doors, exquisitely carved, sprang open to reveal a portrait of the Madonna and Child. 'Daddy, it's beautiful.'

'Not the sort of thing your average merchant seaman carries, I wouldn't have thought.'

'It must be worth a fortune. These are pearls, aren't they?'

'Looks like it.' Lestrade was not well up in jewellery. 'But are they reason enough for some swine to kill the man?'

'But you said . . . where did you find this?'

'In Varushkin's bunk. Sewn into the mattress lining. It was being guarded by an army of bedbugs.'

'So whoever killed him was looking for this. I can't help thinking, Daddy, that this has nothing to do with Paul.'

'You're forgetting two things, sweetheart,' he told her. 'Our friend Varushkin was shot in the back of the head, just like Fallabella Shaw and Monsieur Euperry. And Paul's letter to you was written on Russian stationery.'

'Of course.' She stopped digging.

'And I suspect that Mr Varushkin was no more a merchant seaman than you are.'

'Then what was he?'

'When I know that, I might be a step nearer to the murderer of Paul Dacres. Ibbotson of course was more useful.'

'Who?'

'Ibbotson. First Mate on the *Motley*. Apparently, the Russian was the last of the crew to go ashore.'

'Was he?'

'He was. And do you know what I think?'

'No.'

'I think he never left the *Motley*. At least not alive.'

'Oh?'

'He had a visitor shortly after the others left.'

'Anyone we know?'

'Not personally,' Lestrade told her, 'but I'm prepared to bet a packet of Uncle Gideon's Peek Freans that he's our murderer.'

106

'Did Ibbotson give you a description?' Emma sat beside her father.

Lestrade laughed. 'Yes, a very good one. He was a little under six feet, had a full set, protruding teeth and a patch over his right eye. I even know his name and occupation. Commander Samson of Trinity House.'

'A pilot?'

'Correct.'

'Why should a pilot want to see a merchant seaman?'

'That's what I couldn't understand. Samson went down to Varushkin's cabin alone, spent about a quarter of an hour with him and left.'

'Did anyone see Varushkin afterwards?'

'Well, I did,' smiled Lestrade, 'not to mention Mungo Hyde and an observant constable named Wallace. Unfortunately, he was dead by that time and rather full of water.'

'But at least you've got a lot to go on with Samson.'

Lestrade looked at his daughter and shook his head. 'That's why we haven't any female detectives,' he sighed.

'Meaning?' she said, rather indignantly.

'Meaning that there is no one by the name of Commander Samson who is a pilot with Trinity House, not in the Port of London or anywhere else.'

'But the clear description . . .' she clung on desperately.

'Was a little too clear,' he told her. 'First rule of murder, my dear – A for Anonymity. Your clever murderer, the kind who plans things, the one with malice aforesight, is as bland as that blade of grass.' He flicked it from her hair. 'It looks just like every other blade of grass. Such a man does not have a beard, buck teeth and an eyepatch.'

'At least we know it's a man,' she almost pouted.

'Well, what with the plague of the Spanish Lady and the Lost Generation, that does narrow the field down to only a few million.'

'What about the Russian connection, Daddy?'

'Ah,' he said, 'now I think there we're getting warmer. What time does your new job start tomorrow?'

'Nine o'clock,' she said. 'Madison will drive me to the station.'

'No, he won't,' Lestrade said, 'I will. If my girl is going into the lion's den, I want to be the one to take her there.'

'Thanks, Dad.' She looked at him oddly. 'I knew I could rely on you.'

'So *you're* the new girl?'

Emma Lestrade looked up from her typewriter and instantly recognized the reptilian approach of a lounge lizard.

'Good morning,' she smiled.

'Ravishing,' he said. 'Simply ravishing. Miss . . . er . . . It is Miss, isn't it? Because if it's not, I shall have to throw myself under the nearest tram.'

She looked at her watch. 'Oh, hurry. There's one due.'

'Hah!' His frozen grin never wavered for a moment. 'I'm Archie le Fanu. It's my tragic task to look after the new bugs around her. You must be Miss Lister.'

'Do I have to be?' she asked earnestly. 'I'm very busy.'

'I'm sure,' he beamed, 'but let me tear you away from your Buff Triplicates to show you around.'

'I'm not sure Major Publisher will want me to leave my post so soon.'

'Nonsense,' he held her wooden swivel back for her, 'you'll soon learn the galloping major's bark is infinitely worse than his bite. In fact,' he leaned closer to her, 'I happen to know he's under the thumb of a very domineering wife.'

She removed his hand from her shoulder. 'We're like that, we women. What did you want to show me?'

'Time for that later,' he smirked. 'Let's start with my office, shall we? Ordnance. It also has the best view of the Mall.'

'Very well,' Emma said, 'but I really cannot spare long, Mr le Fanu.'

'Archie,' he crawled.

'Archie. Have you been at the War Office long?'

'Five years or so,' he said.

'Are you a military man?'

'Lord no. Touch of vertigo kept me out of the last show – worse luck. Besides, the tunic does nothing for me. Too well hung, I suppose. Let me see, now, if I remember the roster correctly . . . it's Emma, isn't it?'

'Is it?' she said, and prised his fingers from her waist.

'This way,' and he led her up a flight of stairs. On the landing, he gallantly halted and allowed her to ascend first. Then stood there, smirking and twirling his neat little 'tache as he admired her calves. Much against Fanny's better judgement, Emma had put on her shortest dress.

'In my day,' her stepmother had told her, 'a glimpse of stocking was looked on as something shocking. Now – Heaven knows!'

'Look,' le Fanu said, 'a few of us bright young things are having a little rocking-horse party this weekend at Bayswater.' He opened an office door and let her in. 'Care to come?'

'I really don't know,' she said. 'I had planned to wash my hair.'

'Oh, come as you are.' le Fanu sat in his swivel. 'Oh dear, I seem to be rather short of chairs. And I feel a snatch of vertigo coming on, so I'd better not stand. Come and sit on my lap.'

'Mr le Fanu!' Emma was outraged.

'Archie,' he reminded her. The gap in his teeth was giving her the abdabs and any minute now she'd start screaming.

'Who'll be there?' she asked.

'Anyone who's anyone,' he said, flicking open a side cupboard with what was clearly an experienced hand. 'G and T?'

'No, thank you. Will Fallabella Shaw be there?'

'Who?' le Fanu poured for them both.

'Fallabella Shaw. I understood she worked here.'

'Er . . . oh yes. I remember her. Mannish lass. Hirsute legs. About fifty years too old for me, I fear.'

He patted his rather disreputable lap.

She sauntered to him. 'Which department is she with?'

'Adjutant-General's, I think,' he said, running his fingers up her bare arm. 'But I'm afraid she'd dead.'

'Oh, no,' Emma pulled away.

'Er . . . yes.' le Fanu rose sharply. 'Some time ago. Killed in an air raid. Rather a beastly business, I'm afraid. I say, Emma,' he looked at her in the sunlight from the window, 'you're certainly a bit of a cracker. Makes a chap quite hot under the collar.'

His lips snaked out towards her, but the ex-Superintendent's daughter was faster. At Monsieur le Petomaine's Academy in Geneva, she'd had years of practice avoiding the concierge. 'What about Paul Dacres?' she asked, perching on the corner of a far desk and crossing one delectable leg over another.

'Who?' le Fanu gulped, eyes bulging.

'Captain Dacres. I thought Fallabella spoke of someone of that name when I saw her last. Of course, I could have remembered it wrongly.'

'No, no.' He licked his lips as his hands hovered above her thigh. 'Paul Dacres. Yes. That's right. Old Fally was his secretary for a time. He wasn't here long.'

'In the Adjutant-General's department?'

'Yes. Look, Emma, a chap's only flesh and blood, you know. Couldn't I just . . .?'

She slapped his exploratory fingers. 'Who ran that department? When Fallabella and Captain Dacres were here?'

'You're deuced interested in those two,' le Fanu frowned. 'There are far more interesting topics of conversation. Like me for instance . . .' he closed to her, '. . . and you.'

She flounced off the desk. 'I'm just idly curious,' she said.

'Well, if you must know,' le Fanu, temporarily baulked of his prey, swigged hastily at his G and T, 'they were in some sort of Special Unit. There was a war on, remember. Their boss was Colonel Glass.'

'Still here?' She leaned forward so that her breasts jutted towards him.

'No,' he gulped again, 'retired. Gone gaga. Had a stroke a year ago. He's a vegetable now, I'm afraid.'

'Oh, dear,' she said, pulling back. He stood close to her again. 'What was this Special Unit called?'

He closed his eyes, inhaling her perfume. 'Don't tell me,' he said, 'Femme Fatale.'

'What?'

'Your perfume. It's Femme Fatale.'

'Similar,' she smiled. 'Actually it's called Sow on Heat. Quite pleasant, though.'

'Oh, Emma, Emma,' he squeezed her hand, 'you inflame a man's soul. Kiss me, you ravishing little vixen.'

'Uh-huh,' she held a hand to his lips. 'Not until you tell me what this Special Unit was called and where I can find Colonel Glass.'

'If I remember rightly,' he sighed with impatience, 'he's in Carshalton somewhere. And the Unit was called A.T. One.'

'A.T. One? What does that mean?'

'Now, that's enough,' he snapped. 'If I didn't know better, I'd swear you were some sort of bally female detective. Now,' he sat down, 'come and sit on this till it gets hard.'

'Whatever's this?' Her eyes widened as she glanced down. His pride turned to disappointment.

'It's a paperweight,' he said, following her gaze, 'made, as this is the Ordnance Department, as an exact-scale replica of a nine pounder gun of 1815. Waterloo and all that.'

He patted his lap again.

She smiled, weighing the gun in her hand. 'Isn't it heavy?' she purred, sliding her fingers up and down the barrel. 'And sharp.' And she suddenly swept it with unerring aim into the groin of Archie le Fanu. He howled, his eyes crossed and he clutched his two pounders with both hands.

'As you say, Mr le Fanu,' she paused in the doorway, 'only flesh and blood.'

6

The Wandle brook rose and bubbled in deepest Carshalton before it ran in all directions in search of the sea. Lestrade's quarry, The Oaks, stood like a fortress on high ground above Anne Boleyn's Well. On a clear day like this, with the sky a cloudless blue and the sun sharp on the vermilion japonica, you could see from the great octagonal room the melancholy sepulchres of Highgate and the grey woods of Hampstead, longing for their buds.

The detective and his daughter were shown from the gravel drive where Emma had parked the Lanchester and up a twisting stair to a low, sunlit room. At the far end, a rug across his knees, slumped to his left in a wheelchair, sat their host.

'Colonel Glass?' Lestrade asked.

No response.

'You'll have to speak up,' his man said. 'Since his stroke, the Colonel's left ear has gone completely.'

Lestrade crossed to the pathetic figure, the body sunk and hollow, the face an ashy grey. 'Colonel Glass,' he said again, 'I am from Scotland Yard.'

Slowly the face came up; the dull eyes flickered for a moment.

'Not one of his best days,' the colonel's man said. 'Perhaps if the young lady had a go? Always one for the ladies was the colonel.'

Lestrade looked at Emma and shrugged. She knelt before the paralysed knees and took the hand. She expected it to be cold, but it was as warm as hers. 'Colonel Glass?' she said softly. 'Can you hear me?'

He tried to focus on her hair, her eyes and she thought she

saw the ghost of a smile flutter on the long, lean face. But it was only a trick of the light, the dappling of the birch branches in the sunlight.

'How long has he been like this?' she asked the colonel's man.

'Best part of a year now, miss. Sometimes he'll nod "Hello". Shortly after Christmas I heard him chuckling to himself. But it's mostly useless, I'm afraid.'

'Is it just you, Warmby?' Lestrade asked. 'Are you all he has?'

'I'm afraid so, sir. I was his batman in the Great War, y'see. Oh, not this bit of argie-bargie that's just gone. The *really* Great War, with the Boers.'

Lestrade toyed for one devilish moment with introducing the colonel to Uncle Gideon, but it didn't really seem fair on the colonel.

'No Lady Glass?' Emma asked.

'Bless you, no, miss. Her Ladyship, God Rest her, succumbed to the plague of the Spanish Lady last year. The hinfluenze carried her off just after Christmas. I think it was that that unhinged the colonel here, speaking as I probably shouldn't oughta.'

Lestrade surveyed the vast barn of a place again. 'There must be a housekeeper,' he said, 'other servants.'

'No sir. Just me and the colonel. We get by. Now, sir, madam, I'm sorry the colonel couldn't help, but it's time for 'is mornin' nap. I wonder if you'd mind . . .'

'Of course,' said Lestrade, 'don't trouble, Warmby. We'll see ourselves out.'

'Thank you, sir,' and the colonel's man wrapped another rug around the colonel's shoulders and wheeled him away.

'Oh, Daddy,' Emma linked her arm through her father's, 'how sad. A big, powerful man like that reduced to a hulk.'

'Hmm,' Lestrade nodded. 'Promise me,' he said to her, 'if you see me going that way, you'll put a bullet through my brain.'

'Of course, Daddy,' she smiled, patting his hand reassuringly. 'If I can find it.'

He turned the wrong way at the bottom of the stairs and met the resistance of a locked door.

'No, Dad, over here,' she called, 'this is the way we came in.'

113

'Oh, yes,' he joined her on the sloping gravel where the ground fell away to the lawns and the peacocks swept silently past the fountains. 'That's obviously how Warmby does it. He keeps half the house locked up.'

'So we're no further to discovering the meaning of A.T. One.' Emma clambered aboard her father's car.

'Air Tribunal,' Lestrade tried it out for size. It didn't fit.

'Active Tutorial,' Emma countered. That made no sense at all.

'Absolute Tosh,' was Lestrade's riposte.

Emma pressed the ignition and her father risked serious dislocation by arm-wrestling with the crank handle. He hopped aboard and sat beside her. As they purred out of the grounds of The Oaks and through the high street, the sign of a swinging kettle caught Lestrade's eyes.

'Ah, yes,' he said and snatched the handbrake so that the Lanchester lurched to a halt, 'let's put our heads together over a brew.'

'Brick walls,' said Lestrade, listening to the crinkle of his cigar. 'Didn't I ever tell you about brick walls? All those years I should have been with you, helping you grow up.'

'Daddy,' she swiped him with her napkin, 'you have absolutely nothing to reproach yourself for. And just at the moment, I don't have the time to wallow waist-high in nostalgia. I'm out to get the man who killed Paul. Now, what do you mean about brick walls?'

'Hmm?' He watched the smoke curl to the low beams where the post-War Tudor timbers criss-crossed the ceiling. 'Ah, brick walls. You meet them anytime, anywhere. Just as you think you're getting somewhere – wham! You hit one.'

'And we have?'

He nodded ruefully. 'Is nobody talking at the War Office? Apart from this Archie le Fanny bloke.'

'Well, the Under Secretaries don't talk to the Private Secretaries and the Department heads don't talk to anybody. The only people in the building who are paid to talk are the telephonists and the only ones who do it voluntarily are the cleaners.'

'Ah, yes. Useful people, cleaners. I once solved the Hard Case entirely by talking to a cleaner.'

'Funnily enough,' she sampled her Chelsea bun, 'Mrs Coniston did have a few words to contribute to Fallabella Shaw.'

'Oh?'

'She was certainly Paul's secretary. I established that much. She said what a nice man he was . . .' She tried to smile, but her father knew tears when he saw them and he patted her hand. 'Anyway,' she sniffed, 'Fallabella was a very bright lady.'

'Presumably everybody was to Mrs Coniston?'

'Sholto Lestrade,' she boomed, 'you're just an old-fashioned snob.'

'What else?'

'Well, they were often closeted away for hours, burning the midnight oil in a little room overlooking Whitehall; Paul and Fallabella, that is.'

'A.T. One?' he checked.

'Presumably, but no one – *no one*, mark you – will confess to knowing what that means.'

'And that's it?'

'I'm afraid so,' she grimaced. 'I'm sorry, Daddy, it's not very good, is it?'

'Well, give it a day or two and if nothing else breaks, resign. What do you do, by the way?'

'Do? Daddy, I've signed the Official Secrets Act. I couldn't possibly tell you.'

'That's the trouble,' sighed Lestrade, being mother for the second time that day. 'The whole world is so full of secrets, little girl. And people are dying because of them.'

Norroy Macclesfield, Detective-Sergeant extraordinary, was not delighted to be called out so soon after daybreak. The truth was that he happened to live in that salubrious suburb of north London called Hampstead. Many and famous were the great men and women who had occupied that turf before him. John Keats and Fanny Braune made eyes at each other over a back fence in Well Walk; John Constable daubed his canvases down the road; Lord Mansfield snored away the hours of darkness,

115

dreaming of the wretches he had brought to the gallows; Spencer Perceval left from here the day they shot him in the House of Commons; the hawk-eyed William Pitt dashed from here to assure George II that only he could save England from the French and, curiously, the most cunning Frenchman of them all, old gammy-legged Talleyrand, hobbled his way around its streets too.

But the neighbourhood had certainly gone downhill. The Vale of Health now played host to crowds of holiday-makers at Whitsun and the August Bank Holiday. 'Appy 'Ampstead had become the playground of the riff-raff. Now they let policemen like Macclesfield live there and degenerates like D. H. Lawrence who called themselves writers and opened the door to the milkman with nothing on.

Macclesfield walked when he got the call from the local bobby, past the new houses of Hampstead Garden Suburb where the first sod had been cut on 4 May, fifteen years before. The same sod had been half-cut ever since.

The body lay half-covered by the gorse bushes below the elms and cedars that hedged round Jack Straw's Castle. The arms were thrown wide, the sandalled feet protruding beneath the striped burnous.

'A foreigner,' said Macclesfield, kneeling before the corpse. 'Who found him?'

'I did, sarge. I was comin' off duty and I says to meself "Hello," I says, "there's some silly bugger in fancy dress, sleeping it off." I reckoned he'd probably had a skinful up at the Castle.'

Macclesfield licked his finger in the cold of the morning and carefully drew it down the dead man's cheek. 'Not likely,' he said. 'Either this man is the best made-up Nigger Minstrel I've ever seen or he really is an Arab – in which case, a pint of Bertram's best is not likely to have passed his lips.'

'Not partial to beer, I suppose, the A-rabs,' nodded the constable.

'Not partial to alcohol at all,' said Macclesfield. 'They're teetotal.'

'Blimey!' The constable took off his helmet. 'No wonder they

116

wear frocks an' that. 'Ere, sarge, is there any truth about them and camels?'

Macclesfield looked up at the constable in an old-fashioned way. 'Is there a police doctor this far north? Now that old Simpson's dead?'

'There's Dr Wood, down in Church Row.'

'Get him, then. Then go to the station and put in a call to the Yard. Ask to speak to Inspector Kane. Got it? No one else will do, especially anybody called Quinn or Blevvins.'

'Right, sir. What'll you be doing?'

'Watching.' Macclesfield sat down cross-legged on the dewy grass. 'Just watching.'

'Viscount Allenby of Megiddo?' Lestrade put his grizzled head around the door.

The lantern-jawed man with the clipped moustache was wrestling with his tie in front of a cheval-glass. 'The same,' he barked without turning. 'Frightful handle. You can call me Al.'

'Thank you, my lord.'

'Look, I don't mean to be rude, but I'm late for dinner at Number Ten and I'm straight off to Egypt then. Time and tide waits for no High Commissioner, you know, Mr . . . er . . .?'

'Lestrade. Scotland Yard.

'Ah yes. Well, I can't really advise about motorized transport. I'd heard you fellows were giving up your horses. Damned shame, if you ask me. Or if you don't.'

'No, it's not about the Mounted Branch, my lord, it's about the Arab found dead on Hampstead Heath yesterday.'

'Ah, yes, read about that in the *Daily Blah*. Bad show. Bad show. Don't know much about Arabs, I'm afraid. Could you pass me that?'

He pointed to the scarlet mess-jacket of a Field Marshal draped over a chair. Lestrade passed it to him. 'Let's just check', he looked at the name-tag in the lining, 'that that bugger Wavell hasn't been pinching my kit again. No,' he tugged it on, 'the man to see about Arabs is that little Mary-Anne Lawrence. He lived with the blighters, you know, man and boy. And there were lots of those, I understand.'

'And where might I find Mr Lawrence, sir?' Lestrade leaned back against the door-frame.

'Ah, well, there you have me. Look, be a chum and brush my shoulder would you? Haven't really got enough hair to allow it to drop on to me shoulder cords, but there it is. What do you think?' He dipped his head towards the mirror, pointing to his bald pate. 'Bit of talcum on that? Don't want to dazzle the ladies.'

'Did you say you were dining at Number Ten, my lord?' Lestrade took to batman's duties like a duck to water.

'That's right.'

'Then have no fear. I happen to know that the Prime Minister is as bald as a badger.'

'Lloyd George? Surely not. Got a mane like a Damascus lion.'

'Symphonic,' Lestrade closed to the man and whispered in his ear.

'Eh?'

'Symphonic. Not real. It's actually made of cotton wool.'

'Good Lord!' Allenby was horrified.

'Have a close but unobtrusive look tonight.'

'I will.' Allenby set his jaw as he did when thundering against the Turks at Beersheba.

'Now, Mr Lawrence . . .' Lestrade steered the conversation back.

'Ah, yes. Funny little wog. Don't know where he is now. All Souls, Oxford I shouldn't wonder. There again, he could have changed his name and enlisted in any one of His Majesty's armed forces.'

'So you can't help me, on Arabs, I mean?'

'Well, look, do you mind accompanying me? My man's got a motor somewhere. It'll be faster than a carriage now.'

'Lead on, Field Marshal,' Lestrade said and followed the man past rows of bowing and bobbing servants, one of whom threw a rather fetching military cape over Allenby's immense shoulders. He took his peaked cap and white kid gloves from two others and called back, 'Damn fine body of men. Don't wait up.' Then he leapt into the Daimler with the ageing policeman and they roared into the night.

'Arabs?' Lestrade reminded his man as they screeched around the Aldwych.

'Well, we may have liberated them, and they may have been our allies in the late War, but I wouldn't want my daughter marrying one. Damned ruthless bastards, mind. Eat sheep's eyes and so on. It's the bedouins I remember – dolichocephalic of course.'

'Of course,' nodded Lestrade, unaware that sexually transmitted diseases affected the whole race.

'Your average bedouin stands five foot four and a half inches at the tea-towel, black-haired, scantily-bearded, little and muscular. That's obviously what Lawrence saw in them. They're brave enough, Allah knows, imaginative and seem to know an awful lot of poetry – rather like that bugger Wavell, come to think of it. Never turn your back on one, Lestrade, unless you've taken salt with the blighter. That way you're safe for four days. After that – look out. They're parsimonious in the extreme.'

Lestrade knew about their many wives.

'They cheat for pleasure and can go for days without water. Tough little bleeders, too. They can ride all day with the most chronic piles and still give battle in the evening. Must be all those dates. There again, Arab coffee is something else.'

'Is it?'

'Yes. It's undrinkable.' Allenby leaned forward to his driver. 'Step on it, my man. There might be another honour up for grabs tonight. Has this been of any use?'

'Not really, my lord,' Lestrade spoke as he found. He was far too old to be in one of this man's commands and time was pressing. 'You see, this particular Arab was on his way to see you.'

'Me? How do you know?'

'Well, I am of course merely speculating . . .'

'Go on then.'

'He had your address in his clothing.'

'Really?'

'That's how I found you.'

'Well, I'm buggered.' Allenby turned to face him. 'Got a name, this chappie?'

'Not yet, sir. I was hoping you could help.'

'Where is he now?'

'At Hampstead Mortuary, sir, but I'm afraid I cannot take you there.'

'And I don't have the time.'

'Quite. On the off-chance that that was so I had Constable Lichfield take a photograph.'

He showed it to Allenby who screwed up his eyes in the darkened interior of the Daimler. 'Damn,' he said. 'That bally Palestinian sun. Rots your eyeballs in the end. Good God.'

'You recognize him?'

'Well . . .' He peered again. 'Unless I'm very much mistaken, this is Soheiya Al Haroun, an Emir of some importance in the southern desert. Had the finest camels in the Yemen. He was right-hand man to King Feisal. Of course, I haven't got my specs, it is dark and I've never seen him dead before. Tell me, Lestrade, how did he die?'

'Shot,' Lestrade told him. 'In the back of the head.'

'Well, that rules out another Arab.'

'It does?' Lestrade had not really contemplated *two* bedouins in full dress wandering the deserts of Hampstead.

'Another Arab would have cut his throat, then cut off his meat and two veg for the hell of it. I take it he was intact?'

Tact was obviously not part of Viscount Allenby's repertoire.

'As far as I know,' Lestrade told him. 'A colleague of mine actually found the body and another viewed it without its clothes.'

'Jibbeh?' Allenby asked.

'No. Inspector Kane. So you've no idea why this Al Haroun should have your address in his pocket?'

'None at all. When I saw him last he was hacking some poor bastard to pieces for impugning his ancestors. Tetchy lot, your bedouins. Unless . . . oh, no, that's silly.'

Lestrade sensed a clue. 'May I be the judge of that, my lord?'

'Well, there was some nonsense about the sword of Louis IX.'

'Louis IX?'

'King of France,' Allenby tilted back his peak. 'Saint Louis of the Crusades.'

'A bit before my time, my lord.'

'Mine too. But these Arab johnnies have bloody long folk

120

memories, you know. I think they saw me as some sort of reincarnation of the man, minus the halo, of course. I must say, though, I took Jerusalem when that poor bugger only got as far as Damietta. He surrendered to the Saracens in 1250 and they pinched his sword. It's been passed down ever since, from father to son and I don't think the handle's fallen off.'

'I don't see what this has to do with you.'

'Well, when I first met Feisal, he showed me his camels and his datestocks and his horses and six or seven of his wives. And, his prized possession, the sword of St Louis. Shortly after that, the bloody thing disappeared. Feisal sent Al Haroun round to see if I'd got it. Damn cheek! That's what I mean about the Arabs. Don't give an inch in the trust stakes.'

'Er . . . you hadn't got it, I take it?'

Allenby gave him an old-fashioned, Inspector-General of Cavalry sort of look as the car lurched to a halt in Downing Street.

'No Arab blood in you, is there, Lestrade?' he asked. 'I can't imagine why Feisal should think I've taken it. Give me the good old Wilkinson 1912 pattern any time. Still, I do remember the old goat fornicator thought an Englishman had pinched the damn thing.'

'One of your staff?' Lestrade saw Allenby's moustache bristle. 'I fear I must ask, my lord,' he explained.

'No,' Allenby insisted, 'I don't speak wog myself, but if I remember the gist of the translation, Feisal had given the sword to some British wallah called Zojaaj – for safe keeping in case the Turks got hold of it.'

'And this Zojaaj was not with you in the desert?'

'No. Never heard of him. I promised Haroun I'd look into it, that it was all a misunderstanding . . . and promptly forgot about it until tonight. You don't think this *really* has to do with that sword, do you?'

'How much would you say the sword is worth, my lord?'

'God, I don't know. Haven't a bally clue about money. Doesn't mean a thing to me.' Allenby leapt out of the car. 'My man will drop you somewhere. That'll be eightpence ha'penny for the lift, all right? A cheque will do.'

'Eightpence ha'penny,' said Lestrade. 'I've known men be killed for less. Enjoy your dinner my lord, and thank you.'

Allenby grunted and made for the polished, black door with its sentinel coppers.

'Oh, and by the way,' Lestrade called to him, pointing to the top of his head under the bowler, 'remember!'

It had been some time since John Kane had visited Lestrade's house in Surrey. Actually, it was Fanny's house, as it had been her father's. And so Sholto Lestrade, survivor of everything the world could throw at him, had at last come home.

The four of them sat around the blazing fire in the library where red, leather-bound rows of *The Police Gazette* stood spine by spine with *A Hundred and One Things a Retired Police Superintendent Ought To Know, Volume Thirteen*. Fanny flitted in and out with oatmeal goodies and lashings of steaming cocoa.

'Wouldn't you rather have a brandy, Macclesfield?' Lestrade asked.

'I'm not sure Mrs Macclesfield would approve, sir,' the sergeant answered.

Lestrade shook his head. Six foot two of upright bloke and totally under his wife's thumb.

'Sholto,' Fanny swiped him round the head with a napkin, 'get your foot off the fender.'

'Are you sure you don't mind us pinning bits of paper all over your wall, Mrs Lestrade?' Kane asked, dunking his goodie for the umpteenth time.

'I'm used to it, Mr Kane,' she said. 'And it's all in a good cause,' smiling at Emma. 'Besides, I have to see to Uncle Gideon. He had some tapioca for tea and I just know we're all going to pay the price for that. Emma, darling, Madison is standing by in the kitchen with gallons more cocoa. Goodnight, gentlemen.'

Kane and Macclesfield stood up as she swept graciously from the room.

'Fine figure of a woman, guv'nor,' Kane nodded. 'If I may be permitted to say so.'

'You may, John.' Lestrade was quite prepared to accept such

compliments. It helped that Fanny was twenty years his junior. 'Now, Edwin the bedouin. What do we know?'

'Norroy,' said Kane, 'over to you.'

'Soheiya Al Haroun,' Macclesfield stood to the left of the paper-covered wall. 'We don't know very much.'

'It's not every day that a bedouin Arab in full dress is found murdered on Hampstead Heath, Sergeant.' Lestrade didn't really have to remind him. Without the agility of John Kane, the ex-Superintendent left his goodie that fraction too long in the cocoa and it plopped into the murky depths.

'No-one seems to have seen him, sir, not since he arrived at the Port of London.'

'Which was when?'

'Last Wednesday.'

'Right. So he'd been in the country nearly a week. Where had he been? Who had he talked to? Did he just tie his camel to a nearby bush and pitch his tent?'

'Guv'nor,' Kane reminded him, 'you know the problem. It was luck that Norroy here was the first plain-clothes man to view the body. That gave us a day's grace.'

'By the time I'd done the paperwork, three,' Macclesfield explained with a wink.

'Good man.' Lestrade knew carefully-planned dilatoriness when he saw it.

'But then Patrick Quinn moved in and it was hush-hush, softlee, softlee catchee coldee,' Kane said. 'I was ordered to pass all relevant papers over to him.'

'Including Allenby's address?' Lestrade was fishing for the soggy remains of his goodie.

'Yes. But I gather you got to him first?'

'I gather so,' Lestrade said, 'in that he made no mention of any other police inquiries. And by the time Quinn would have got to him, he was hopefully half way to Egypt.'

'Can someone tell me', Emma broke in, 'why you people can't work together on this? After all, you're supposed to be on the same side.'

There was a stunned silence. Kane looked at Lestrade. Macclesfield found an intensely interesting drawing-pin to scrutinize.

'The same side?' Lestrade repeated. 'I blame myself,' he sighed, 'all those years you were growing up and I wasn't there.'

'Daddy!' She threw a napkin ring at him. 'Not back to that again!'

'The point is, oh fruit of my loins,' he held a carafe of water to the rapidly darkening bruise the ring had raised, 'that once the Branch take over an investigation, the rest of us – and I use the word neurologically – might just as well go and play in the traffic.'

'Your dad's right, Emma.' Kane nodded. 'Patrick Quinn has the Branch sewn up tighter than Lloyd George's wallet. I blame the War. I mean, they were always bad, but secrecy became an obsession with them in 1914. It's never gone away.'

'Sholto,' Fanny burst into the room, 'those two nice young men outside. I've given them some cocoa. Is that all right?'

'What nice young men?' Lestrade asked.

'The one who's been following you and the one who's been following Inspector Kane.'

'Oh, Marks and Spencer,' Lestrade remembered, 'they must be a bit on the frozen side.'

'It is quite bitter for March.' Fanny unwrapped her cape. 'And they did return Uncle Gideon.'

'Return Uncle Gideon?' Lestrade frowned.

'Yes, he'd wandered off again. They found him down by the lake. He told them he'd seen a hand in the water, holding a sword.'

'And they returned him?' Lestrade scowled. 'If I was still on the Force, they'd be in Lost Property by now. What about the sword, John?'

'Norroy?' Kane asked.

'Well, the British Museum have never heard of it. The Victoria and Albert said it probably wasn't genuine. But I did better at the Fitzwilliam.'

'Where?'

'Cambridge, Daddy,' Emma said.

'They certainly knew of its existence and showed me a drawing.' Macclesfield rummaged in his Gladstone and produced it for Lestrade.

'Hmm. Did they give it a value?'

'Priceless they said. It disappeared in the last century for a while, but apparently it was exhibited at the Paris Exposition of 1889. The French demanded it back. There was quite a scene. Running punch-ups in the Bois de Boulogne. But the Arabs kept it. It was returned to Feisal.'

'Anything known on him?' Lestrade asked. 'John?'

'Norroy?'

'I had a word with Charlie Dickens about that,' the long-suffering sergeant said.

'Dickens?' Lestrade interrupted. 'I haven't seen him for years. Is he still with "P" Division?'

'They sent him over to France, didn't they?' Emma asked. 'At the start of the War?'

'That's right,' Lestrade remembered, 'as one of two Metropolitan policemen who spoke the lingo.'

'Well, he's back home now,' Macclesfield assured them, 'and very knowledgeable on Feisal.'

'Of course,' Lestrade chuckled. Detective-Sergeant Dickens was very knowledgeable on everything. 'Go on, then.'

Macclesfield crouched by the fire, referring to his notes. 'He was born in 1883, the third surviving son of Hussein, King of the Hejaz. He spent eighteen years in Constantinople and fought in the Arab contingent of the Turkish Army. His dad sided with us in the Great War and he attacked Aqaba with Colonel Lawrence and led the right wing of Allenby's force in Palestine. He's recently been made King of Syria by the terms of the Sykes-Picot treaty.'

'What?' Lestrade was astounded. 'Didn't Dickens know the man's inside leg measurement?'

'I asked him that, sir,' Macclesfield explained, stony-faced, 'but Sergeant Dickens did point out that as Arabs didn't wear trousers, the information was a little superfluous.'

'And nothing on the sword of St Louis?'

'Nothing,' Macclesfield shrugged.

'All right. John, did you get back to Robert Churchill?'

'Norroy?'

'Mr Churchill, the gunsmith,' Macclesfield flicked over his notepad. 'Yes. The bullets embedded in both Monsieur Euperry and Mr Haroun were fired from the same gun – a .455 Webley – and yet . . .'

'And yet?' repeated Kane.

'And yet there's something else, don't tell me,' Lestrade explained. 'The same something else he told me about after Paul's death, unless I miss my guess. Ridges on the bullets he couldn't explain. You haven't still got the bullets, I suppose?'

'I had to return them both to Special Branch, sir,' Macclesfield said. 'You know how it is.'

'Sergeant,' said Emma, 'did anyone ever tell you you're wonderful? And Mr Kane, how dare you work this man so hard?'

'All our policemen are wonderful, Emma,' Lestrade grinned, 'you know that. And I don't suppose young Macclesfield is all that busy. Whereas in my day . . .'

'Don't listen to him, sergeant.' She wandered past and patted his hand. 'I am very grateful,' she said, looking him steadily in the eyes.

'Just doing my job, Miss Lestrade,' he blushed.

'All right,' Lestrade clapped his hands, staring as he was at the overlapping bits of paper on the wall, 'where's our thread? Our common dilapidator? John?'

This time Kane did not turn to his overworked sergeant. 'One,' he began on his thumb, 'the same gun killed all five victims. Two,' the index finger sprang up, 'Chummy shot all but one in the back of the head. Three . . . ah.'

'That's what I feared,' Lestrade said. 'The thread soon breaks, doesn't it? We've got more differences than similarities.'

'What does that tell us?' Emma asked.

'God knows,' Lestrade said. 'Let me ask you,' he lit a cigar without offering one to Kane or Macclesfield, 'what did Euperry, Varushkin and Haroun have in common?'

'They were all foreign,' she said.

'And?'

'And they were visiting the country.'

'How did they arrive?'

'By ship, via the Port of London.'

'Anything else?'

Emma screwed up her face. 'They were all found dead in London.'

'Anything else?'

'Is there a treaty or something between Belgium and Iraq, or wherever the bedouin came from? And does the *Dreikaiserbund* still exist?'

'Possibly,' nodded Lestrade, 'but there's something else.'

Now, Lestrade's daughter was nobody's fool. She had inherited her mother's brain as well as her mother's looks. That already put her well ahead of her father. 'No,' she shook her head, 'you've lost me.'

Lestrade held up the drawing of St Louis's sword and he fumbled in his pocket to fish out something else. It was the little Russian icon.

'Er . . .' Emma jabbed the air, the answer on the tip of her tongue.

'Old things,' her father helped her. 'Old valuable things. A priceless sword and a fairly expensive . . . thing.'

'But . . .' Kane interrupted.

'I know,' Lestrade held up his hand, 'Euperry doesn't fit that pattern – quite. But consider this. The man may be a translator, but his abiding interest is paintings. He visited the Keeper of the King's Paintings a few days before he died. Varushkin, who we can assume, I think, was not actually a merchant seaman, has this sewn into his mattress. And Haroun appears to be on his way to visit Viscount Allenby to get his boss's sword back.'

'Do we know that Allenby's got it?' Kane asked.

'He says not,' said Lestrade. 'It appears to have been commandeered by somebody called Zojaaj.'

'Zojaaj?' Kane repeated. 'Who's that?'

Lestrade shrugged. 'A British officer in Palestine during the War.'

'A *British* officer.' Kane wasn't sure he had heard properly. 'Funny name for a British officer.'

'Probably Anglo-Arab,' Lestrade suggested. 'I gather some funny things go on in the desert.'

'It'll be the sandstorms,' said Kane, as if that said it all.

'So, Daddy,' Emma had been puzzling it out, 'are you saying that this man Zojaaj is our murderer?'

'Well,' Lestrade sighed, 'it's a long shot, but John, I'd send young Macclesfield here tomorrow to the Fitzwilliam Museum. It's in Cambridge, apparently. The long nose of Paddy Quinn hasn't found this icon thing yet and that gives us a head start. Macclesfield, tell the curator johnnie that we know it's by some French bloke, but we want to know more and how much it's worth. Emma, can you get into the army files?'

'With my eyes shut,' she smiled. 'Major Publisher is a push-over for a pretty ankle. You don't think there'll be somebody called Zojaaj, do you?'

'Well, there can't be many in the Zeds,' Lestrade said. 'Look in the Staff section.'

'What about the other two?' Kane had been concentrating on the pieces of paper, too.

'Hmm?' Lestrade said.

'Paul Dacres and Fallabella Shaw – the other ends of our broken threads.'

'Ah, yes.' Lestrade stirred the residue of his cocoa, draping the skin carefully around the rim of the cup. 'All right. They knew each other. Both worked for the War Office in the late War. And bearing in mind that Paul said nothing to anybody about it, it must have been something hush-hush.'

'Department A.T. One,' said Emma.

'And we can't find out exactly what that was,' Lestrade added.

'Though we will,' she assured them.

'Quite.' Lestrade was sucking his teeth, a sure sign he was staring a brick wall in the face. 'Macclesfield, are you sure Mr Churchill said the same gun killed all five?'

'He was adamant, sir,' the sergeant said.

'It's just that they don't fit. Fallabella Shaw is found buried in a field in Hertfordshire. Which means . . . John?'

'Er . . .' Kane frowned in concentration. 'Which means that Chummy didn't want her found.'

'Right. Paul Dacres was found in a hotel bedroom in London. Which means . . .?'

'That Chummy *knew* he'd be found.'

'Yes,' Lestrade agreed, 'but he didn't think it would matter because he hoped it would pass for suicide – and with Blevvins in charge it nearly did – and because without the body of Miss

Shaw and her inscribed cigarette lighter, we'd have no reason to make a connection. It was just our man's bad luck that they were making a town in the middle of nowhere – the same middle of nowhere in which he had chosen to bury his victim.'

'It also proves something else,' said Emma defiantly. 'He didn't know Paul Dacres very well if he thought any of us would fall for that.'

There was a silence. Four tired people had run the gamut of speculation for one night and the embers had turned to ash in the grate.

'Well,' Lestrade crossed to his little girl, squeezing her round the shoulders, 'we've got a little further tonight. Miracles? Well, they take a little longer.'

Emma Bandicoot-Lestrade spent rather less than a minute on the lap of Major Publisher before she had lifted the key to the files from his inside pocket and he had had to lie down with a glass of water. As she had feared, there was no one by the name of Zojaaj listed as a staff officer in the British Army. There was a Clement Zoroaster, of the Buckinghamshire Zoroasters, but he'd bought it while observing with the Chinese Army in Tibet in 1904. And there, the trail went cold.

Norroy Macclesfield had fared better. It was well worth the train fare to Cambridge and the slight derailment at Baldock, because the curator johnnie of the Fitzwilliam Museum was very excited. When Macclesfield had calmed him down, however, with the quiet, soothing delivery of an officer of the Metropolitan Police, he was quite forthcoming on the Russian icon. It had been made by one Agathon Fabergé, the younger brother of the more famous Carl Peter and they were not, as Lestrade had supposed, French, but Russian. They were the official Court Jewellers to His Imperial Majesty Nicholas II, Tsar of All the Russias, but precisely where anyone connected with the Russian court was now, the Fitzwilliam declined to say. The icon, it transpired, was one of a pair given by the Little Father to his youngest daughter, Anastasia. Its value on its own made Norroy Macclesfield go quite weak at the knees. The value of the pair made him feel, just for a moment, decidedly criminal.

But finer feelings prevailed and the sergeant resisted all offers from the curator johnnie to buy the object and tucked it away carefully into his inside pocket before making the journey south.

It was a Friday – Madison's day off. Emma had caught the seven thirty-eight for Town, to see what else she could wheedle out of Archie le Fanu and Major Publisher. Lestrade himself had gone on a wild-goose chase to the Russian Embassy. He needn't have bothered. A peasant on the door told him in halting English that it was the day of St Gregori and everybody but he had the day off. He was only there, he explained, because he had the misfortune to be born in Tobolsk. Lestrade thought it unwise to ask any more of him. And it was a dejected, geriatric ex-Superintendent who stumbled off the bus at the bottom of the road and staggered through the daffodil beds of early April for the comfort of his fireside.

He noticed the French windows were thrown back, the curtains billowing wide. His wife was spring-cleaning again. God alone knew where she would have put his slippers this time. It wasn't until he got nearer that he saw the broken pane, heard the glass crunch beneath his feet. His heart thudded in his chest, his mind raced. He'd seen too many of these to think the window-cleaner had been a little over-zealous in the pursuance of his duty.

He hurtled through the library, papers flying in all directions, crashing through the hall and into the kitchen. No sign. He tried the drawing-room. Empty. And everywhere he went, furniture had been overturned and drawers ripped out.

'Fanny!' he bellowed, racing for the stairs. 'Fanny!'

He reached their bedroom, his heart in his mouth. Fanny Lestrade lay across the bed, the counterpane clenched in her fist, her head thrown back, her day dress torn. A trickle of blood ran like a crimson worm across her forehead and down her cheek. With frantic fingers he ripped at her cuffs to find a pulse. He couldn't. He threw his bowler at the wall and crushed his ear on her chest. It was the last thing he did for the next six hours, for then darkness hit him.

*

There was a dim pool of light swimming, eddying above him, like a bubble he couldn't catch. There was a shape, willowy, golden-haired, a long, long way away. The shape spoke to him, as though down a tunnel of sound. 'Daddy? Daddy? Are you all right?'

'Aarggh!' He sat bolt upright. 'Who are you?'

'Oh, my God.' The shape's hand shot up to her mouth. 'His memory's gone. It's Emma, Daddy, your Emma.'

'I know that,' he snapped, then noted her expression. 'I asked you where I was – didn't I?'

She shook her head.

'Steady, old chap,' a second shape said. 'You've had a nasty crack on the head.'

'Where am I?' Lestrade asked him.

'It's me,' the shape said. 'George Alexander, your family doctor. You know, you're lucky to be alive.'

Lestrade sat blinking at him. No one was answering his questions. And why were they all so blurred? Alexander appeared to be twice his former width and surely, Sarah Lestrade hadn't given birth, those twenty-seven years ago, to twins? What was going on?

'What's going on?' he asked.

'You've had a nasty bang on the head,' the doctor said.

'I know that!' Lestrade realized it anew with the force of the shout. 'What happened?'

'You tell us, old chap,' and Alexander stuck something cold and glass under his tongue.

Lestrade gurgled incomprehensibly.

'That's easy for you to say, Sholto,' the doctor said. 'How are the stools today?'

Lestrade whipped out the thermometer. 'The same as the rest of my furniture. My God!' he ripped off the bedclothes. 'Fanny!' and he hauled Alexander out of the way.

'Daddy!' Emma dragged him back by the tail of his nightshirt. 'She's all right. She's got what you've got.'

'Yes, irritable patient syndrome.' Alexander was searching the carpet in vain for the collar-stud Lestrade had just ripped off.

'She's sleeping in the guest-room.'

'Emma,' Lestrade swayed by the bed, trying to focus on her

131

face, 'you're not lying to me, are you? About Fanny, I mean? She is all right?'

'Of course, Daddy,' his daughter said.

'I must see her,' Lestrade said, but Emma and the doctor lowered him gently to the pillows again.

'Not now, Daddy,' she said. 'Fanny needs rest and so do you.'

His head swam and the pool of light from the electric lamp hurt his eyes. He closed them, feeling the bandage tightening as his head swelled. 'What happened?' he asked, calmer now.

Emma looked at the family doctor, who had given up searching for his stud and trying to take Lestrade's temperature. 'Well,' she said, 'a Boer Kommando had crept up on the British positions and there was a short exchange.'

'What?' Lestrade was worse than he feared.

'Well, you did ask,' Emma said. 'That was Uncle Gideon's version of events. He obviously saw you crouching over Fanny and assumed you were ravishing the woman. He fetched you a nasty one with the sideboard.'

'The sideboard?' Lestrade fell back, exhausted.

'Well, a bit of it, anyway,' she explained. 'It must have been broken off by the rest of your command.'

'Emma!' he scolded. 'Will you stop talking nonsense? What *really* happened?'

'We don't know yet, old chap,' Alexander fussed with a poultice, 'but I must get that bruising out. Fanny woke up briefly and told us she startled an intruder going through her drawers. She doesn't remember any more until young Emma here brought her round.'

'I came home from Town and found the police here. Your shadow, Constable Spencer, had called them and they called Dr Alexander. You were slumped apparently across Fanny on this very bed. The place looked as if it had been bombed.'

'Where was Gideon?'

'Standing guard by the front door, posing for photographs.'

'Photographs?' Lestrade couldn't believe his ears. 'Who was taking them?'

'Nobody,' Emma explained, 'but he was in his full dress uniform, shading his eyes from the glare of the flash.'

'He'll have to go,' mumbled Lestrade. 'The mad old bugger could have killed me.'

'He thought he was doing the right thing, old chap.' Alexander was kindness itself. It was part of his technique.

'Will you stop calling me old chap, George?' Lestrade hissed. 'I am nearly three years younger than you are.'

'Sorry old . . . Sholto.'

'An intruder?' Lestrade was talking to Emma again. 'Yes. Yes. I remember now. The place had been ransacked. I found Fanny on the bed. She'd been hurt.'

'Just a headache, the doctor says.' Emma patted his hand. 'She'll be all right. You both will.'

Lestrade sat slowly up in bed. 'It was Chummy, wasn't it?' he asked his only daughter. 'We've flushed him out at last. I don't know how, or why, but we're on to him now.'

7

Inspector Blevvins broke the habit of a lifetime two days later and sniggered out loud.

'Look at this, Green,' he said, uncrossing his feet from the desk. 'Somebody's burgled old Lestrade. Coshed him and his missus over the head. I don't know what the world's coming to, I really don't. You'd think the police would do something, wouldn't you? Helpless old git like him. Mind you, if I remember his missus right, I wouldn't mind giving her one myself.'

'There's a call coming in, guv'nor,' Greeno said, adjusting his headphones.

'Why are you wearing a Victorian lady's wig, Green?' Blevvins felt he had to ask.

'Oh, sorry, sir,' the young constable turned carmine and pulled the thing off. 'It's the Police revue, sir. I'm Mrs Lovett – you know, the accomplice of Sweeney Todd.'

'Who?'

'The demon barber of Fleet Street, sir. He cut people's throats and slid them down into the cellar where Mrs Lovett cut 'em up and made them into pies.'

Blevvins shook his head. 'Before my time,' he said. 'What's the call?'

Greeno hauled at various plugs and wires. 'It's a body, sir. At Boreham Wood. Local constabulary would like a hand. They're asking for Inspector Kane, sir.'

'Are they?'

'Or failing him, Inspector Bower.'

'Is that right?' Blevvins had downed his paper and was reaching for the tube that speaks.

'At a pinch, they might make do with Chief Inspector Dew.'

Blevvins snatched the equipment from Greeno, whose neck snapped backwards with a jerk. 'Hello?' the inspector snapped too. 'Who's this?'

The telephone crackled in his hand.

'Never you mind who it is at this end!' Blevvins bellowed. 'If you country bumpkins can't handle things, we'll send you our best man – Inspector Edward Blevvins. That's right, Blevvins. B for buggery, L for larceny, E for extortion, V for vice, V for vice, I for intimidation, N for nocking shop and S for . . . Funny, they've rung off.' Blevvins slammed down the receiver. 'Well, don't just sit there holding your ear, Green. Find a map and get me a motor. I'd like to know where bloody Boreham Wood is before I start drawing my pension.'

Bloody Boreham Wood lay in that complicated little bit south west of Barnet, and up a little bit from Elstree, with its paper-mill and reservoir. Young Constable Greeno tried to draw a veil over what happened there on that sixteenth day of April, in the Year of His Lord 1920. From the time the black police van lurched uneasily onto the open heathland until the Hertford-shire Constabulary were called in to break up the fight, Greeno would remember only the barest essentials. And when it came, in the years ahead, to writing his memoirs, 1920 was curiously omitted from them.

Yet some sense of impending disaster drove him later that night to pedal south through the pouring rain, drips bouncing like bullets off his sou'wester, in search of a legendary policeman whose name was never spoken at Scotland Yard. Norroy Mac-clesfield had given him the address.

'You poor man,' Fanny had said, 'you must be drenched. Come in.'

The first sight the dripping policeman saw was a gaunt, white-haired old man in a slouch hat.

'It's the Relief Column, Uncle,' the lady turned to reassure him.

'From Colenso?' Uncle Gideon asked warily.

'Er . . . yes, sir,' Greeno said, vaguely aware of Fanny nodding furiously to his right.

Uncle Gideon shook his hand warmly. 'Well done, my boy. Well done. How's Ian Hamilton?'

Greeno looked in desperation over the old man's shoulder to catch Fanny's mouthings. 'Very well, sir. He sends his best.'

'Good. Good.'

'Now, Uncle,' she manhandled him towards the stairs, 'time for the Last Post.'

'Good Lord, is it really?' He checked his hunter. 'I shall expect your report, son, first thing in the morning.'

Greeno saluted in accordance with Fanny's silent instructions. 'Yes, of course, sir.'

The second sight he saw was a gorgeous young lady who looked rather familiar. 'Miss?' he gasped.

'Constable Greeno, isn't it?' Emma said. 'My goodness, you're drenched. Get out of those bicycle clips at once.'

He did and the water cascaded all over the carpet. 'Come and sit by the fire. Daddy won't be long. I assume it *is* Daddy you've come to see?'

'Er . . . I've come to see Superintendent Lestrade, miss,' he explained.

'Well, it amounts to the same thing. Would you like a nip of brandy?'

'No, thank you, miss,' Greeno said, 'I'm in charge of my vehicle, viz. and to wit, my bike.'

'Quite.' She reached for a silver case. 'Cigarette?'

But before the horrified constable could decline, an apparition in a dressing-gown floated into the library. 'Who are you?'

Greeno leapt to his feet and stood steaming in front of the fire. Before him stood the great Lestrade, the face yellow as parchment, the sad eyes dark and circled, the nose-tip missing, a bandage round his head. There was something in his bearing, yet nothing in what he was wearing.

'Detective-Constable Greeno, sir,' he said. 'Scotland Yard.'

'Ah,' Lestrade gestured to the lad to sit down, 'you're Blevvins's man, aren't you?'

'Yes, sir.'

'Don't tell me he sent you.'

136

'No, sir,' Greeno said quickly, 'I'm here on my own initiative.'

'Initiative?' Lestrade chuckled. 'Write that one down, Emma. There's something new at the Yard since my day. Oh, you've met my daughter, of course.'

'Er . . . yes, sir,' Greeno said, 'twice.'

'Constable Greeno was kind enough to show me around the Yard, Daddy, when I toyed with enlisting . . . you remember?' She looked at him hard.

'Yes, of course,' Lestrade smiled. 'Well, lad, you've come a long way in the rain. What do you want?'

Jonquil de Ville stood with his arms folded, his jodhpurred legs planted in the furrow, the winds of mid-April blowing through his lion's mane of hair. He lifted the megaphone for the umpteenth time that morning, carefully draping his cravat first.

'Lovies, lovies. That was fine, lovies. But Claude, we're not making *Birth of a Nation*. I don't think we really need all that angst with the custard pie, do we? And Petronella, darling, look, you've just lost both your children and your husband has been killed in a duel. I'm not sure *that* much thigh is appropriate, is it?'

He lowered the thing and a little man dashed out across the set and straightened the canvas backcloth. Another one operated the clapper-board.

'Take Nineteen,' shouted de Ville. 'Quiet on the set.'

Petronella steadied herself against the bedstead and flung an anguished hand across her forehead. Claude perched gingerly on the window-sill, a new custard-pie plate in his hand.

'Oh, lord,' groaned de Ville, 'I asked for Tom Mix and Tony and got Don Quixote and Rosinante. Who the bloody hell . . .?' The megaphone was lost for words as de Ville watched an old man in an older Donegal wander into Petronella's bedroom, gazing confusedly about him.

'Cut! Cut!' the director screamed and slapping his boots with his riding crop strode across the Hertfordshire field. Grabbing the old man by the collar, he hauled him out of camera shot. 'Do you mind?' he shrieked, the annoyance mingling with the rouge to give him a very red countenance. 'We're trying to make a film, here. What the hell do you think you're doing?'

The man with the Donegal smoothed down the garment, affronted. 'Unhand me, sir.'

'Please!' an outraged female voice made de Ville spin round.

'I am Emma Mackintosh,' She said, 'You are manhandling that great thespian, Sir Mortimer Lister.'

'Who?' de Ville frowned.

'Come, Emma,' said Lestrade, haughtily, 'I told you we were wasting our time. The legitimate theatre is the only true art form.'

'Just a minute,' de Ville called them back, rather more impressed with the turn of Miss Mackintosh's ankle than Sir Mortimer's purism. 'Forgive me, Sir Mortimer,' he took her hand and kissed it, 'it's the strain. I have to make another four pictures by Thursday. Which part had you in mind?'

'*The Destruction of Sennacherib*,' said Lestrade with a flourish. Greeno had briefed him well.

'Ah, yes, yes,' de Ville pushed the girl aside and took the actor by the shoulders. He turned him first one way, then the other. 'Of course,' he said, 'Sir Mortimer, darling, I see it. You're a natural for Hammurabi. Pop over to make-up, will you? I'll fill you in on the story later. We should have an Angel of Death by tea-time.'

'Mr de Ville.' A shout broke up the reverie. 'Mr Fairbanks on the field telephone.'

'Oh, God, that boring old fart.' He crossed to the cased machine. 'Just an incy-wincy seccy, lovies.' He waved to the girl and her old man.

'Who's Hammurabi?' Lestrade whispered behind his collar.

'He's some Old Testament king, Daddy,' Emma said. 'Invented a code or something. I had chicken-pox that term, I'm afraid. Everything from the Fertile Crescent to Vespasian is as a closed book to me. Who's the Angel of Death?'

Lestrade looked around the open-air set at the hastily rebuilt and repaired furniture, bearing out what Greeno had told them. 'Ned Blevvins, I wouldn't be surprised,' he said.

'Douglas, darling!' they heard de Ville screaming over the phone. 'Oh, no, oh, how dreadful! Can't she? Oh, lovey. Well, another time, then. Give my love to Mack, Charlie, Fatty and the others. Yes. Yes. Will do. Toodlepip!' He threw the receiver to his lackey. 'Thank God for that. Mary Pickford can't make it. She's got about as much talent as a removals van, anyway. Er . . . Miss Mackintosh?'

The girl not of that name turned to him.

'Emma, darling,' he cradled her hand in his, 'look, can I have a word? Er . . . over there, Sir Mortimer, the caravan on the end. That's make-up,' and he led the girl to the shade of an elm tree. 'I can make you a star,' he said.

'Really?' she smiled, gazing up into the clear blue of his hair.

'I've got rather a plum part . . .'

'Oh, good,' she snuggled against him.

'It's Salome in *The Destruction of Sennacherib*. Lots of sinewy movements,' he pressed against her, 'sensuous undulations,' she felt her back against the bark, 'steamy situations.'

'Ooooh!' she gasped.

'Oh, I'm sorry,' he said, removing the offending article from between them, 'it's my riding crop.'

'I'm glad to hear it, Mr de Ville,' she said.

'Jonquil,' he said. 'Call me Jon-Jon.'

'Very well,' she purred, 'Jon-Jon. But I should warn you, I've never acted before. I am merely Sir Mortimer's Johanna Factotum.'

'Yes, well, the old boy looks as though he needs as many of those as he can get. Don't worry, lovey', he held her at arm's length, 'the punters won't be looking at your thespian qualities. Could you . . . er . . . could you do it topless?'

'I beg your pardon?' She sprang away from him.

'Don't worry,' he said, 'I know April in Hertfordshire can be beastly, but there'll be an entire crew standing by with hotties. And of course, all we chaps will close our eyes.'

'Will the male cinema audiences do the same?' she asked, raising an eyebrow.

'Oh, I'm sure of it,' he grovelled. 'I wouldn't ask it of you, but I'm a stickler for realism, you see. It's the "*nouveau* cinema", the *cinéma-vérité*. Put that cigarette out, Beerbohm. That set will be the Temple of Baal in half an hour. You see.' He turned to her again.

'I'll think about it,' she said.

'Good,' he smiled, 'that's what I do, most of the time. Right, come and sit with me while I direct this love scene. Claude, when you're ready. Petronella, darling, take the jumper off, could you? Who the bloody hell's in charge of continuity?'

Lestrade sat in front of a mirror surrounded by powerful lights as a tiny woman at least four hundred years old painted his jaw with glue that smelt like an abattoir and pressed black curls around his face.

'Murder, isn't it?' he heard a voice behind him. In the mirror he saw a middle-aged man with a neat moustache and a centre parting. He looked like a professor of ancient history.

'I'm William Barnstaple, Emeritus Professor of Ancient History, Oxford University.'

'Sh . . . Shir Mortimer Lister,' Lestrade slurred, temporarily off guard.

'Are you in this wretched film?' Barnstaple asked, lighting his pipe.

'Er . . . yes, I'm Hammurabi.'

'Oh, God,' the Professor buried his face in his hands.

'Don't I look much like him?' Lestrade peered forward as the little woman piled on the black cotton wool and began to tug his hair backwards.

'No one knows what Hammurabi looked like,' Barnstaple told him, 'but he had about as much to do with the destruction of Sennacherib as Mr de Ville out there has to do with art.'

'Well,' Lestrade shrugged, 'it's a job. Are you an actor?'

Barnstaple chuckled. 'Lord, no. I'm de Ville's historical adviser, would you believe? But every time I suggest something or point out the error of his ways, he says he's on a tight budget, tight schedule and so on. If it weren't for the twenty pounds a week he's paying me, I'd walk off the set. Who's the ravishing girl he's ravishing at the moment?'

Lestrade craned under the Babylonian wig to see in the mirror what Barnstaple could see through the open door. Emma was sitting as far away as she could from the director, who was leaning to one side like a man with a double hernia. 'My secretary,' he said. 'She can take care of herself,' and he crossed

140

his fingers under the shawl the old crone had draped around his shoulders. 'Have you been here long?'

Barnstaple leaned back, blowing smoke rings to the ceiling. 'It seems like years. Actually, I suppose it's only been a week.'

'You were here when they found that body, then?'

'Oh, the Frenchman,' Barnstaple said. 'Yes, I was.'

'Odd business,' Lestrade fidgeted as huge black eyebrows were stuck over his own.

'Very.' Barnstaple leaned forward. 'You'll never get those off, you know.'

'I read about it in the paper. Did you know him?'

'Who?'

'The deceased.'

'Vavasour? Only in passing. He was the historial adviser on de Ville's epic of last week.'

'What was that?'

'*The Sea-Green Incorruptible* – a story of everyday revolutionary folk.'

'And what did Monsieur Vavasour have to do with that?'

'Oh, he's the leading expert on Robespierre, the central character of the film. Or he was. That post is wide open now, I suppose.'

'The paper was very sketchy,' Lestrade pointed his lip as the crone fitted a moustache over his own.

'You look just like George Arliss when you do that,' she said and went back to sucking her teeth.

'Well, we passed like ships in the night, really,' Barnstaple said. 'I got here, let's see, on Tuesday and they found him two days later.'

'You said you knew him in passing.'

'Oh, by reputation,' Barnstaple explained. 'I believe we nodded once. We're a rather pompous breed, Sir Mortimer, we historians. You seem very curious about all this.'

'Well,' Lestrade could feel the heat from the bulbs ungluing his beard already and it suddenly pinged off his right ear, 'it's not every day a corpse turns up in Hertfordshire.'

'No, I suppose not. Well, a lot of us saw it – the body, I mean.'

'Oh?'

'I think it was old Smithers who found it.'

'Smithers?'

'The night-watchman at the studios. He patrols the grounds and literally fell over him.'

'Tut, tut. How did he die?'

'Well, somebody said he'd been shot. I'm afraid I don't know one end of a gun from another.' He brandished a walking-stick. 'I rely on this to beat my way through the bracken of a spring evening. De Ville called the police – or rather got someone to do it for him. Mind you, it's the police that amaze me – falling over themselves, they were. First, we had the local bobbies.'

'Trampling all over the place, I expect,' Lestrade grinned.

'Yes. How did you know?'

'Oh, I once played a detective on the stage, some years ago now, of course – in *No, No, Nanette*. Do you know it?'

Barnstaple shook his head. Lestrade was relieved. 'Then the Yard were called in. I mean, they're supposed to be the experts, aren't they?'

'So I believe,' Lestrade hedged, while the crone began to paint purple frown-lines across his forehead. 'Is this really necessary?' He struggled under the wax stick.

'It's Leichner,' the crone said.

'Bless you,' Lestrade hissed.

'Well, anyway,' Barnstaple went on, 'the chappie in charge of the case was an oaf called Bevin or Bevan or something . . .'

'Blevvins,' Lestrade put him right. 'Er . . . unless the *Sketch* got it wrong, which is always likely.'

'Yes, well, he was a perfect pig. He hadn't been here five minutes before he'd quarrelled with the local force, ordering them off the site – er, set – and then he picked a fight with a group of extras.'

'Really?' Lestrade's false eyebrow rose dramatically until it reached his crown. The *Sketch* hadn't mentioned any of this and even Greeno had been coy.

'Well, it cut de Ville's crowd scenes by half. All looked a bit silly, really, three chaps and one old crone sitting around the guillotine.'

'And I didn't need make-up,' the crone said triumphantly. 'Chin up, sonny.'

'No, quite,' said Lestrade, doing as he was told with as little grace as he could muster.

'He even blacked de Ville's eye.'

'I didn't notice,' Lestrade said as the crone whisked away the shawl. He looked slightly incongruous, the pressed curls and tiara of a Babylonian king above the tie-knot of a rather scruffy ex-detective below it. 'Thank you,' he said to the old girl, who reached for her own pipe from a rack near the mirror.

'Make-up,' winked Barnstaple. 'His is so discreet, isn't it?'

On the set, as the tragi-comedy of *Death by Custard Pie* came to an end and technicians scurried in all directions to set up the cardboard blocks of the Temple of Baal, Emma was plying Jon-Jon de Ville for all she was worth.

'And this beastly man punched you in the face?' She squeezed his hand.

'I shall sue, of course,' he told her, interspersing their conversation with shouts over the megaphone. 'This isn't Mrs Holland's Palace of Light,' he bawled to a lighting technician, 'get a key grip, man. It's nearly half past three. Where are the widows of Ashur, for God's sake? You can't get the staff anymore.'

'What happened then?'

'Well, no sooner had the imbecile Blevvins wrecked the Place de la Concorde than he broke Robespierre's jaw.'

'Wasn't that rather useful?' Emma summoned up her school history. 'Didn't Robespierre shoot himself in the jaw on the eve of his execution?'

'Did he?' de Ville was caught off guard, rather as he had been when Blevvins put one on him. 'Oh, yes, of course he did. But we'd done that bit already. I shall be sending him the hospital bills. Then that other lot arrived.'

A lackey whispered in his ear and they both turned to survey a sorry-looking cart-horse that shivered and twitched like a mobile sofa in the field behind them. 'Is that it?' de Ville asked. 'The cavalry of the Assyrians? That's not going to come down like a wolf on the fold, is it?'

'It's the best I can do at short notice, Mr de Ville,' the man told him.

'All right,' sighed the magnate, 'I suppose we all have to make sacrifices. Talking of which, the farmer does realize we'll have to kill it, doesn't he? And make sure there's lots of foam white on the turf from his gasping – I don't want to see one dry eye at the Palaceadium a week Tuesday. Oh and get a letter off to the RSPCA – as far as they're concerned it's a rubber horse, remember, and all proceeds will go to the Retired Quadrupeds Home at Saffron Walden. Where was I?'

'The other lot,' Emma reminded him.

'Yes, that's right. Special Branch. Some Irish chappie in charge. That muscle-bound oaf had gone by then.'

'So what happened to the body?'

'Lord knows. They threw a screen round it. I tried to get them to let me film it. It would have been quite useful for *The Masked Terror Strikes Again*, but the Irish chappie was quite adamant that we couldn't do it. So much for *cinéma-vérité*. Kenneth, Kenneth, darling; cohorts.' He patted Emma's hand and moved to direct from the front. 'Let me have a little word about cohorts.' He put his arm around a man in a ludicrous frock, carrying a bow. 'They're supposed to gleam, lovey, for a start. Now, you and I know it's only in black and white, don't we, but the script, lovey? The script calls for purple and gold. We want the audience to live this, don't we, darling? So, realism. Please? Look just a little as though you're anti-Semitic. You're trying to knock Jerusalem down. All right?'

Kenneth mumbled something inaudible and de Ville returned with his stately mince to the director's chair.

'Did you know the dead man?' Emma asked.

'Yes, darling, I hired him,' de Ville told her. 'Between you and me, he wasn't very good.'

'No?'

'No. Now, I'm no expert on the French Revolution, I'll be the first to admit. Clinton! Clinton, lovey,' he called to another bowman nearby, 'no smoking on the set, dear. It's not only contrary to everything the Assyrian Empire stood for, it's downright dangerous, isn't it? Celluloid, dear. Remember the celluloid.' He looked at his watch, 'Tut. Where *is* that wave-machine? We'll never create deep Galilee by nightfall.'

'What was wrong with Vavasour?' Emma was as tenacious as her old man when she had to be.

'My dear, he was dead,' de Ville explained. It merely re-affirmed his deepest convictions. Whether secretary or actress, women were not intellectually on a par with men. Still less film magnates.

'No,' she smiled, 'I mean his views on the French Revolution. I thought you said he was your historical adviser.'

'That's right. That's right. But he had that old crone who does the make-up knitting at the foot of the guillotine.'

'Not right?' she asked.

'Lord, no. That old humbug Dickens made that up. That reminds me,' de Ville turned back, lolling on his chair, to a team of script-writers behind him, 'how's my *Little Dorrit* coming along, Truman?'

'Very well, thank you, sir, but are you sure you want it as a musical?'

'Yes, of course I am,' de Ville insisted. 'And put a move on with those lyrics, Tim. I'm lunching with Paderewski tomorrow. He's doing the score.'

'Art twenty, de Ville nil,' Emma muttered under her breath. 'Can you think of any reason why anyone should want to see him dead?' she asked.

'Good Heavens, lovey,' de Ville said, 'anyone would think you're a policeman. I really haven't the faintest idea. Ah, here's Sir Mortimer. Oh, yes, darling. The living embodiment of Hammurabi.'

Emma took one look at her father, in glittering crown and flowing frock with huge outsize sandals on his feet and it was all she could do to stay upright for laughing. 'Excuse me,' she giggled, 'I think this is where I came in.'

'What's this?' Lestrade sat in the snug of The Best Boy, merci-fully back to his bowler and Donegal. As Barnstaple had predicted, however, the eyebrows had refused to budge and he looked like George Robey.

'It's the script for *The Sea-Green Incorruptible*,' Emma told him. 'I lifted it from de Ville's caravan.'

'But it's only two pages long.' Lestrade riffled through both of them.

'It *is* a silent film, Daddy. Anyway, from what I've seen of Mr de Ville's pictures, plot isn't exactly paramount. Isn't it your shout?'

'Oh, is it?' he groaned, clicking his fingers. 'Mine host. Another pint and a . . . what *is* that?'

'A G and T, please,' she beamed.

Lestrade tutted. 'If your mother was alive today . . .'

'. . . She'd be sitting there having one with me,' Emma said, smiling.

'Ha! You're right,' Lestrade laughed. 'All right, Miss Mackintosh, what did you learn at school today?'

'Well, Sir Mortimer, it went something like this. Monsieur Emile Vavasour is a rather enigmatic character – a history expert.'

'No, he isn't.'

'What?'

'He isn't an expert. That's one lecture I did go to – "Knitting Through the Ages" – and at no time did old women sit and knit at the foot of the guillotine.'

'In other words?'

'In other words, Monsieur Emile Vavasour was not all he seemed.'

'Ah.'

'Stumped, little lady?' Lestrade was enjoying this.

'Not in the least,' she beamed. 'Daddy, I'm going to have a cigarette, *with* a cigarette holder. I think this could be a three cigarette problem.'

'Emma,' he growled, looking furtively to left and right.

'I just don't care, Daddy. This is 1920. Women of thirty have the vote, ivory is now made of benzoline, there's been another attempted *putsch* in Germany and hot cross buns have gone up to threepence. The writing's on the wall for civilization and I'm loving every minute of it. So there!' And she blew a series of smoke rings at him.

'Well, what a retiring little blossom you are,' he said, taking refuge in the newly-arrived pint. 'All right, then Miss Flapper, your deductions?'

'So Emile Vavasour is not an historian – then why did Mr Barnstaple say he knew him?'

'He said he knew the name not the man. He'd only nodded at the man.'

'Wouldn't de Ville know him?'

Lestrade shrugged. 'Why should he? Did he know the great Sir Mortimer Lister? Well, thank God he didn't. Come to think of it, I rather wish he had. Tomorrow, I'm taking part in a moving picture,' and he gulped at his froth again.

'How many people did you talk to today on the set, about the murder, I mean?'

'Half a dozen, why?'

She sipped the G and T. 'I talked to eight, once I'd extricated myself from de Ville.'

'That's fourteen.' Mr Poulson's Academy for the Sons of Nearly-Respectable Gentlefolk had done Lestrade proud all those years ago. 'What's your point?'

'Well, there must be at least another thirty to go. It could be any one of them.'

'Or none of them,' Lestrade said.

'What?'

'If our man was not, as I surmise, actually an historical adviser, but something else, then whoever wanted him dead could have been trying to reach him for some time before he caught up with him in the shrubbery a little to the south of the Place de la Gréve, by way of Boreham Wood.'

'So the film company is a red herring?' she chewed the end of her cigarette-holder.

'Don't do that, dear,' he said, 'you'll wear your teeth away. Very possibly, but I'm not ruling anything out at this stage. What else have you got?'

'If . . .' she pointed her cigarette at an imaginary target swirling in the smoke, '. . . if Vavasour was not an historical adviser . . . if Varushkin was not a merchant seaman . . . if Euperry was only a translator in passing . . . then what were they really?'

'Well?' he said, suddenly on the edge of his seat. 'I'm on the edge of my seat. Out with it, girl.'

'Secret agents.'

'Emma Bandicoot-Lestrade,' he leaned back, smiling, 'we'll make a detective of you yet. And don't worry. I'll have a word with Mr Lloyd George about getting the vote for you. I'm sure he'll be understanding.'

'Won't you have to shoot Winston Churchill first?'

'Yes, of course,' Lestrade shrugged, 'but that's merely a formality. Still, the penalty would be horrendous. A man was fined £5 the other day for using foul language about him. If we shot him, I hate to think what the fine would be.'

'So you like my theory then, Daddy?' Emma was being just a little smug.

'How much notice do you have to give at the War Office?'

'A week. Why?'

'Do you know Stanley Accrington, Harry's chum at the Foreign Office?'

'I think I met him once. Why?' A note had crept into the voice of Lestrade's daughter, a note that spoke volumes.

'How long do you think this Salome part of yours will last?'

'Well,' she said, 'I signed on on my day off. Having read the script it should take a morning, perhaps a full day. If de Ville insists I do it the way he wants it done, it will take about three minutes.'

'Why?' Lestrade was confused.

'Never mind,' she told him. 'I'm not sure your arteries would stand it. What are you getting at, Daddy?'

'Where would you go to find out about the presence of foreign agents in this country?'

'Er . . .'

'Two places,' he prompted her.

'Er . . . the Foreign Office?' she asked.

He nodded sagely. 'And?'

'Er . . . Scotland Yard?' she proffered.

'More precisely?'

'Special Branch.'

He nodded again and leaned forward. 'Now, tell me honestly, Emma Lestrade, do I look anything like Sir Patrick Quinn?'

*

'But he's not due back off leave for another two days.' Sir Basil Thomson quaffed his Martini.

'You know Sir Patrick, sir,' John Kane told him, 'salt of the earth. It's hard to keep a good man down.'

'Knocked down, you say?'

'Keep down, sir,' Kane repeated, as though to an idiot. 'It's an old English saying.'

'No,' said Thomson, equally convinced of Kane's imbecility, 'you said he was knocked down by a motor car.'

'Oh, yes indeed. He was just rushing out to buy some of those enormous stocks of frozen mutton we keep reading about for Lady Quinn when a Morris Cowley caught him amidships. If it hadn't been for the mutton he was carrying, I'm afraid we'd all be in church about now, sir.'

'Hmm.' Thomson ruminated briefly on the transience of life. 'Did you know that eight thousand, three hundred and eight-eight people were knocked down in London alone in the last year by motor vehicles?'

'Eight thousand three hundred and eighty-nine now, sir,' Kane pointed out.

'Quite. Quite. Between you and me, Kane, I wonder what those buggers on the second floor are doing about it. Unprofessional of me to say so, I know, but I ask you. Public Carriage Office indeed! They're supposed to be policemen! But tell me, Kane, how is it you're carrying these glum tidings about Paddy? You'll forgive me for saying so, but you're not exactly one of us, are you? You've never ventured beyond the Green Door.'

'Oh no, sir. I just happened to be in the Casualty Department at St Mary's when they brought him in, sir. My youngest got his toe caught in the bath tap. It wasn't only his toe that was smarting by the time I got him home, I can tell you.'

'Quite right,' approved Thomson, who belonged to the muscular school of parenthood. 'Give children a healthy respect for an S-bend, that's what I say. So Paddy sent his regards.'

'Yes. I . . . I feel I should warn you, sir, that Sir Patrick is . . . well, changed.'

'Changed?' Thomson held the glass in mid-swig, appalled by the catch in Kane's voice.

The Inspector nodded, his jaw tense, his brow heavy. 'He'll be wearing an appliance, sir, when he comes in later today.'

'An appliance? I wonder how Lady Paddy is taking it?'

'Not lying down, sir, if I know Lady Quinn.'

'You're right, by God. They're curious cattle, Kane, but that one's made of sterner stuff. That woman has a heart of asbestos.'

'Sir Patrick also said he'd like to come towards nightfall, sir. He feels a little . . . sensitive . . . about his appearance and wants to work alone, after most of the boys have gone. He hoped you'd understand.'

'Understand? Understand? I'd go through a typewriter for that man. It's his kind that made Scotland Yard what it is today. Not like that snivelling Bolshie . . . whatsisface? Lestrade. He isn't fit to walk in Paddy Quinn's shadow.'

Paddy Quinn's shadow hobbled on crutches into the lift and along the carpeted corridor towards the Green Door. Superintendent Fred Wensley rarely ventured that far north at the Yard. The atmosphere on the top floor was all too rarefied for him. But today was an exception. Needs must when the paperwork drives, and even a man destined for the exalted office of Chief Constable was given short shrift at the Green Door. A mysterious hand took the relevant form from him and returned a grudging receipt.

'Sholto?' Wensley peered at the apparition before him, the neck and lower face immersed in a surgical collar, the head swathed in bandages. The apparition walked on.

'Sholto Lestrade?' Wensley said again as he became surer he was right.

Lestrade looked behind him. 'Where?' he growled in a manner he assumed an Irishman would adopt having been hit by a car.

Wensley looked down the corridor too. It was empty.

'Trick of the light, me boy,' Lestrade brogued. Wensley swept past him.

'Yes, I must have been mistaken, Sholto. Sorry.' And he vanished into the lift.

Lestrade tapped on the Green Door. Rumour had it that there was an old piano and that someone played it hot here, but he heard nothing but the surprised gasps of Quinn's underlings as they opened doors. Now he had a problem. He had no idea where Quinn's office was.

'Could you help me?' he wheezed. 'I fear the old legs aren't very chipper at the moment, begorrah.'

Detective Constable Marks did the honours. His surveillance of Inspector Kane effectively ended when that officer reached the Yard and 'Twenty-Twenty' Johnson was briefed to let the Branch know if he stirred again. Marks's oppo., Spencer, was at that moment not surveilling Lestrade either. Whether by accident or design, the long-suffering undercover man had been buttonholed by Uncle Gideon, who insisted that the constable dig a trench to repel a Boer attack. Surrey County Council had taken umbrage that two maniacs were digging up their roads and not laying gas pipes and both men were explaining things to a magistrate as Lestrade spoke.

He lowered himself into Quinn's chair – a damn sight more comfortable than the one he had vacated three floors below not eight months since.

'Can I get you anything, Sir Patrick?' Marks found himself staring at the eyes with their polished purple rims. The bruising looked decidedly waxy, but then Marks had never seen a car-crash survivor before.

'Er . . . yes,' said Lestrade, 'the files on Euperry, Varushkin, Al Haroun and Vavasour.'

'They're classified, sir,' Marks reminded him.

'Bejaysis,' Lestrade croaked, 'must I remind you who's in charge around here.'

'Sir Basil Thomson, sir,' Marks understood hierarchy.

'Operationally!' hissed Lestrade. 'On a day-to-day basis.'

'All I mean, sir, is that you and Sir Basil have the only keys.'

'What about the spare?' Lestrade took a leap in the dark.

'I'll need your signature, sir,' Marks frowned. The accident must have jarred Quinn's brain. He seemed to have forgotten all procedures. The constable slid the relevant chit under his guv'nor's hand and Lestrade lifted his right arm with his left and with trembling fingers wrote 'Patrick Quinn'. Marks looked at the signature – it was like Guy Fawkes's after torture. 'I'll just be a moment, sir.'

While the man had gone, Lestrade hopped over to the nearest filing cabinet and riffled through its contents. He was still chuckling at the information contained in the Winston Churchill file when his telephone rang. For as long as he dared, he ignored it and flipped through the Indian Dissident file. 'What did you do in the War, Gandhi?' he read, and the answer, 'I drove an ambulance'. He tutted to himself. They didn't come more dissident than that, did they?

But the phone would not go away. If he didn't answer it soon, someone else might come in and catch him without his crutches. He collapsed into the plush leather of the chair and snatched up the receiver.

'Who's that?' a disembodied voice asked.

'Special Branch,' said Lestrade.

'I know that,' the voice crackled. 'To whom am I speaking?'

'A senior officer,' said Lestrade. 'I fear I can't say more.'

'Well, what the bloody hell are you doing in my office?' the voice exploded.

Lestrade slammed the phone down. It was Sir Patrick Quinn, on his day off, checking the ship. How long would it be before he turned up, incensed at the intrusion? And how long could Lestrade bluff the men who worked with Quinn every day?

'Sorry, sir,' Marks was back, file-less. 'It's Inspector Qualtrough in Records. He says he's very sorry, but he can't accept your signature. He'll have to come up to verify you.'

Lestrade sagged back in his chair. 'I couldn't bear being verified at the moment, Marks,' he lilted. 'Look, it was clearly a mistake me coming in so soon. Get me to the lift, will you? I shall be all right from there.'

'Very good, sir.'

So it was that Sholto Lestrade, civilian, found his way briefly into the inner sanctum of the Yard. And on his way out, he collided equally briefly into the hurtling form of Superintendent Patrick Quinn. The paranoid little Irishman had rung from just around the corner. Both men looked oddly at each other and went their separate ways. It was what they had done all their working lives together.

*

John Kane grinned like the Cheshire Cat. 'You do realize guv'nor,' he said to Lestrade, 'that I can't possibly do that – though you might.'

'I might indeed,' Lestrade agreed, 'but not a word to my good lady wife.'

'Mum it is,' promised Kane and he and Norroy Macclesfield clambered aboard the inspector's car and drove west.

Lestrade put his head around the drawing-room door a few moments later. 'Still bound over?' he asked.

Fanny nodded. 'It's those scrambled eggs he had for breakfast,' she said. 'But thank you for speaking to the magistrate, dearest. I couldn't bear the thought of poor old Gideon being in an institution.'

'Couldn't you?' Lestrade wrinkled up his face. 'No, I suppose not.'

'Tell me,' she said, 'will we be seeing that nice young man again? The one who kept posing as a window-cleaner?'

'Detective Constable Spencer? Not for a while.' Lestrade began throwing things into his Gladstone. 'I assumed you'd have no objection to his being in an institution.'

'Sholto,' she put down her sampler, 'you didn't!'

'Oh, they'll put him in a rubber room for a few days. Then they'll realize his ravings about being in Special Branch are quite correct and they'll let him go. End of his career, of course.'

'Oh, the poor boy,' she tutted. 'He was only doing his duty.'

'No, he wasn't,' Lestrade countered. 'He was snooping on an honest, upright citizen at the behest of an Irish megalomaniac. That's not quite the same thing.' He glanced out of the window to see a motor-cab carrying Detective Constable Marks purr past. 'He'll have to step on it to catch Norroy Macclesfield,' he murmured.

'Who will?' she asked.

'John Kane's shadow,' Lestrade told her. 'One down, one to go.'

'Do you think someone else is out to catch Norroy Macclesfield?' she asked him, raising an eyebrow.

'Someone else?' Lestrade paused in mid-pack. 'You mean there are *two* tails on Kane?'

'I was talking about that daughter of yours.'

'Emma?'

'She's been asking a lot about him recently. Hasn't she mentioned him to you?'

'Not a word,' he shrugged.

'After Paul . . . well, she must be lonely.'

Lestrade nodded. 'I suppose you're right.'

'It's a pity in a way that he's married. By the way, where are you going, husband mine?'

'Spot of sleuthing, dear,' and he kissed her forehead. 'Now, are you sure you'll be all right – after the break-in and all?'

She ignored him and patted his pocket.

'Please, madam,' he held her at arm's length, 'I am a married man.'

'You're carrying your knuckles, Sholto Lestrade,' she said flatly, 'that always means trouble.'

'No, it doesn't,' he kissed her again. 'Wherever did you get that idea? Back tomorrow,' and he made for the door. 'And he isn't, by the way.'

'Who isn't what?' She'd lost his thread.

'Married. Norroy Macclesfield.'

'But he talks about Mrs Macclesfield.'

'I talk about retiring, too,' he smiled, 'but I haven't done it yet. Norroy Macclesfield.' He thought about the huge, easy-going sergeant of detectives. 'Mrs Emma Macclesfield . . .'

'That's why she hasn't mentioned him to you, Sholto,' Fanny told him. 'She doesn't know what you'd think.'

'Quite right,' said Lestrade. 'Neither do I.'

He knocked on the door of The 43. A colossus in evening suit barred the way. 'Are you a member, sir?' he inquired.

'Not especially,' said Lestrade, feeling decidedly uncomfortable in the tails he had just hired from the Brothers Moss. 'Can I do anything about that?' He waved a five-pound note under the giant's nose.

'Life membership, Mr . . . er?'

'Lister,' he said.

'Lister.' The doorman wrote the name solemnly under the sixteen Smiths who had unimaginatively joined the previous evening. 'Roulette to the left, sir, dice to the right, cards in the centre. Special services . . .' he looked Lestrade up and down, 'but you won't be needing those.'

'A friend of mine', Lestrade handed his topper and cane to a scantily clad flapper, 'mentioned a certain Miss Dominatrix . . .'

'Ah, my mistake,' the giant grinned. 'First floor, sir. Third door on the right.'

'Thank you.' He followed another girl to a large foyer hung with misty red lights. A band in one corner was hammering out one of those new ragtime tunes from America, which Lestrade scarcely recognized as music at all. The twisting balls on the ceiling sent out showers of sparks, myriad points of light that bounced and flashed on the glass floor. For a brief moment, Lestrade wondered why the floor was glass; then the reflection of his little blonde guide told him all. Well, with the price of silk underwear these days, he wasn't surprised. Even so, his spectacles steamed up.

'Good evening.' A voluptuous lady in shimmering backless evening gown suddenly stood before him. 'I'm Kate Meyrick. Welcome to The 43. We haven't seen you here before, Mr . . . er.'

'Lister,' Lestrade bowed.

'No relation to the carbolic man?' she asked with a flutter of diamond fingers.

'On my mother's side,' Lestrade smiled.

'Enjoy your evening, Mr Lister.'

'Thank you, Mrs Meyrick. I shall.'

Now Lestrade, it had to be said, was no stranger to these places. Since he was a green rookie copper in Flower and Dean Street, an eternity ago, his dubious calling had brought him into close contact with various naughty nymphets of the night. From Fifi la Bedoyere who had patched his broken ribs one night when he'd been pursuing his duty a little too arduously to Catherine Walters, known to men and boys as 'Skittles', he'd known his share of the rough and smooth trade. The girl who stood in front of him now, behind the bland third door on the right, was what? Sixteen? Seventeen? She wore the uniform of a French maid, black skirt clinging tightly around her hips, tiny white apron over a delicious pair of breasts stretched taut under a blouse. In her hand she carried a rattan cane and her eyes shone with anticipation.

'Would you like to bend over, ducks?' she asked him. 'We can talk about the money later.'

'I'd just like to talk,' he told her.

'Ah,' she said, 'I'm not very good at that. You want Felicity next door but one.'

He sat carefully on the pink, satinned bed. 'No,' he said, 'I mean I want to talk about one of your clients.'

'Clients?' she shrilled in what was thinly disguised Walthamstow. 'You mean guests.'

'Of course,' he said, patting the bed beside him. 'Guests.'

'I can't tell you nuffink about them,' she said. 'I got my pride, you know.'

'I know,' said Lestrade, solemnly. 'Shall we say ten bob?'

She snatched it from him. 'Well, I first done it when I was twelve. There was this vicar . . .'

'Yes, yes,' Lestrade interrupted, 'but it's a *specific* guest I want to know about.'

'Well, who?' she frowned.

'That I don't know,' he said. 'He might have gone by the name of Vavasour. A Frenchman certainly.'

She looked vague. He fished in his pocket for the morgue photograph John Kane had been able to half-inch from the Yard. 'This man. Have you see him before?'

'Oh, 'im. Yes. Flamin' nuisance 'e was. 'Ere,' she frowned at the photo, ''e don't look too chipper in this picture.'

'He hasn't been well,' Lestrade told her. 'He *was* a guest?'

'Oh yeah.'

'When?'

'Er . . . lor, now you've asked me, darlin'. Wait a minute. It was the night after that nice Mr Randall Thomas Davidson come.'

'The Archbishop of Canterbury?' Lestrade hadn't read anything about this in Patrick Quinn's file.

'No,' she slapped his arm, 'not *that* nice Mr Randall Thomas Davidson. But 'e was funny.'

'Mr Davidson?'

'Mr Vavasour.'

'So he did use that name?'

'Yeah. Look, mate, wassis all abaht?'

'For ten bob, you don't need to know,' Lestrade assured her. 'In what way was he funny?'

'Well, 'e wanted me to do it, you know, *that* way.'

'*That* way?' Lestrade repeated. Man of the world though he was, he wasn't sure how many ways there were. So much for the ways of the world.

'Yeah, you know. Hunnish practices an' that.'

'Oh, *that* way,' Lestrade smiled. Clearly the world had not totally passed him by.

'Well, I said to 'im, I said, "I'm not a bloody Turk," I said.'

'Turk?' Lestrade repeated.

'Well, I had that nice Colonel Lawrence in 'ere the other day. 'E told me all about it.'

'Did he? Tell me, did Vavasour say anything?'

Miss Dominatrix thought for a while, 'Well, he said "Ooh" a few times and a couple of "Aahs". The rest was in French. Quite filthy, I shouldn't wonder.'

'I see.'

'Can I do you now, sir?' she bared her right arm a little more and scythed through the air with her cane. The candlewick bounced on the coverlet.

Lestrade rolled sideways as though to avoid the swipe and hooked open a side cupboard as he hit the floor. A pile of wallets fell on to the carpet.

''Ere,' she screamed, 'you ain't got no right.'

But Lestrade's eagle eye had hit on the right target. He had been to the lecture on 'Instant Wallet Recognition' years ago and the old skills had not deserted him. He snatched it back from the vixen's grasp and opened it. 'Hmm,' he said, 'Emile Nougat de St Etienne Vavasour, late of the Quai d'Orsay. He's not carrying many francs, is he?' He shook the wallet upside-down and a single piece of paper fluttered to the ground.

While Miss Dominatrix was gathering up all the other spillage, he stooped to read the missive. Damn. It was in French. No matter. He slipped it into his pocket, then held out his hand.

'Are you ready now?' Miss Dominatrix, her indignation gone, recognized submission when she saw it.

157

'No,' he assured her, 'I just want *my* wallet back.'

Grudgingly, she handed it over. 'You're an old bugger you are,' she scowled.

'Rather like Mr Vavasour,' he nodded.

'Look,' she purred, running her fingers under his dickie, 'you're probably embarrassed because you're so old. I'm sure I can do sunfink abaht that, eh? Wotya say?'

Lestrade was about to say goodbye, when the door crashed back and an ox-like oaf of vague familiarity stood there.

'Blevvi,' she scampered over to him, 'you're early tonight.'

Inspector Edward Blevvins placed the girl to one side. 'So I see,' he snarled, not taking his eyes off Lestrade.

'This gentleman was just goin', wasn't you, ducks?' she said.

'Yes,' he told them, 'I think I've got what I came for.'

Blevvins stopped him. 'Is that so, *guv'nor*? You know, I've been longing for a chance like this.' And he prodded Lestrade in the chest, so that the older man jolted backwards.

'Ooh, are you gonna 'it 'im, Blevvi?' Miss Dominatrix clapped her hands. 'Can I 'old your coat?'

'No need, darling,' he grunted. 'One thump and Mr Lestrade here won't be getting home with his lower jaw.'

'Lestrade?' she was confused. 'Nah, 'is name is Lister. Or so Mrs Meyrick said on the blower while 'e was on 'is way up.'

'Oh yeah? And mine's Ramsay MacDonald.'

He swung a right at Lestrade, who back-stepped nicely. He swung again, using his left this time. Again, Lestrade *pas de deux*'d. By now, however, he was against the wall and there were no more back passages to escape down. Blevvins straightened. 'You've had this coming, Lestrade,' he hissed, 'for a bloody long time.'

He thrust his head forward to crack Lestrade's skull with his own. Lestrade snatched up his topper and wedged it between their foreheads. The hat crumpled like paper, but for Blevvins there was no second chance. Lestrade's shin came up and caught him a nasty one in his wedding tackle. Simultaneously, the fist with the brass knuckles snaked upwards, splitting the inspector's lip and loosening two of his teeth. He crashed backwards on to the bed, only marginally less sensible than when he came in.

''Ere,' purred Miss Dominatrix, 'you're bloody good for an old geezer, aintcha? Would you like a job on the next floor? Wiv the boys, I mean? I could have a word with Mrs Meyrick.'

Lestrade rummaged through the fallen policeman's pockets. 'That's *Mr* Lestrade to you, Blevvins,' he said and folded the knuckles away, 'and you'll never get to be Leader of His Majesty's Opposition with a left hook like that. *And* I'll just take thirty bob to pay the Moss Brothers for one rather battered top hat. Hello, hello, hello,' the old police habits died hard, 'what have we here?'

He held the paper up to the light, together with a large wad of used notes. 'Tsk, tsk, Inspector,' he said. 'Take some advice from an old copper,' he chuckled at the paper. '*If* you're going to take bribes, *never* keep a carbon copy of the receipt.'

Lestrade stood up. 'Miss,' he said, 'thanks for the offer of a job, but I've already got one. Do one thing for me, will you?'

She knelt on the floor.

'No, no, not that,' he said. 'When Mr Blevvins comes round, tell him I shall expect to hear that his resignation is on the Commissioner's desk bright and early Monday morning. Got it?'

'Yeah,' she said dumbly.

He kissed her hand. 'You've been very helpful,' and he swept out. In the ragtime corner outside, a large, upright sergeant of detectives nearly bowled him over.

'Mr Lestrade, sir. Mr Kane thought you might need a little help.'

'Help, Norroy?' Lestrade frowned at him. 'Not a bit of it,' and he sauntered off down the corridor. 'Anyway, half of Vine Street police station's in here tonight. Funny there are always so many around when you don't want them, isn't it?'

8

The verdant foliage that Lestrade remembered from earlier
sorties into the Foreign Office had given way, in these days of
depression and war economy, to a single, rather wilting, aspidistra. It was up this still-extraordinary staircase that Emma
Lestrade glided that Monday morning in search of her new
office. For all that she was a girl brought up to the leisured
classes, she had obtained three jobs in as many weeks and had
therefore never failed an interview in her life.

She had in fact been at work for nearly an hour, and had
already realized that one government department was very
much like another. They all had the capacity to bury people
under tons of paper and most of them had views over parkland
pleasant enough to make the humble filing clerk long to be
elsewhere. It was also spring and Emma's heart did tend to
dance with the daffodils.

She knocked on the oak door and an oaken voice boomed
from within, 'Enter.'

'Baron Curzon of Kedleston?' she asked.

'At the moment,' he said. 'Who are you?'

Behind an enormous desk and before a wall festooned with
maps sat a man with the deep-set eyes of a viceroy of India. The
high-domed forehead and the oddities of spine made Lord
Curzon a most peculiar person.

'Emma Lister,' she bobbed.

'How refreshing,' Curzon staggered over to her. 'Not only are
you female, you're actually less than sixty.'

'Considerably,' she assured him.

'Sit down, my dear. Do you have shorthand?'

'As short as you like, my lord,' she said, perching on the cold leather of the chesterfield.

'Wretched nuisance, my permanent under-secretary going down with his old trouble again. Still,' he patted her knee, 'probably a blessing in disguise. He hasn't got your ankles,' and he winked at her.

At least Emma was grateful to discover that having twenty-seven-year-old female ankles wasn't the permanent under-secretary's old trouble.

'How long have you been at the Foreign Office?' Curzon asked.

She looked at her watch. 'Sixty-three minutes, sir,' she told him.

'Oh, dear. Have you been vetted?'

'Positively,' she assured him, although in the stables at Bandicoot Hall, such things were achieved with red-hot pincers.

'Where were you before?'

'The War Office,' she said, omitting her brief role in *The Destruction of Sennacherib*. Lord Curzon didn't look the type to guzzle tea and biscuits in the back row of the Troxy. She'd be quite safe.

'For how long?'

'Nearly two weeks,' she said.

'Ah. And before that?'

'I was a lady of leisure, sir.'

'I don't really think you're quite what I had in mind for this morning's . . .'

'Sir,' she sat bolt upright, holding her notepad towards him, 'I hope you won't think me forward, but may I have your autograph?'

'Autograph?' he blinked, moving slightly away.

'My godfather, Donald Corleone, was with you at the Durbar of 1903. He never forgot it and was so impressed that he named all three of his sons after you.'

'Really?'

'Yes. George, Nathaniel and Curzon. Stout fellows all.'

'Oh, I say.' Curzon turned a shade pinker above the Eton collar. Emma secretly hoped it wasn't the *actual* one he had worn at school. 'Oh, very well,' and he scrawled his name. 'Tell me, Miss Lister, how did you obtain this post?'

'Mr Stanley Accrington, sir,' she said, truthfully. 'A friend of my godfather's.'

'Accrington?'

'In accounts, my lord. On the first floor.'

'Ah, yes. Well, I suppose it will be all right. I have a letter of a rather confidential nature I would like you to type. When you have, of course, you will burn your notepad and erase every word of it from your memory.'

'Every word of what, sir?' she asked, wide-eyed.

He patted her knee again, a little higher this time. 'That's the ticket, my girl,' he leered. Then he hobbled over to his desk again. 'To Captain Vernon Kell, Military Intelligence, National Portrait Gallery; Vernon: colon . . .'

'Vernon Colon?'

'No, no, I'm doing the punctuation, my dear. What with declining educational standards these days.'

'I *can* manage, comma, my lord! Exclamation mark,' she purred.

'Quite. Quite. Well, then, Vernon: Re the murders of various foreigners in and around London in the past few weeks, what the bloody hell is going on? I know you are short-staffed and money is tight, but hang it all. I am being besieged by embassies and plenipotentiaries. Who is behind it? Is it the Bolshies? What is Basil Thomson doing? By the way, I hate to remind you at a time like this, what with over 800,000 men unemployed, but when can I have that 3/6 you borrowed off me? Obediently yours, et cetera, et cetera. Got that?'

'Every word, sir,' she told him.

'Right. Now, I don't trust the postal service. In India there was a nigger in a loincloth and he got through come hell or Rajputana. Over here, the blighters are striking every five minutes. Besides, I haven't forgotten Cleveland Street. So, type it up and take it round yourself.'

She rose to go. 'By the way,' he adopted his slimier tone, 'what are you doing for dinner tonight?'

'I'm washing my hair, my lord,' she told him and turned

sharply on her heel before he had the chance to fondle her knee once more.

She did not come at evening. She did not come by dark. Fanny was coping with Uncle Gideon at the time and it was Sholto Lestrade who roamed the house, pacing back and forth. True, the girl had only lived with them for just over three years. It was shortly before Paul Dacres disappeared that she had left sleepy Somerset where her childhood years had been spent. True, she was twenty-seven and quick and clever and brave. True, she was Lestrade's daughter, with his iron in her soul. Yet she was his only daughter. And because he had not been there when she was growing up, he felt her absence all the more keenly now.

Madison made him up a flask of tea and he drove his Lanchester round to the station and sat in the cab for a while. He paced the cold, dark platform as the commuter trains whistled in and whistled out. He got funny looks from the men with flags and a little before midnight, he gave up and drove to Town. He stopped to telephone Fanny. No, there was no sign. No, there had been no message. Fanny would wait up with Madison. Gideon was on full alert anyway. Ladysmith may have been relieved, but Mrs Lestrade certainly wasn't.

He drove with gears crunching through the moonless April night, rattling north east through sleeping Merton and on to Kew. It was lilac time, but he couldn't see it in the dark. He crossed the river and found a few. 'Am I all right for the Foreign Office?' he asked. 'St James's?'

One of the beat coppers saluted. 'Indeed you are, sir,' he said. 'Just take the next left, the sixth right, the fourth left and you'll come to a junction. Go under the bridge, sharp right and up the hill. There's a level-crossing on your left and a pub called The Lost Traveller. I should ask again when you get there.'

'Thank you,' Lestrade said, 'I will.'

The Italianate vulgarity of the Foreign Office loomed eventually out of the early hours, its reflection black in the pearly haze of the pond. A crunch on the gravel told Lestrade of the presence of a Park policeman. 'You can't park that 'ere, you know.'

Reflecting that that was obviously why they were called Park policemen, he reversed the Lanchester and drove it unerringly into a rhododendron bush around the corner.

The air hit him like a brick wall and he pulled up the collar of his Donegal. More feet padding down the path. It was like Piccadilly Circus. 'Now then, Mr Chiozza, sir,' he heard a constable say. 'You put that young lady down and get off home, there's a good gentleman.'

He didn't hear the answer, but the ingratiating tone of the constable rather gave it away. 'Oh, really, sir, I couldn't. No, no. Not that much. Oh, well, all right, then.'

But with Inspector Blevvins as a model, it was hardly surprising. He crossed by the little bridge and the ducks stirred in their still-winter plumage and quacked at him, shifting from webbed foot to webbed foot. He slipped momentarily on the Canada-goose shit, but steadied himself and reached the building. There were no lights burning. All was locked and barred. Whichever door he tried, the same result. Shut fast. A weary cabman on his way to his rank sauntered by, leading one of the last cab-horses in London. 'They've all gone 'ome, mate,' he growled.

'Thank you,' Lestrade called. It wasn't the news he wanted to hear, but he knew the man was right.

'Wanna lift?'

'No, thanks. I've got my motor round the corner.'

He trudged back to it. At least his shadow had fallen by the wayside. The long-suffering Constable Spencer, released at last by the Surrey police, had shivered in the shrubbery all day near Lestrade's house. Unfortunately, Superintendent Quinn had neglected to give his man any transport and all Spencer could do was to ring in to the Yard. The man they had sent had forgotten to bring his map, and so Lestrade was on his own.

Morning brought no joy. For a start, drizzle set in from the west. Lestrade entered the Foreign Office with the cleaners and sat among mops and buckets until anybody real arrived.

'You poor old bleeder,' one of them said to him. 'Cuppa tea while you're waiting? Or d'ya fancy a nip of the 'Onourable Curzon's brandy?'

'Does he let you help yourself?' Lestrade asked her.

'What 'e don't know, don't 'urt 'im,' and she tapped the side of her nose. "'E might know all there is to know about foreign affairs an' that – an' 'e's 'ad a few of them in 'is time, I can tell yer – but 'e don't know bugger all about the levels in 'is decanters. Bleedin' shame, ain't it?'

'Mr Accrington?' Lestrade lunged gratefully for a face he thought he knew crossing the entrance hall.

'Mr Lestrade, isn't it?' the accounts man said.

'Yes. Can I have a word?'

'Of course. Shall we go to my office?'

Lestrade was grateful for a soft chair and a cup of coffee. As the accounts department came to life around him, with the comforting noise of double-entry book-keeping scratching in his ears, the ex-policeman got down to business.

'Emma,' he said.

'Yes?' Accrington was an Old Etonian of the Bandicoot school. Except that he wore glasses and lacked Bandicoot's bulk. Lestrade remembered Harry saying that Stanley was something of a swot at school. Won the prize for hendiadys-spotting and so on. Arsehole Accrington, they had called him. Behind his back of course.

'Do you know where she is?'

'Ah,' Accrington raised a clerkly finger and rattled out a series of keys on a monstrous machine to his left. 'At this precise moment, she's on the eight thirteen. It'll just be leaving Vauxhall as we speak.'

'No,' Lestrade shook his head.

'Not another derailment at Balham? Whatever *is* becoming of Southern Region?'

'She didn't come home last night,' Lestrade told him.

'Not? Oh dear. That's odd. Isn't it?' It had to be said that Accrington didn't know Emma Lestrade all that well. 'By the way, now that you're here, I have to say I'm not all that happy about this little subterfuge – the alias and everything.' He closed to Lestrade. 'This is a very sensitive department, you know.'

'When did you see her last?' he asked.

'Let me see. It must have been yesterday morning. That was her first day, wasn't it? Something of a flap on. The Old Boy was screaming blue murder.'

'The Old Boy?'

'Curzon. The Foreign Secretary. His staff has been decimated. Well, it's the 'flu. We've none of us been right since last year. He wanted a secretary urgently to take a memo and Emma was the first thing I laid eyes on.'

'So she was working with him?'

'Oh, only for a few moments. Then she came back and went out again.'

'Out?'

'Yes. Put her hat and coat on.'

'Where did she go?'

'Er . . . let me see. She had a letter in her hand.'

'The Post Office?' Lestrade's deductive reasoning was still like greased lightning.

'No. The National Portrait Gallery.'

'The . . .'

'Don't ask me why,' shrugged Accrington, 'but that's what she said.'

'How long was she there?'

'Er . . . oh, lord. Come to think of it, I didn't see her again. Spot of shopping, d'you think? Not strictly on, you know, except on Thursdays.'

'Dammit, Accrington!' Lestrade was on his feet. 'My daughter has disappeared in the centre of London, under your very nose and you accuse her of surreptitious shopping! If anything has happened to that girl, I shall be back and, depend upon it, I shall be placing that machine up a certain part of your anatomy.' He paused at the door amid bewildered clerks. 'Arsehole!' he shouted.

The National Portrait Gallery was founded by Act of Parliament at about the time our brave chaps were getting off the ships from the Crimea. Mind you, it had moved about a bit since then – Westminster, South Kensington, Bethnal Green. And finally, when Lestrade got there, Trafalgar Square. Like every other visitor before him and since, he went to the wrong entrance and had to trudge round to the side door in St Martin's Place.

He nearly collided, in one of Ewan Christian's elaborate doorways, with men in uniform hurrying out with bulging

166

briefcases and men in overalls hurrying in, carrying paintings under their arms.

'Who's in charge?' he asked the man on the desk.

'War Office or Gallery?' The clerk did not look up.

'I have a choice?' Lestrade asked.

'The Gallery was taken over during the War by the War Office.' The clerk was busying himself with a rubber stamp. 'They're only just moving out.'

'I'll ask again,' sighed Lestrade. 'Who's in charge?'

'Sir Eustace Bishop for the Gallery, Captain Kell for the War Office.'

Now Lestrade had already met Sir Eustace Bishop. And although in Sholto Lestrade's mental Book of Handy Hints to Catch Criminals, page thirty-eight had dealt with the fact that if a name turned up twice in the course of an inquiry, that name was worthy of further nosing, he remembered Bishop's offer to show him his Beardsleys and he opted for Captain Kell.

'I've got no instructions about that,' the clerk said. 'I'm a civilian. I can only tell you where Sir Eustace Bishop is.'

'Where?'

'Out.'

Lestrade made to go out, then suddenly veered around the clerk's counter, catching himself a nasty one on the turnstile, and poked his finger through his pocket into the man's ribs. 'Do you know what this is?' he asked.

The clerk stepped back, glancing at the protuberance in Lestrade's pocket. 'I hope it's a gun, or something,' he said.

'You do not hope in vain,' Lestrade told him. 'Now, you will take me to this Captain Kell and you will do it now. And remember, my finger and I have a hair-trigger. One slip, one nod to any passing soldier or removals man and the best-known painting in here will be *Gentleman in Red*. Savvy?'

The clerk savvied. And he had no wish to antagonize an obvious madman.

'Well, put your hands down, then,' muttered Lestrade. 'Let's not make this too obvious, shall we?' And he followed the clerk up the stairs. They passed a cross-eyed vicar preaching on the wall, three weird sisters from Haworth and a crook-backed king of England who looked for all the world like Sir Henry Irving.

167

At the top of the stairs, a corridor turned a sharp right and they came to a door marked M15. The clerk knocked.

A dapper little man with glasses, greying hair and a rich, brown voice opened it. 'Yes?' he said.

'Captain Kell, please,' Lestrade said.

'Yes?' the man repeated.

'Oh,' said Lestrade. 'I expected someone in uniform.'

'Who are you?' Kell asked.

'My name is Lister,' Lestrade lied. 'I've just been seconded to . . . M Fifteen.'

'Ah, you must be Eric Smiley's replacement,' Kell beamed. 'Come on in.'

'Yes.' Lestrade's luck was running with him. 'Yes, Smiley, that's right.'

The clerk began gesturing as wildly as a man feels he can with a loaded index finger where he hopes his vertebrae will still be in a few minutes' time. 'That's all right,' said Kell. 'No need to call security. Back to your desk now, there's a good chap. Won't you come in, Mr Lister?'

Lestrade took in the office at a glance. Kell was alone in a cramped little room, from floor to ceiling filled with filing cabinets. 'What happens now?' Kell asked.

'My name's not Lister,' Lestrade said, poking his finger forward.

Kell hesitated for a moment, then sat down. 'I know,' he said. 'And that isn't a gun in your pocket either. Either you're very pleased to see me or that's your finger.'

Lestrade uncocked it. 'Do I assume you're not Captain Kell?' he said, not moving from the door.

'Assume what you like, dear boy. Now, Mr Lestrade, what can I do for you?'

'How do you know who I am?'

Kell put his feet up on the desk and lit a cigar. 'No half measures,' he said. 'It's the logical processes, the minutiae of the little grey cells that I love. Let's decide first how I know you weren't actually Smiley's replacement, shall we?'

If this was an intelligence test, Lestrade was likely to fail. 'Don't tell me,' he said, sitting opposite his man and placing the bowler on the desk between them. 'There is no such person as Mr Smiley in your organization.'

'Of course not,' Kell said. 'What a ludicrous name. No one in . . . my line of work . . . would have such a handle. But there was something else.'

'Oh?'

'You misread the door. It's not M Fifteen. It's Em Eye Five.'

'Ah.'

'So, Mr Lestrade, two mistakes in one morning. You're not going to make any more, are you?'

You haven't told me how you know who I am,' he said.

'Sholto Joseph Lestrade, born January 18th 1854 in Pimlico, London. Mother Martha, washerwoman, deceased. Father, Joseph, police constable, deceased. Only surviving child of three. Married Sarah Manchester 1892. She died as a result of childbirth the following year. Only daughter Emma, born . . .'

'It's about Emma that I've come,' Lestrade interrupted.

'But I haven't started on your cases yet,' Kell said.

'She came here yesterday,' Lestrade told him.

'Under the alias of Smiley or Lister?' Kell asked.

'Where is she?'

'My dear Lestrade,' Kell kicked his feet off the desk, 'I'm afraid I have no idea.'

Lestrade leaned back. 'How do you know about me?' he asked again.

'It's my job,' said Kell. 'The initials on the door don't stand for Mixed Infants, Lestrade. They stand for Military Intelligence.'

'You've seen my file at Scotland Yard,' Lestrade realized.

'Seen it?' Kell chuckled. 'My dear boy, I probably wrote it. People like you don't break wind without us knowing about it. Now, I'm sorry you've had a wasted journey. Good morning.'

'What does A.T. One mean?' Lestrade asked him.

Kell's eyes narrowed. 'A.T. One,' he murmured. 'That's the War Office proper. Not in this annexe. It stands for Allied Transport. Does that help your case?'

'What case?' Lestrade did what came naturally. He looked blank.

Kell chuckled. 'You know, you're pretty fly,' he said. 'About as good as Roger Casement.'

Lestrade stood. 'I know,' he said, 'I've met him.'

'I know you have,' Kell smiled and he saw Lestrade out.

When the door had closed, a wooden panel in the wall slid sideways with a scrape. Sir Basil Thomson emerged from the gloom.

'Should we call in Sir Reginald, Naval Intelligence?' Kell asked.

'Contradiction in terms, Naval Intelligence,' Thomson said. 'Well?' he asked. 'Does he know anything?'

Kell shook his head. 'No, but he'd like to,' he said. 'And such men are dangerous.'

For a while, Lestrade sat on the little bench that used to stand by the railings in St Martin's Place. A tramp sat on the far end, snoring, so Lestrade ate one of his sandwiches. He dropped some money into the old man's hat; after all, he'd been poor himself once. Come to think of it, he'd been poor several times. He telephoned Fanny and toyed with telephoning the Bandicoots. Then he thought better of it. It had still only been seventeen hours since Emma should have been home. No point in worrying them yet.

In the end he went back to the Yard. He stood on the Embankment, glowering at the side entrance he knew so well. His shadow had found him again, sauntering casually in the guise of a knocker-up; a bad choice as it was half past three in the afternoon. He was grateful to John Kane and his man Macclesfield who drove out at that very moment.

'I've got to do something about Constable Spencer,' Lestrade said, momentarily resting his elbow in Kane's groin as he clambered into the car. 'He's beginning to get up my nostrils.'

'What news of Monsieur Vavasour, guv'nor?' Kane asked, once his eyes had stopped watering.

'Never mind him,' said Lestrade, 'I've got more pressing business, John. Emma's missing.'

'Emma?' Kane and Macclesfield chorused.

'Keep your eyes on the road, Norroy. We don't want this

police motor wrapped around a lamp standard, do we, or we'll all be back to horses. What happened, Sholto?'

'Damned if I know. It was her first day at the Foreign Office. I thought she might get a lead on the murdered foreigners. She was last seen on her way to deliver a letter to the Military Intelligence branch of the War Office.'

'To whom was it addressed?' Macclesfield asked, without, this time, taking his eyes off the road.

'Haven't a clue,' shrugged Lestrade. 'But the letter was dictated by Lord Curzon.'

'The Foreign Secretary?'

'That's the boy,' said Lestrade.

'Did you ask him?' Macclesfield suggested.

'You don't ask Foreign Secretaries who they write to, Norroy,' his guv'nor told him. 'It's a bit like asking if a chap dresses to the right or to the left.'

'I thought politics would be behind this somewhere,' the sergeant said.

'We'll get the Divisions moving,' said Kane, 'I don't know how far we'll get against Military Intelligence, but we'll have a damned good try. Macclesfield here will issue a detailed description of Emma, won't you, Norroy?'

'I don't know what you mean, sir,' the sergeant said.

'Anything else, guv'nor?' Kane asked.

'Oh, one thing, John.' Lestrade dug deep into his inside pocket. 'You might pass this little billy doo on to Fred Wensley. It's a copy of a receipt for a pretty hefty bribe kindly offered by a Mrs Meyrick who runs the 43 Club in Gerrard Street to one Inspector Ned Blevvins, Spinster of this Parish.'

'Got him!' Kane thumped the leather upholstery.

'Yes,' smiled Lestrade, 'I can't tell you how wretched I feel having narked to the coppers. If only all our boys in blue were as wonderful as Mr Blevvins.'

'Yes, indeed,' chuckled Kane. Then he caught his old guv'nor's eye. 'And don't worry,' he slapped the man's shoulder, 'we'll find her.'

*

There had been a phone call by the time Lestrade got home. Kane and Macclesfield had dropped him in the Park and he had collected his Lanchester. A distraught Fanny had run out to meet him and had thrown herself into his arms.

'They've got Emma,' she had sobbed. 'You're to go to this address. Alone. No tricks or . . . or . . .' and she had soaked his collar with her tears.

He had looked at the address she had written down and had smiled grimly. 'What sort of voice was it?' he had asked. 'Man? Woman?'

'Man,' she managed. 'An accent. Was it Irish?'

'Irish?'

And so Lestrade faced another brick wall. In reality, it was a privet hedge, twenty feet high. The maze at Hampton Court. Getting in, of course, was no problem. He simply showed his ticket to the man at the entrance. The man had grinned at him. He looked very young for a Royal Pensioner and something large and ugly was protruding under his trenchcoat. 'Top o' the morning,' the man had said – hardly the traditional greeting of a man from Hampton Wick.

Lestrade began well enough, turning left and right in search of the heart of the maze. The sky was a leaden grey and his feet crunched on the new gravel of the footpaths. In the distance he could make out the palace which Cardinal Wolsey had built in 1515 and had passed a trifle petulantly to Henry VIII, whose Tudor greyhound leered down from the brickwork of the main gate. He had sauntered through the William-and-Mary gardens with their symmetry and precision, past the grape-vine and the Long Water. In the distance he had seen the fallow deer cropping the lush grass of Bushey Park. What he had not seen, and their absence struck him as odd, were any tourists. The spring season had just begun and there ought to have been the odd old dowager, wallowing in the nostalgia of the place. There ought to have been the hideous cackle of a party of underprivileged school children soaking up its culture. Nothing. Just a darkly handsome man on the gate with what might have been a sub-machine-gun slung under his coat.

'Over here, Mr Lestrade,' a lilting voice called. He turned, fingers curled on the knuckles. No, he had promised Fanny, of course he wouldn't go alone. He had declined her offer of help, and with difficulty had persuaded Uncle Gideon to put his sword away. Kane and Macclesfield would be there, he had lied to her. There was absolutely no danger, either to himself or to Emma. He had never been convinced of that. Now he was still less sure.

There was no one behind him. The voice chuckled. 'Unnerving, these mazes, aren't they?'

He turned again. Surely the voice was behind him? Ahead of him?

'Haha, you're getting warmer.'

He spun for a third time. He was the mouse. The maze was the trap. Emma was the cheese. But somewhere in the green entanglement there was a cat.

'Here, Mr Lestrade.'

He spun for the last time, the blade in his fist slashing the air. But he was too slow. Was it the years? Was it the loneliness of the maze? Was it the fact that his daughter's life was in danger? Or was it the fact that he found himself staring down the muzzle of a loaded revolver?

'You're very slick with that,' the ex-Superintendent said.

The gunman cocked the weapon and slid it back into the holster of his Sam Browne, strapped low on his right thigh.

'Theatrical, isn't it?' the man's thin lips broke into a smile. 'Too many dime novels as a boy, I'm afraid.'

'You carry a Webley, Mr . . . er.'

'Collins,' said the gunman. 'Michael Collins. I'd shake your hand, only it appears to be full of a switch-blade.'

Lestrade clicked the blade back and pocketed it. 'Where's my daughter?' he said levelly.

'Ah yes,' Collins put an arm round his shoulder. 'I'm not quite sure – yet.'

'Meaning?' Lestrade pulled away.

Slowly, from all blind corners of the maze, trench-coated, trilby-hatted gunmen emerged.

'Mr Lestrade,' Collins tilted the Homburg back on his head, 'I've gone to considerable trouble to arrange this meeting. I

173

couldn't manage a nicer day for it, I'm afraid, although we do have our people at the Met. Office. Would you care for some Irish coffee?'

Lestrade was afraid that that would turn out to be made from seaweed, but the man's entourage bristled with firearms and he wasn't likely to find Emma by antagonizing them. 'Delighted,' he said. 'Some of the boys?' He jerked his head in their direction.

'They were summoned from the hillside, they were summoned from the glen,' Collins told him. 'Seamus, Sean, Padraic, Padraic, Seamus, say hello to Mr Lestrade.'

'Hello,' the gunmen brogued.

'Would I be right in assuming that you gentlemen are members of the Irish Republican Army?'

'Well, now, Sholto me boy – er, you don't mind if I call you Sholto? "Army" is such an emotive word, isn't it? I prefer the term "Brotherhood". It puts matters in perspective.'

'And the Brothers are your execution squad?' Lestrade asked.

Collins stopped walking, 'Oh, Sholto, that's a terrible harsh thing to say about them. Seamus,' he turned to one of his men, 'do we have anything to do with executions?'

The gunman opened his coat to reveal a hanging arsenal of grenades, pistols and knives.

'There you are,' Collins smiled with his bee-sting lips. 'Not a thing. Ah, coffee.'

In the centre of the maze was an open square and a table was spread there with Irish linen, silver jugs and steaming glasses of coffee with delicious Kerry cream floating on the top. Collins clicked his tongue. 'Such an unfortunate combination of colours,' he said, 'black and tan. Won't you have a seat, Sholto?'

Lestrade slid the chair back, carefully checking for booby-traps as he did so. 'You're a suspicious one, Sholto Lestrade,' Collins chuckled, 'but I admire that.'

'And you're a killer, Mr Collins. Can we get down to business?'

'A killer, is it?' Collins dipped his lips into the frothy coffee. 'Ah, you shouldn't believe all you read in the papers.'

'So you didn't break Eamonn de Valera out of Lincoln Jail?'

'Well, I happened to be passing,' Collins admitted.

'And you didn't riddle Lord French's car with bullets at Ashtown Station?'

'What have I got against the motor-car industry?' Collins asked.

'And you weren't in the Post Office in O'Connell Street, Dublin, in the Easter of 1916 when the shooting started?'

'Indeed I was,' Collins said proudly. 'A terrible beauty was born. But sure, wasn't I just getting the pension out for me sainted mother? I thought you wanted to talk business?'

'I do,' Lestrade risked the coffee. It was quite pleasant, with a kick like a mule. 'Emma.'

'Ah, the business I had in mind was of a rather different nature.'

'Did you or did you not telephone my wife with a threatening message concerning my daughter?'

'Well, that depends on your definition of the word threatening. Padraic . . .' Collins turned to another of his henchmen, who grinned and opened his coat to reveal a sawn-off shotgun and what closely resembled a medieval mace. 'Now *that's* threatening,' said Collins. 'No, my job for the Brotherhood is largely financial. I am the Secretary of the Irish National Aid Association.'

'How nice,' said Lestrade.

'Well, it has its moments,' Collins agreed. 'But it has its limitations, too. You see, for various reasons, we can't exactly do street collections. The British public will put up with a lot – witness the fact that Lloyd George is Prime Minister – but contributing to what they see as a terrorist organization? No, that they will not do. It is, as always, Sinn Féin.'

'I beg your pardon?'

'Ourselves alone,' Collins translated. 'But you see that sort of Celtic pride is all fine and dandy, but it doesn't buy the weapons – er, the things we need for our cause. That's where you come in.'

'I do?'

'Oh yes.'

'Ah, I see.' Lestrade leaned back with one arm over the back of the chair. 'So, the idea is, I pay you a small fortune in ransom for my daughter?'

'Sholto, would you like a job in the Brotherhood? You'd be a damn sight more use than Cathal Brugha anyway. His idea of furthering our cause is to blow up the Cabinet. It didn't work in 1605 with that good old broth of a Catholic boy Guido Fawkes – I can't see it working now, to be honest. But you have the ruthless mind of a financial tactician.'

'There's one snag to that,' Lestrade said, as though considering Collins's offer. 'I am a retired Superintendent of police. My pension wouldn't pay for young Patrick there's cartridges.'

Collins chuckled. 'You're richer now than you've ever been, Sholto,' he said. 'Your pension is not vast, I know, but there's Fanny's house as well as the little bit put away by her Da for a rainy day, which, with compound interest, computes at £3,408 17s 11d as of the close of the banks yesterday.'

Lestrade was astonished. 'How did you know that?'

Collins laughed. 'Man,' he said, 'I have been on the run from the British army for the past three years – all of course on a case of mistaken identity. And yet here I am sitting with you in the middle of Hampton Court in broad daylight. And it's all ours. I've hired the place for the day.'

'Can you do that?'

'I can,' Collins assured him. 'I've got the best intelligence network in the country. By the way, I *do* like that new pink wallpaper Fanny's got in the bathroom.'

Lestrade's face came up darkly from his coffee. 'So it was *you* who ransacked my house? Beat my wife senseless?'

'No,' Collins told him, 'that's not my style. I'm fighting a war, Sholto, but I don't wage it on women.'

'All right.' Lestrade knew when he was beaten. 'How much do you want?'

'Want?'

'For Emma. Name your price.'

'All right,' Collins lolled back in his chair, 'I'll make it easy for you. One Russian icon by Agathon Fabergé and we'll call it quits.'

'You know about the icon?' Lestrade frowned. 'How?'

'As I said, Sholto, the best intelligence network in the country. I am its director.'

'That's what you were looking for in my house?'

'I told you, we didn't do that,' Collins repeated. 'Do you have it on your person?'

Lestrade nodded.

Collins held out his hand.

'First, my daughter,' Lestrade said.

Collins sighed. 'Yes, well, there's the real snag, of course. I haven't got her.'

'You're a liar, Mr Collins.'

Lestrade heard the snick of rifle bolts behind him. 'No, no,' Collins smiled, holding up a hand to his men. 'We don't want any unpleasantness. Why, it was in this very garden that Dutch William, the Protestant bastard, came a cropper off his horse. I'd hate to stain this sainted placed with red on such a promising morning.' He looked up at the sky. 'It'll be sunny later, I shouldn't wonder. In the meantime,' he looked back at Lestrade, 'here we are, two gentlemen sipping our coffee and engaging in a simple friendly business transaction.' He leaned forward. 'You have the word of Michael Collins, if you'll take it, that I do not have your daughter.'

Lestrade looked at him for a long time.

'But I know a man who has.'

Lestrade started. Collins raised a hand. 'If I tell you who has her, will you leave it there?'

'What do you think?'

'I think you're getting in over your head, Sholto, that's what I think. Take it from me, this thing isn't quite bigger than both of us, but it's bigger than you. You're a retired copper, that's all.'

'With friends,' Lestrade said.

'Yes, but they're not in sufficiently high places.'

'You tell me who has her,' said Lestrade, 'I give you the icon.'

'I can take the icon anyway,' Collins told him flatly, 'with or without your consent. And if I have to put a bullet in your head first, then you may rest assured, I will do just that.'

'Isn't the back of the head more your style?' Lestrade fished.

'Tut, tut, Sholto,' Collins chided him. 'This isn't getting us anywhere. The icon?' He held out his hand again.

'The name?' Lestrade sat his ground.

Collins sighed. 'Vernon Kell,' he said.

Lestrade blinked. 'Captain Kell of MFI?'

'Very nearly.'

Lestrade got to his feet.

'Hold your water,' Collins waved him down again. 'You won't find him at the National Portrait Gallery.'

Lestrade stood up again, his brain whirling. No. Kell would have gone back to Whitehall by now.

'And you won't find him in Whitehall either.'

'Where then?'

Collins poured them both another coffee. 'If I assure you that she's safe – more than that, she's very comfortable – isn't that enough?'

Lestrade looked at the solid Irishman with his mutton cheeks, his dancing eyes. 'Do you have children, Mr Collins?' he asked.

Collins returned the stare. 'All Ireland, Sholto,' he said softly. 'And I do know what you mean. If you go to the War Office, all you'll get is a brick wall of bureaucracy. Kell will have her somewhere in the country, is my guess, out of your reach.'

'But why?'

'Ah, well,' Collins chuckled, 'that's the three-guinea question, isn't it? And only two men in the country have the answer.'

'Oh?'

'One is Captain Kell, Head of MI5. The other is Sir Basil Thomson, Director of Intelligence at Special Branch.'

'Special Branch?' Lestrade repeated.

'Oh, and perhaps Paddy Quinn knows a thing or two, depending on how much Sir Basil has seen fit to tell him.'

'Right!' Lestrade was on his feet again.

'Sholto!' Collins stopped him again. 'A brick wall at the War Office is astonishingly like a brick wall at Scotland Yard, you know. And you're not exactly the flavour of the month there, are you? Oh, I know it was misunderstood, but most of them there think you resigned on behalf of mutinous bobbies. Then there was that unfortunate business in Queen Mary's bedroom – I do like her chamber-pot, don't you? – and how long do you think it will be before Paddy Quinn realizes it was you who impersonated him – very badly, by the way – the other day? Not only will they not tell you anything, they'll have you locked up as a lunatic or hanged as a traitor. Either way, you'll never see Emma again.'

Lestrade stood there. 'Do I have an alternative?' he asked.

Collins thought for a moment. 'I'll see what I can do,' he said.

The ex-Superintendent fumbled in an inside pocket and produced the icon with its silver and pearls. He leaned over Collins. 'Mr Collins,' he said, 'I will give you forty-eight hours. If I've heard nothing from you by then, for all your private army, I'll be coming to look for you.' And he threw the icon into the man's lap.

'Ah, Sholto,' sighed Collins, 'I have a rendezvous with death at some disputed barricade. It'll come soon enough without your help,' and he tipped his hat. 'Thanks all the same. Boys, see the nice gentleman out.'

Detective-Sergeant Dickens was a difficult man to find. Like all clever policemen, he had been allowed to obtain a little rank and then had found all doors closed. Certainly a man of his encyclopedic knowledge could have been invaluable in the Criminal Record Office, which was probably why he was still administering horses at Imber Court.

'But they can't,' Lestrade heard one mounted copper say to another as he crossed the courtyard. 'They can't just scrap our horses and give us motors. What about football hooligans?'

'What are football hooligans?' the other asked him.

'Tearaways who cause trouble at football matches,' the first one said.

'But they don't.'

'Well, no. I know they don't. But what if they did? I'll bet you one bloke on a white horse could control thousands. You couldn't drive out on to the pitch at Wembley in a motorized Maria, could you?'

Lestrade smiled grimly. He had been a young copper once. In those far-off days he had had such important things to worry about, like the new pub closing-times and the tax on matches that everybody refused to pay. Now, there were more pressing matters.

'Guv'nor!' Charlie Dickens emerged from a mountain of paperwork. 'It's been years. How's retirement?'

'I've no idea,' Lestrade told him, 'but I could use your help.'

'Fire away. I have to confess, though, I'm a bit rusty on detection.'

'Translation,' Lestrade explained. 'I was rummaging through my pockets this morning trying to decide whether they were full enough to buy a new coat or not and I came across this.'

He held out the slip of paper to his former sergeant.

'It's French,' said Dickens.

'Yes, I gathered that.' Lestrade moved a pile of horse returns from the desk and perched himself. 'What does it say?'

'Where did you get this?' Dickens asked.

'Does it?' Lestrade was confused.

'No, I mean, where did you get this?'

'Oh, I see, well, apart from the fact that I'm asking the questions, it's none of your business. But since you're doing me a favour, it fell out of somebody's wallet at the 43 Club, Gerrard Street.'

'Ho, ho,' Dickens beamed. 'I had no idea, Mr Lestrade.'

'I hope you have; that's why I'm here,' his old guv'nor said.

'All right. Let's see.' And Dickens read aloud, ' "Parlez au Duc au sujet de verre." Roughly, talk to the Duke about glass. Does that make sense?'

'Glass?' Lestrade repeated.

'That's what it says. Does it help?'

'It might,' said Lestrade, 'if I knew who the Duke was.'

'You don't want me to reel off *Debrett's*, do you?' Dickens asked, afraid to hear the answer.

'No,' said Lestrade in all seriousness, 'I don't think it would help. Oh, how's your Arabic?'

'Himyarite or Sabean?'

'Just Arabic,' shrugged Lestrade.

'Sketchy,' confessed Dickens.

'Does the name Zojaaj mean anything to you?'

Dickens frowned. 'Well, it's not a name exactly. It means a drink.'

'A drink?'

'Yes, as in a glass of something.'

'Glass!' they both chorused and Lestrade dashed for the door.

'Charlie,' he paused in mid-dash, 'remind me to recommend you for promotion to Commissioner.'

'Thanks, guv'nor,' the sergeant said and went back to his statistics.

From Imber Court you drive south-east, through the newly-budded, still-rural lanes of Surrey, past Esher and the Wrythe until you come to Carshalton. Lestrade's number was taken down by many an astonished copper, wobbling on his bike in the wind created by the Lanchester.

'Somebody'll write a bloody highway code one of these days!' one of them bellowed at him. 'Road hog!' So much for the courtesy cops.

He hauled the wheel around the final bend and snatched at the handbrake before stumbling out on to the gravel drive. He didn't notice the sign over the door, the wrinkly old men, much like himself, wandering the grounds with sticks or rolling deadly in their lethal Bath chairs. The door stood ajar on this lovely spring day and he found himself facing a desk that had not been there before.

'Yes?' A little Scottish lady peered up at him, wearing the white starched frontage of a Sister of Mercy. 'Admission or visit?'

Lestrade had long ago learned never to admit to anything. 'Er . . . isn't this Colonel Glass's residence?' he asked.

'Residence?' the matron repeated. 'This is the St Ignatius Loyola Home for Only Partially Responsible Officers.'

'I see,' said Lestrade, wildly taking in the fact that the decor had changed considerably since he was here last. 'Well, in that case, I've come to visit Colonel Glass.'

The matron perused her ledger. 'I don't believe we have anyone of that name,' she said. 'Do you know when he was admitted?'

'No,' Lestrade told her, 'except that he was here in March.'

'Oh, but we weren't open in March,' she explained.

'Yes,' he said, 'I was coming to that. How long *have* you been here?'

'Since Mafeking night,' she said.

'But you weren't here in March?'

'No. We were closed for refurbishment. From December until early last month.'

'But there *were* some patients here?'

'No. We were able to move into the Police Officers' Rehabilitation Hospital at Hove. Not one of our charges missed their Christmas dinner, thanks be to God.'

'Yes, indeed,' Lestrade said. 'But I was here in March. There was a what-not in the corner there and a monk's bench thing behind you. You've had the fireplace boarded up.'

The matron smiled. 'There is indeed a fireplace behind that partition, but it hasn't been in use since before the Boer War, Mr . . . er?'

'Never mind. Are you telling me the place was closed in March?'

'Bolted and barred,' she assured him. 'I expect you've mis-remembered the month.'

'Nonsense, madam,' Lestrade hissed. 'Check your ledger again. If Glass isn't there, what about Verre?'

'Where?' she tried to follow his pointing finger.

'No – Verre. v-e-r-r-e. It's French. Or Zojaaj perhaps. That's Arabic.'

Unbeknownst to Lestrade, the sturdy little matron rang a silent bell under her counter. 'I assure you we have no foreigners here,' she said. 'Now, I really think . . .'

'What about a Duke?'

'A Duke?'

Lestrade was clutching at straws. 'Yes. Do you have any titled patients here?'

'I'm afraid, sir, that I cannot divulge any information concerning our patients. Ah, Sister Clarissa, Sister Eunice, could you show this gentleman out, please?'

To his dying day, Lestrade wasn't sure whether the old trout had said 'show' or 'throw'. It amounted to much the same thing, however, as he felt himself lifted off the ground by two burly nurses and hurled into the seat of his Lanchester. He was aware of some of the dodderers looking at him. Any one of them could have been Colonel Glass but to pin his man down he first had to pin down his assailants. And anyway, for all their similarity to Sumo wrestlers, they *were* Sisters of Mercy. What would it look like? He could just see the screaming headlines. 'Maniac Who Exposed Himself to Queen Attacks Nuns.'

Discretion, as ever, was the better part of valour and he turned the Lanchester's tail and fled.

9

This time John Kane not only got there first, but he was actually allowed to stay. For the first time since they found the body of Fallabella Shaw, Special Branch was not on his tail. Detective Constable Marks had been, for a while, but he had tripped over a well-placed foot belonging to Detective-Sergeant Macclesfield and had known no more until he came round in the cottage hospital the following day. John Kane castigated his clumsy Number Two by giving him a large Havana and increasing his expenses.

'I've got another for you, guv'nor,' Kane said over the telephone. 'Same *modus operandi* as the others – bullet to the back of the head. I know your mind's on other things, but shall I send a car?'

The car, with Macclesfield at the wheel, had taken Lestrade via his back door a little after breakfast. Fanny had sat in her husband's favourite armchair, a little self-conscious as she was wearing his bowler, in full view of the library window. From there, Detective Constable Spencer, who had been told to shape up or ship out, had a perfect view of his quarry, dozing as presumably old people did. And so depleted was the Branch in good men in those days that he in no way thought it odd that Lestrade should still be wearing his hat indoors. A little after eleven thirty, by which time she assumed her husband had a reasonable head start, Fanny Lestrade took off the bowler, shook her hair free, got up and waved to the hideously embarrassed constable who stood open-mouthed, staring dismissal in the face. It was perhaps a little gratuitous of her to slide up the sash and offer him twopence for his phone call.

Macclesfield gave Lestrade the basics as they rattled north in the black, cramped police motor. By the time they'd reached Swain's Lane, the ex-Superintendent had it all by heart. At the Victorian wrought-iron gates, they stopped. Lestrade looked across at the mausoleum, dark even in the early-May sunshine. His eyes lingered wistfully on the entrance to the Egyptian Avenue where he had lost the tip of his nose in a duel an eternity ago. Perhaps if he looked hard he could still find it. But then, British surgery had not really progressed since the real Mr Lister and they did not have the technology to sew it back on.

In any case, their search took them to the other side of the lane, to the newer part of Highgate Cemetery and to a perfectly hideous grave belonging to Karl Marx. Above a blue cordon and a knot of policemen, in and out of uniform, the squat, neckless bust of the German Jew, who once lived here and who had changed the world for ever, stared out with defiant, granite eyes. At the base of the pillar lay a corpse, already covered with a Metropolitan Police blanket – a unique shroud in this field of shrouds; a body among so many bodies.

John Kane was brushing the soil from his hands. 'Not a foreigner this time, guv'nor,' he said, as Lestrade approached. 'At least, all his clothes are English.'

'Norroy here tells me the grass-cutter found him,' Lestrade said. 'What time was that?'

'About six this morning. He'd come in for the first scything of the season and here was the deceased draped over Marx's grave.'

'Odd place,' Lestrade commented. 'At the feet of the great man, so to speak. How did you get here?'

'It's Eric Cameron's patch,' Kane explained. 'We were in "L" Division together a few years back. He put through a call to me.'

'Good thing you weren't in the same division as Paddy Quinn,' nodded Lestrade. 'But then, nobody's in his league. Can I have a look?'

One of Kane's constables flicked back the blanket. There lay a man the wrong side of sixty, his thin grey hair swept back on to the stone slab, his mouth slightly open and his grey eyes staring sightlessly at the sky. There was a dark patch of blood over his chest, covering the tell-tale exit wound of a bullet.

'We've found the bullet,' Kane told Lestrade. 'It was embedded in the gravel over there.'

Lestrade walked the path with his protégé and looked back to the corpse. 'So he died here,' he turned the loose chippings carefully to find the drops of blood, dried and brown now in the May morning, 'and Chummy carried him and laid him out. Was he in that position when he was found?'

Kane nodded. 'His arms across his chest, like some sort of sacrifice. I'd give my right arm to know who he was and how he got in on the act.'

Lestrade turned, the hairs bristling on his neck. He brushed past the various officers standing around and crouched again beside the body. Then he stood up sharply. 'My God,' he murmured.

'What is it, guv'nor?' Kane was beside him.

'Only the other day I was talking to Emma, John,' Lestrade said. 'About brick walls. Well, we've just met another one.'

'Oh?'

'This', Lestrade nodded at the dead man, 'is Colonel Glass.'

They sat in the snug of the Tollgate Inn, three stumped coppers over their pints. In accordance with the pathological tightness of the Yard's more senior officers and ex-officers, it was Norroy Macclesfield's shout.

'Colonel Glass,' muttered Kane, 'I can't believe it.'

'Well, I'll be an appliance invented by Major Condom.' Macclesfield stared into his froth.

'I have to confess,' Lestrade said; the others leaned forward, 'I thought he was our man. Still, it does leave one or two unanswered questions.'

'One or two!' Kane agreed.

'First,' Lestrade refused to resort to his fingers, 'how is it that a man almost totally paralysed by a stroke can get all the way from Carshalton to Highgate and kneel or crouch beside a grave before getting himself shot in the back of the head?'

'What if he was taken?' Kane asked. 'By car or ambulance?'

'That's possible,' said Lestrade. 'But why? Why didn't

Chummy kill him in Carshalton? Why bring him all the way up here? It must be fifteen or twenty miles.'

'You visited him at his home,' Kane said. 'Anything amiss there?'

'Funny you should mention that, John.' Lestrade shook his empty glass at Macclesfield. 'I'm carrying the bruising still.'

'Trouble?'

'Not exactly. But the missive I found in Emile Vavasour's pocket carried a rather curious line. It said, "Talk to the Duke about glass."'

'So that's why you thought Glass was our man?'

'Yes, especially when you realize that Zojaaj is Arabic for the same thing.'

'You don't say.' Kane lit up another cigarette while Lestrade practised throwing the beer mat off the back of his fingers and catching it in mid air. He missed every time. 'I see now why you were nonplussed. Glass was a brick wall.'

'Right.'

'So,' Kane took the new pint brought by his sergeant, 'we now have three members of the Allied Transport One Unit – isn't that what Captain Kell called it? – dead. All by the same hand.'

'It looks that way.'

'What was your second question?'

'Hmm?' Lestrade was miles away.

'You said the death of Glass raised one or *two* questions.'

'The second question is why Colonel Glass rented an empty hospital for at least a day.'

'Eh?'

'I went to The Oaks in Carshalton again yesterday, the home of the late colonel,' Lestrade told him. 'It's a nursing home, appropriately enough for old codgers who have gone gaga. I think I'll enrol myself later – cheers, Norroy,' and he raised the amber nectar. 'Yet when I was there last in March it was the private residence of the said Glass.'

'What now?' Kane saw the end of a road in view. The annoying thing was, it went nowhere.

'Get a photographer up here at the double, John,' Lestrade said. 'I want copies of Glass's face everywhere. And let the Press in. No names. "Unidentified" will do. It's about time those buggers in Fleet Street earned their keep.'

'Amen to that,' said Kane. 'Norroy.'

The sergeant downed his pint and dashed to put the wheels of the Metropolitan machine in motion. In the doorway he paused.

'Any news of Miss Lestrade, sir?' he asked.

Her father shook his head.

It was the next day that the *Graphic* got some results. A telephone call to Inspector Kane at the Yard. This time there were no crossed wires. Inspector Blevvins was suspended pending a full public, but internal and actually private, inquiry into his surprisingly lucrative lifestyle. A deliriously happy Constable Greeno was transferred to John Kane's office and made highly respectable cups of tea for him and Norroy Macclesfield. True, the inspector had been summoned to Superintendent Wensley's office and asked to explain, in front of Superintendent Quinn, the charade of a few days earlier concerning the curious accident the Head of Special Branch was supposed to have been the victim of. Kane had explained, from his position on the carpet, that he too had been the victim, probably of a late April Fool's joke of cruel proportions. Somebody had masqueraded as Sir Patrick in the Casualty Department of St Mary's Paddington and he had been genuinely duped. He studied the reactions of the superintendents before him, and faced frank mistrust and suspicion. Still, that was all they could get out of him and in the end, with Quinn's venom ringing in his ears and Wensley's wry smile before his eyes, he was allowed to resume his place among the human race.

But his tail had doubled. Constable Marks was a trifle conspicuous, what with the head bandage and all, and Constable Spencer was back in uniform at Hyde Park Corner, his pitch having been decidedly queered. Their places had been taken by Constables Philby and Vassal, but both of them shadowed Kane this time. Lestrade was left unmolested. And so it was that Kane's phone call had that Grand Old Metropolitan scurrying round to the *Graphic*'s offices in Fleet Street.

Lestrade's assignation was at the Wayzgoose, a little before eleven thirty. A rather seedy character from the wrong side of the tracks in Golders Green sidled up to him. He looked like a man about to interest Lestrade in some artistic poses of Miss Isadora Duncan, in which case he was wasting his time. Lestrade had seen those already and the lady in question seemed to be displaying little else but a very long scarf.

'Mr Kane?' the man whispered.

'The same,' lied Lestrade.

'Inspector John Kane?' the man wanted to be absolutely sure.

'Indeed.' Lestrade offered a seat.

'Hymie Ibizit, Theatrical Agent. My card.'

Lestrade took it gingerly. 'Can I get you a drink, Mr . . . Ibizit, is it?'

'Thank you, no. I shouldn't even be out before sunset.'

'Ah, I see.' Lestrade had met the Chosen People before. They were not as other men. 'Is that why you wanted to meet me here rather than at the Yard?'

Ibizit nodded. 'You don't mind?'

Lestrade was delighted. It would have posed certain problems for him otherwise. 'I believe you have some information for me?'

The theatrical agent ferreted in his voluminous pockets. Lestrade's first guess had been right. It *was* a photograph. But one from the *Graphic* of yesterday.

'Colonel Glass,' Lestrade said when he saw it.

'Colonel Glass, *schmass*,' Ibizit confided. 'If he's Colonel Glass, I'm Friedrich Nietzsche. His name is . . . was, my life . . . Tamburlaine San Marco.'

'Tamburlaine . . .?'

'Oh, all right,' Ibizit shrugged, 'Bert Philpotts.'

'What are you telling me, Mr Ibizit?'

'He was one of my stable,' the agent said. 'An actor *manqué* – and they don't come much manquier than him, I can tell you.'

'An actor,' Lestrade repeated.

'That's right. He specialized in panto, mainly. You know, Widow Twanky, Mother Goose, that sort of thing.'

'Do you have a list of his engagements?'

'List, he says,' chuckled Ibizit. 'On the back of a postage stamp, I could write that.'

'No luck?'

'No talent. Not to mention the stutter.'

'A stuttering actor?'

'In the business, he was known as the Strolling Mummer. Whenever he said he was playing Mother Goose, that's as far as he got – Mummer. Good thing he wasn't Jewish, or he'd have been called the Yiddisher Mummer. Still, Mr Kane, what a way to go, eh? Quite a death scene, already.'

'Towards the end of March,' Lestrade said, 'do you happen to remember who hired him? Perhaps for one day?'

'Let me see. Sybil Thorndyke was doing *Cinderella*. Edith Evans and Gladys Cooper were in *My Lady's Dress*. C. Aubrey Smith was in *Why Marry?*. A. Teeny Sailor was in *Not in My Conservatory, You Don't* at the Aldwych. That's right. It's all coming back to me . . .'

Lestrade moved away.

'There was a phone call. The gent said he needed somebody to play a vegetable. I immediately thought of *Chicken Soup With Barley*. Philpotts was hired to sit in a wheelchair and act as though he'd been paralysed. Well, it was perfect for him, you see. No lines. I did offer it to little Donnie Wolfit, but he had a previous engagement in York.'

'So he went?'

'Yes. Bloke paid him handsomely too. Well, times are hard, Mr Kane. Ten per cent goes nowhere these days.'

'Did he say anything about the day?'

'Hush hush, he said,' Ibizit explained. 'It was all top secret.'

'Did he say where he performed?'

Ibizit closed his eyes behind the bottle-bottomed glasses. 'Car-car-car. I'm just reliving it in my mind. Carleton? Carlingwark?'

'Carshalton?' Lestrade prompted him.

'Carshalton!' Ibizit triumphed. 'That's it.'

'When did you see him last?'

'Ooh, it must have been before Christmas. He was a bit miffed because I knocked him up on Christmas Day. I can never get used to the gonoph festivities; no offence, Mr Kane.'

'None taken,' Lestrade said.

'Has any of this helped?' Ibizit asked. 'When I saw his picture in the paper,' he clutched his heart, 'oy vay, I had to sit down. Why should anybody want him dead?'

Lestrade shrugged. 'Critics,' he said. 'Murderous.'

'Tell me about it,' Ibizit said. 'It's killing my business, Mr Kane. Well, if there's nothing else . . .'

'Did the gent who hired Philpotts give a name?' Lestrade asked.

'Er . . . now you've asked me,' Ibizit assumed correctly, 'it was a foreign name. Acres? Shakers?'

Lestrade sat upright on the edge of his seat. 'Not Dacres?' he asked.

Ibizit clicked his fingers. 'That's right,' he said. 'Shaw Dacres.'

The circulation of the *Graphic* wasn't wide enough. Lestrade needed a more prestigious journal for the next part of what he laughingly referred to as a plan. He sent Norroy Macclesfield, courtesy of John Kane, to the offices of *The Times* to place an advertisement. He sent him from there to the offices of *The Connoisseur* and finally to the offices of *Exchange and Mart*. From one of these three, he hoped to receive a reply.

Meanwhile the forty-eight hours of Michael Collins came and went. For all his brash promises, Lestrade could not in fact find the Irishman to carry out his threat. He had vanished like a will-o'-the-wisp. Like the post-boxes in the institution in which Collins had trained, he was never around when you wanted him. Lestrade knew there was no point in going back to the maze at Hampton Court. This time it really would be full of little old ladies and giggling girls. And other than that, nothing. No word of his little girl. No glimmer of hope. He and Fanny wandered the house, careful to avoid each other's eyes. Madison went about his domestic duties with the *bonhomie* of an under-taker. Even Uncle Gideon was subdued, waiting as he was for news from Laing's Nek.

Then came the letter.

Lestrade read it in the library, where the sun filtered through the stained glass in red and gold. 'Sir,' it read, 'I would be most interested to inspect the item offered for sale in *The Times* of

191

yesterday and will call at midday on Wednesday, hoping that this will be acceptable with a view to purchase.' It was unsigned and there was no address, but there was something far more interesting. The letter was written on Russian stationery.

Michael Collins sat in the Reading Room of the British Museum with its great circular dome. He and the boys often used it to come in out of the rain and peruse the day's papers, to see what they were wanted for this time.

'Have you seen this, sir?' one of his trench-coated henchmen asked.

'*Exchange and Mart*?' Collins glanced up from his paper. 'Don't tell me Lloyd George is flogging any surplus military hardware? The odd second-hand submarine might come in extremely handy one of these days.'

'No, sir. It's this, look.'

Collins read the ringed advertisement. '"Unusual icon. Believed one of pair. Silver and pearls, by Agathon Fabergé. Offers." Hmm,' he threw it back to his man, 'I've just been reading the same thing in yesterday's *Times*. It's a trick by Lestrade to smoke somebody out into the open. Ignore it, Padraic.'

'Well, he won't smoke us,' crowed Padraic, 'we're on to him.'

'We are indeed,' Collins said, 'but the broth of an ex-Superintendent is playing with fire all the same. I hope his insurance is fully paid up. Pass me the Dublin *Gazette*, will you? I want to see how poor old Ireland is and how she stands.'

Lestrade waited at midday in an upstairs room, close enough to the landing to hear conversation and handy enough should the visitor be even uglier than he turned out to be. A tall, bearded man in an old-fashioned frock-coat and topper, he stayed for just a moment. Lestrade heard Fanny say that her husband, who had the icon, was not at home, but if he cared to call back tomorrow at the same time, he was sure to be in. He saw the tall man tip his hat and go to where a large, black car waited at the end of the drive.

192

Lestrade winked at Fanny as he dashed past her at the bottom of the stairs, kissed her briefly on the cheek and was into the cab he'd paid to wait out of sight around the corner. True to his word, the driver asked no questions. Lestrade kept his eyes fixed on the limousine ahead, with its shaggy chauffeur and the mysterious man in black. He had not heard him speak, but one thing was certain. The proud bearing and stately stride made it unlikely that he was an antique dealer. Even Bond Street jewellers didn't come as haughty as him.

Years of surveillance gave Lestrade the edge. He switched cabs three times and took two short cuts before the limousine reached its destination, a large Victorian pile in obsolete Gothic, set well back from the road behind a high fence, cedars of Lebanon and rhododendron bushes brilliant in their colour. He tipped his last cabbie and began to reconnoitre.

He soon thought better of that, though. This was, after all, Chertsey in the middle of Surrey and people might complain. He skirted the outer fence for a while. The place was ominously impregnable, no cover for yards around the house and no blind side to the building. While he stood dithering, uncertain of his next step, the answer to a private detective's prayer came whistling round the corner in the form of the mid-afternoon post. Lestrade tampered with the Royal Mail by offering the bloke five quid for his uniform and bag. The postman was a thoroughly conscientious and upright member of the community. He wouldn't part with either for less than six pounds. Lestrade didn't have time to argue. His daughter's life might be tied up with the icon, the one he didn't have, and no expense could be spared. He beat the postman down to five guineas.

It was while crossing the lawn that he felt his bottle going. Two extremely large dogs loped around the side of the house and stood there, black and salivating, their pink tongues trailing the ground, their beady eyes watching every move he made. He wished now he hadn't chosen this particular disguise. After all, wasn't it traditional for dogs to bite postmen?

He kept the whistling going, both to keep his spirits up and because a change of key now or a deadly silence might be his last conscious move. The curs lowered their heads again and their foreheads wrinkled, snarling and growling as they watched him. He rang the bell. For what seemed an eternity, no one answered, then a huge, bearded man in a peculiar shirt, baggy trousers and boots stood before him.

'Yes?' he said in fractured English.

'Er . . . parcel for you,' Lestrade chirped in what he hoped sounded like a postman's delivery.

'For me? There must be some mistake.'

'No, no.' Lestrade played for time, trying to see beyond the huge man. 'Could you sign here, please?'

The huge man looked closer at the parcel. 'Nyet,' he said, 'this is not me.'

'Isn't it?' Lestrade looked as well.

'I am not Mrs Mavis Mablethorpe,' the giant assured him.

'Ah, no.' Lestrade looked his man up and down. 'No, of course not. It must be for the lady of the house,' and with a monumental shove, pushed the bearded man aside and hurtled into the hall. It had to be said that Sholto Lestrade was past his best. He was twenty years too old to be mixing with ruffians and in this case about five stone too light. The doorman caught his ankle as he tried to rise and hauled him backwards. Lestrade swung his mailbag for all he was worth and caught his man a nasty one in the groin with Mrs Mablethorpe's parcel. He didn't notice the shattering sound as Mrs Mablethorpe's tea-service disintegrated on impact. His man wouldn't be slowed for long however. Lestrade clawed his way upright and drove his right boot into the giant's kidneys. But no sooner was his man writhing on the floor than Lestrade heard the scream of steel and, looking up to the great curving staircase, saw a sight that made him jerk backwards against the oak panelling. Two Cossacks, each as large as the man Lestrade had felled, were descending the stairs towards him, their long coats to the floor, their spurs ringing as they walked. What he noticed especially were the flashing curved swords in their hands – that and the quiet homicidal fire in their eyes.

He looked to left and right. A door at each side. But before he could try for either, the Cossacks had pre-empted him and blocked his escape. Even the doorman was struggling to his feet, more than a little intent on revenge. He slowly pulled out the brass knuckles and clicked out the blade. Four inches against a total of six feet of steel was not much of a contest. He could just imagine the letter of complaint to the Post Office. There was still one avenue of escape, however, and he took it. Slicing wildly to the left, where the nearest man crouched, he bolted for the stairs. He was horrified as he ran to realize that the Cossack had leapt high in the air *over* Lestrade's swipe which had been at chest height. In the agility and fitness stakes, Lestrade sensed he was just a little outmanoeuvred.

'Stop!' a booming voice echoed above him. Eight eyes turned to the tall man that Lestrade had been following. He stood at the top of the stairs with a revolver aimed at Lestrade's head. The ex-Superintendent felt the sting as a Cossack sword hacked the knuckles from his hand. He felt his head being wrenched round to the left and his right arm being forced up in the air behind him. A Cossack boot crunched down on his neck, pinning him to the stair.

He heard orders barked in a harsh, guttural tongue and he was allowed to roll clear, nursing his neck, head, back, chest and all points north and south.

'Thank you,' he said to the Cossacks who now sheathed their scimitars. 'I think we're all a little too old for this.'

'Who are you?' the tall man asked in a voice that throbbed in Lestrade's temples.

'Sholto Lestrade,' the postman said. 'Who are you?'

'Lestrade?' the tall man repeated. 'You aren't a postman.'

'And you aren't a collector of objay dar,' Lestrade said.

The tall man had reached the stairwell by now. 'Collector?' he said, clicking back the hammer of the gun.

'I see you carry a Webley revolver, Mr . . . er . . .?'

'For the time being,' the tall man said, 'I will ask the questions.'

He waved the pistol in the direction he intended Lestrade to go.

'Your accent,' said Lestrade. 'Russian, isn't it? Like your notepaper.'

'Notepaper?' the tall man said, prodding Lestrade into an ante-room and on to a horsehair sofa of hideous proportions. He sat opposite him. 'Who *are* you?'

'The man whose house you have just visited,' said Lestrade.

'But then, you know that already, because you or your friends here', he jerked his head in the direction of the Cossacks and immediately wished he hadn't, 'had already visited it in search of the icon I have for sale.'

'You have the icon?' the tall man asked.

'You haven't mentioned a price, yet.'

The tall man clicked his fingers, careful not to take the gun off Lestrade. One of the Cossacks disappeared, only to return a moment later with a bulging suitcase. He put it down on the floor between Lestrade and the tall man. The tall man flicked it open with his boot. Lestrade's eyes bulged like the case. He had never seen so much money in one place in his life.

'There are one hundred thousands of your British pounds there,' the tall man said. 'I regret I cannot go higher.'

Lestrade paused for a moment to allow his heart to descend to its rightful place. Then he leaned back. 'You and your friends are armed, Mr . . . um . . . and you outnumber me four to one. What's to prevent you from taking the icon, assuming that I have it, without giving me this money?'

'Nothing,' the tall man said. 'But I did not come down with the last shower of snow, Tovarich. Does Daniel walk into the lion's den? I am prepared to wager that you do not have the icon with you. But why did you follow me?'

'You wouldn't like to point that thing the other way, would you? I can explain things so much more easily that way.'

The tall man uncocked the gun and placed it down on top of the money, the butt towards him. 'You don't have the icon,' he said.

'No,' Lestrade confessed, 'it is currently in the hands of an Irishman named Michael Collins. Though I suspect it won't be there for long.'

'Is this the Michael Collins who is in your English newspapers?'

'Newspapers, post offices, police stations, mazes. To use an English phrase, he is iniquitous, everywhere.'

'This Michael Collins. He is a collector of art works?'

Lestrade shrugged. 'I doubt it. Though he is undoubtedly a man of many parts.'

'Then why does he want it?'

'He wants to buy guns, Mr . . . er . . . He'd give somebody else's right arm to get his mitts on the contents of your suitcase. It's all in a good cause, he'd say. But that's what madmen always say, isn't it? Tell me, . . . er . . . why you are prepared to pay so much for the icon?'

'You object?' the tall man asked.

'No,' said Lestrade, 'but I am surprised.'

'Why?'

'Because the icon is worth perhaps ten thousand pounds. The pair – shall we way, thirty thousand? You are very generous, you Bolsheviks, Mr . . . er . . .?'

He heard the scrape of steel to his right and saw the Cossack's blade winking in the afternoon sunlight. The tall man waved a hand and the blade slid back.

'May I ask', said the tall man, 'where you obtained the icon?'

'Certainly,' said Lestrade. 'From the mattress of a merchant seaman named Varushkin.'

'Varushkin?' the tall man repeated.

'You know that name?' Lestrade probed, aware how inscrutable the Slavs could be.

'It was not his name. Neither was he a merchant seaman. Where is he?'

'In a pauper's grave somewhere on the Isle of Dogs – St Botolph's, probably.'

The tall man leaned back against the sofa. 'How did he die?'

'He was shot in the back of the head by a Webley revolver,' Lestrade told him.

'Do you know who killed him?'

Lestrade leaned forward. 'I rather assumed you did,' he said.

The tall man blinked, once. 'A moment ago you said that my friends and I had visited your house twice. What did you mean by that?'

'My house was ransacked some days ago. My wife and I were clubbed senseless. We could have died. All because you wanted that icon. You haven't told me why you're prepared to pay so much for it.'

The tall man stood up. 'Mr Lestrade.'

Lestrade stood up too.

'I am going to – what is it you English say – put all the cards

197

on my table. I am going to show you something that only three other Englishmen know about. And one of those is dead. I will be watching your reactions the whole time. If I decide I cannot trust you, I will give the signal to my men here and they will hack you to pieces. Do you understand this?'

Lestrade nodded. It would make a mess of the carpet, but he sensed that the tall man was prepared to make certain sacrifices. He followed the man in black up the curved staircase, the Cossacks clattering in his wake. At the top of the stairs, the little party turned left and the tall man knocked on a door. He motioned Lestrade to stay outside and the ex-Superintendent heard muffled voices. Then the tall man came back and the Cossacks stood sentinel on each side of the door.

'Speak in hushed tones only, Lestrade,' the tall man said. 'Make no sudden moves. Speak only when spoken to.'

Lestrade followed the man into a room heavy with the smell of incense. For all that the May sunshine flooded the world outside, in here it was near darkness. The English furniture of the ground floor gave way here to rich carpets and tapestries of an Eastern pattern. Seven candles guttered in the draught as the men entered. The tall man bowed and stayed with his head down. He flashed a glare at Lestrade who did the same thing. Glancing up under his eyebrows, Lestrade first took in the photographs of a happy family, of a little boy in a sailor suit and a pair of ice-skates. A cluster of dolls with blue eyes and golden hair sat on a chair to his left. But what held his attention most was a figure, pale in the candlelight, moving with difficulty towards him.

'Mr Lestrade,' a young female voice said, 'I am the Grand Duchess Anastasia. Welcome.'

Lestrade's hand came up involuntarily. Out of the shadows stepped a girl of perhaps twenty. Her face was beautiful, her hair cascading over her shoulders. Only her eyes were dark and sad and a cruel scar ran from one corner of her mouth under her tresses, giving her a permanent and twisted smile.

'I believe from Strogovitch that you have my father's icon, one of a pair.'

'Alas, Your Royal Highness,' said Lestrade, 'no longer. I had it, yes. But I was forced to give it away.'

Her eyes clouded. 'That is a pity,' she said. 'Tell me, Mr Lestrade, is the sun shining today?'

'Yes, Your Royal Highness,' he said, 'it is a lovely day.'

She smiled at them both. 'Strogovitch, it is May.'

'It is, Anastasia Nikolaievna.'

'The blossom will be out at Tsarskoe Selo.'

'It will,' he said and held her hands in his.

'And will we see them again, Strogovitch, the flowers?'

He nodded. 'When the summer comes,' he said, 'I will take you there myself.'

'And the songs – will we sing the old songs?'

All he could do was nod.

'And the icon?'

Strogovitch looked at Lestrade and his eyes burned into him.

'I will . . . get the icon to you as soon as I can, Your Royal Highness,' Lestrade said.

She held out her hand for him to kiss. 'You are very kind, sir,' she said.

A nudge from Strogovitch and Lestrade bowed again. He noticed that the tall Russian was moving backwards, bobbing as he went. He, too, walked that way.

Strogovitch led the way back to the ante-room. Lestrade sat near the money again and the loaded Webley.

'What you have seen, Lestrade,' the Russian said, 'you must not divulge to a living soul.'

'That the youngest daughter of the Tsar is alive and well and living in Chertsey? Do you know what Fleet Street would pay for that?'

'I have a pretty shrewd idea,' came the dark answer, 'but I assure you, you would not live to spend it. And let me correct you on one point; the Grand Duchess is far from well. Doctors in Switzerland gave her less than a year to live.'

'I see,' said Lestrade. 'Does she know that?'

Strogovitch nodded.

'What happened?' Lestrade asked. 'May I know?'

The tall Russian crossed to the sideboard and pulled from a drawer an Orthodox Bible. He placed it on the table beside the ex-policeman. 'Are you a religious man, Lestrade?' he asked.

'If you mean, do I leave my two bob in the collection plate of

199

a Sunday, the answer is no. If you mean, do I believe in a Great Commissioner in the sky, then . . . yes, I suppose I do.'

'Put your right hand on that book, then,' Strogovitch ordered, 'and swear by your Great Commissioner that what I am about to tell you you will repeat to no man on pain of death.'

Lestrade hesitated, weighed up the melodrama of the moment and laid his hand on the cold leather. 'I so swear,' he said.

Strogovitch poured them both a colourless drink that Lestrade had tasted once before, on board the *Motley*. Its kick hadn't lessened and it brought the colour back to his cheeks.

'When the Bolsheviks overthrew the Provisional Government,' the Russian said, 'the Tsar Nicholas, his family and servants were moved from place to place. What the traitor Lenin had in mind for them, I do not know, but they ended up in a house in Ekaterinburg.'

Lestrade nodded.

'Three British agents traced them that far in the spring of 1918. My country was and is torn by civil war, Lestrade. There were bands of marauding peasants everywhere, the rabble that Trotsky has the nerve to call the Red Army. God alone knows how those agents got as far as they did.'

'What happened?'

Strogovitch looked into the clear bottom of his glass, as though into a crystal ball. 'This I heard from one of these agents. Anastasia herself remembers nothing of Ekaterinburg – God is merciful. One morning in March, a little before dawn, the Tsar, the Tsarina, the children, the doctor, the sailor who carried little Alexei and a nurse were ordered down into the cellar of the house that was their prison. There they waited, as though posed for a photograph, the Tsar and his wife holding hands. As the clock struck six, the door opened and armed men entered the room. They fired on our beloved royal family at point-blank range with pistols and rifles. The agent who told me this saw the room afterwards. The back wall was riddled with bullets, the wallpaper hung in shreds. The floor was a heap of bodies. All that was left of Nicholai Alexandrovitch and his family lay like broken marionettes amid the smoke. If there was a twitch of a muscle, a dying spasm, the guards went forward and smashed their limbs with the butts of their rifles. No one could have survived. Except . . .'

'Except Anastasia,' said Lestrade, watching the tears roll down the Russian's long, gaunt cheeks.

'Somehow, the British agents got into the house before the burial party came. They found little Anastasia still breathing and they smuggled her out, like Cleopatra, in a carpet. How they got her to Switzerland, through the Reds and the Germans, I will never know, but they did. Her jaw was shattered with a rifle butt. Her left arm is useless. She is afraid of the sunlight. She is afraid of the dark. Loud voices terrify her. Sometimes a car backfires in the street outside and she screams. My God,' he closed his eyes, 'such screams. She carries a bullet near her heart. They dare not operate.'

'That place she mentioned,' Lestrade said, 'Tsarsk . . .'

'Tsarskoe Selo,' Strogovitch nodded. 'It was the Romanov summer home in the warmth of the Crimea. It is the one shining memory she keeps. That and the icon.' He hung his head. 'She will not see either of them again.'

'Who was Varushkin?' Lestrade asked. 'We both know he wasn't what he claimed to be.'

'He was a White Russian. Like me, an officer in His Majesty's Imperial Guard. They don't come more loyal. I remember once one of the children slammed the carriage door too hard. It could have trapped the hand of the Tsarina, but . . . Varushkin, you know him . . . caught it in time – and lost a finger into the bargain. He must have come in search of the Tsar's jewels.'

'The Tsar's jewels?'

'Oh, yes. During the early months of the War, it became dangerous to leave all that in the Winter Palace at St Petersburg. After Tannenberg, our army was fighting a retreating war. Oh, we did all we could, but only one man in three had a rifle. The others carried clubs, threw rocks. I know, I saw it. Such was the wealth of the Winter Palace that arrangements were made to ship some of the crown jewels by sea from Archangel.'

'To where?'

'To Britain,' said Strogovitch. 'To London.'

Lestrade's eyebrows rose slowly towards his hairline. 'Have you any idea how much is involved?'

'One crown of Nicholai Romanov would be in your English pounds, seventy-five million.'

Lestrade felt and heard his jaw drop. 'Tell me,' he squeaked after a while, 'who was responsible for it at this end?'

'A British officer named Glass,' Strogovitch told him. 'Colonel Glass.'

'But Colonel Glass disappeared, am I right?'

'Yes,' frowned Strogovitch. 'So you knew about this all along?'

Lestrade shook his head. 'No,' he said, 'I'm only just finding out.'

'News comes through slowly from the Motherland,' Strogovitch said, 'but in the war against the Bolsheviks, we needed the money those jewels represented more than ever. That I am certain is why Varushkin was sent across. He had managed to find one of the pair of icons somewhere *en route* and was after the other one, but . . .'

'But Colonel Glass found him first.'

Strogovitch nodded. 'Perhaps,' he said. 'Anastasia only wants the icons back. She doesn't care about their worth. They are a living link with her dead father. She knows she cannot bring him back. But the icons. One would be enough.'

'Tell me,' said Lestrade. 'These agents, the men who rescued Anastasia, do you know their names?'

'Their leader was one named Reilly. Another was Lockhart. The other I knew only as the Duke. He it was who arranged this safe house for us. He visited once and I never saw him again. Now you tell me, Lestrade, why you placed your advertisement knowing that you could not provide the icon?'

'"It's not bigger than me, but it's bigger than you",' Lestrade remembered Michael Collins saying.

'Pardon? I do not follow.'

'I placed the advertisement in the hope of flushing out a murderer, Mr Strogovitch. Instead, I stumbled on . . . sadness.' He stood up. 'I have a daughter . . . somewhere,' he said. 'Not much older than your Grand Duchess. If it's humanly possible, I'll get her icon back. And as for your secret,' he smiled at the Bible, 'it's safe with me.'

The Duke, he said to himself as the Cossacks saw him out and gave him back his brass knuckles. What was it the Frenchman's note had said? 'Talk to the Duke about Glass.' Deeper and deeper.

Kane and Macclesfield plodded up Primrose Hill a little before sunset, the lights of the metropolis twinkling like stars below them. There was a third man with them, younger probably than Lestrade but without the ex-Superintendent's clarity of eye and firmness of jaw. For a brief moment, as Lestrade watched them from the park bench on which he sat, he fancied he looked like God, his wild white hair and beard flying sideways with the deceptively treacherous gusts of May.

'Guv'nor,' Kane hailed him, 'how goes it?'

'Tolerable,' nodded Lestrade.

'Can I introduce Professor Havelock Ellis?' the inspector said. 'Mr Lestrade.'

'Professor,' Lestrade took the outstretched hand. It was firmer than he had expected.

'Mr Lestrade,' the Professor's voice was rather piping. 'Ex-Yard, I understand.'

'Er . . . yes,' Lestrade sat down, 'John . . .?'

'I should explain, Sholto,' Kane said. 'The Professor has recently been appointed by the Home Office to . . . well, perhaps you can explain, Professor?'

'Well, I'll certainly try. I believe that you gentlemen have what I should term a serial killer on your hands?'

'He's nowhere near our hands, Professor,' said Lestrade. 'That's our problem.'

'Well, the chappies at the Home Office think I may be able to shed some light, so to speak, by creating a psychological sketch of the man you call Chummy.'

'A si . . .?'

'. . . Cological sketch, yes. Metaphysical profile, if you will, based on the pathological and psycho-sexual information at our disposal.'

'I see.' Lestrade narrowed his eyes. He found it easier to do that when he was lying. 'Sandwich?'

'No, thank you. I never partake after three.'

'Does the Branch know about this, John?' Lestrade asked.

Kane shrugged. 'I've heard no word,' he said, 'but I appear to have lost my shadows. Unless Norroy . . .?'

'No one, sir,' the sergeant said. 'I haven't seen Philby and Vassal for days.'

'Sandwich, Norroy?' Lestrade couldn't stand cucumber.

'Thank you, sir,' and he fell upon it with the voracity of the bachelor.

'Mr Kane has apprised me of the attitude of the Special Branch,' Havelock Ellis said. 'Acute paranoia. You've read my "Philosophy of Conflict" of course.'

Lestrade realized in a horrified moment that the mad old bugger was talking to him. 'Ah,' he said, shrugging embarrassedly, 'in a busy life . . .'

'Oh, quite, quite. What we have here, gentlemen, if I read aright what Inspector Kane has told me is a father-fixated homicidal deviant. I wrote about him comprehensively in "The Criminal" a few years ago.'

'You wrote about Chummy?' Lestrade was astonished.

'Not the specific man, no,' Havelock Ellis explained, 'but the type. The psychosis.'

'The . . . er . . .' Lestrade squeezed the bench's woodwork momentarily to reassure himself of his grip on reality.

'Professor Havelock Ellis has a theory, Sholto,' Kane said. To the inspector, any straw looked pretty hopeful at that moment. He was nearly forty-two years old. Life was passing him by.

'Father fixation,' said Havelock Ellis, 'but father revulsion. The horns of the buffalo, the wings of the swan, the dark and light side of the moon.'

'Mmm.' Lestrade found himself nodding in the gathering dusk, his fingers interlocking ever tighter in their grip around his shin.

'The relationship between George II and his son Frederick exemplifies it typically. The boy constantly smoked his pipe in bed – a phallic ano-masochistic reflex, of course – and called his father a Hanoverian cyst. George in his turn of course died "at stool in his closet" as the chroniclers have it – what they used to call Irritable Bowel Syndrome when I was at St Thomas's. I prefer to think of it as an involuntary release of hyperbolic suspectibility.'

Lestrade looked at Kane. Then they both looked at Maccles-field who sat rooted to the spot, staring intently at the mad Professor with a piece of cucumber sticking out of the corner of his mouth.

'So, our man . . .?' Lestrade tried to hold the threads together.

'. . . Is probably short. Five foot two, three, with a fetish about feet. He almost certainly wears ladies' brassières, possibly two at a time, and had an unnatural liaison with his choirmaster at school. He was afraid of his mother, but hero-worshipped some transient uniformed figure like the postman or a railway ticket-inspector.'

'Clever?' Lestrade probed deeper. Madam Petulengro at Bat-tersea could have told him what the Professor had.

'Fiendishly,' said Havelock Ellis. 'But there's Methodism in his madness.'

'A Nonconformist?'

'In every sense,' Havelock was certain. 'The double brassières alone.'

'Of course. Tell me, Professor, has he finished? Will Chummy kill again?'

'Ah.' The Professor closed his eyes as the sun went down. 'Who can predict the unpredictable? It's in the lap of the gods, of course, but I feel he may, yes. At least once.'

A strange silence fell over the two policemen, the ex-police-man and the Home Office expert. The shadows lengthened across the Hill until they sat in darkness and a little man hobbled up the path, lighting the lamps with his long stick.

'Any luck with the ad., guv'nor?' Kane asked at length. 'The one Norroy placed?'

Lestrade remembered the sad girl with the shattered face and her shattered dreams. 'No, John,' he said, 'not yet. We'll give it a day or two longer, shall we?'

The next morning a telegram came from Michael Collins. He assured Lestrade that his daughter was not in Hertford, Hereford or Hampshire. It was not the best of news, but it was a start. And it reassured Lestrade that the Irishman was at least as good as his word.

He sent Fanny away that Friday. If ever a sixth sense hung like a cloud over Sholto Lestrade, this was it. No, he told her, the phone would not do. It had to be done face to face. Emma had been missing for six days now. It was time Harry and Letitia were told. Yes, they would be furious that the Lestrades had not told them earlier. Yes, they would drive like maniacs through the night. No, Harry would not leave one stone upon another to find his adopted little girl. That was Bandicoot's way. A bull in a china shop. And that was why Lestrade had put it off until now.

He had told Fanny Lestrade all that, but it was not the reason why. And he told Madison to take the rest of the day off, too, slipping him a few bob to take a train up West if he so desired. He waited for the real reason as the fire died down in the grate. It was a chill evening, for all it was May and Uncle Gideon had retired after a hard day's scouring the veld.

Lestrade sat in the library, in his favourite armchair, his slippers on his feet, a glass of brandy near his right hand, the curtains drawn. It was the moment he knew only too well, the moment he was born for. The moment when he looked death in the face. When it came, it came on silent wings, like the barn-owls he had often watched swooping silent and deadly over the low woods. And again, he was the mouse, alone in the dark.

'You don't mind if I switch on the lamp, do you, Lestrade?' The voice was one he thought he knew.

'Colonel Glass,' the ex-Superintendent said, 'I've been expecting you.'

'I know you have,' and Chummy moved into the light. He was a six foot, square-looking gent wearing an Astrakhan collar topped off with a fedora.

'You've led us all a merry dance,' Lestrade said.

Glass smiled. 'Well, it's the last reel, Lestrade. Look,' he raised a finger, 'the band's going home.' He glanced at the decanter. 'One for the road?'

Lestrade poured for them both. 'A glass, Colonel Glass.'

The Colonel sat down in the chair opposite Lestrade's, the firelight glowing on the firm features. 'Your very good health – at least for the next few minutes,' and he sipped from the glass, careful to see that Lestrade did it first. 'Delicious,' he said. 'Now, the icon.'

'How do you know I've got it?'

'Come, come, Lestrade. I've been all over this place with a fine-tooth comb. It's not here.'

'Ah, yes.' Lestrade rubbed his head. 'We have a score to settle on that account. You can knock me around as much as you like, but you touch my wife, Glass, and you'll pay the price.'

'Come off it, old man,' Glass chuckled. 'You're about as frightening as a Girl Guide. I read your advertisement. Oh, I know it wasn't genuine – that you had no intention of parting with the icon. It was designed to flush me out and it did.'

'All right,' said Lestrade. 'You show me yours. I'll show you mine.' And he reached into his pocket.

Glass was faster and the cane he carried jerked up horizontal, pointing at Lestrade's head. 'Slowly,' hissed the colonel.

'Of course,' said Lestrade. '*That* was what Robert Churchill saw on the murder bullets. Something he hadn't seen before, couldn't place. The extra grooves caused by the stick. I'll bet that makes it pretty quiet, too, doesn't it? Which is why the clerk at the Cedar Hotel didn't hear a shot. But Paul Dacres' gun *had* been fired. Quite clever that. What did you do, fire it out of the window?'

'Up the chimney,' Glass said. 'Has a surprisingly deadening effect. If you aim for the brickwork, the echo effect resembles dropping a banana skin. And you slipped on plenty of those in this case, didn't you, Lestrade?'

'Oh? Perhaps you'd like to humour a dying man and tell me about them.'

Glass laughed. 'And give you time to summon Kane and Macclesfield? I don't think so.'

'You know about them?' Lestrade removed his hand slowly from his pocket.

'Only in the psycho-sexual ramifications of the case,' Glass said, his eyes taking on a curious twinkle and his nose becoming more hawk-like. 'You've read my "Serious Limitations in the Intelligence Quotient of ex-Superintendents of Police" of course.'

'Professor Havelock Ellis!' Lestrade sat bolt upright.

'No,' said Glass. 'Oh, he is an old buffoon all right and no doubt he does talk the kind of nonsense I talked to you on Primrose Hill last night. I'm afraid it was a little subterfuge on my part. You see he doesn't actually work for the Home Office.'

'Then why . . .?'

'Use your head, man,' Glass said. 'I knew you were on to me. But I didn't know how close you were. A bit of Leichner wax, some false hair and some long words. It's amazing how easy it is to pull the wool over the eyes of an inspector and sergeant of the Metropolitan Police. Kane was help itself. Told me every nuance, every wrinkle of the case. He was also very informative on you. I asked him how you'd tackle me – or rather Chummy – if ever we met face to face. Alone, he said. Seemed quite proud of the fact. No supporting cast? I asked, no team of big-footed bobbies? No, he assured me, alone. And here you are. So I will humour you a little while longer. But you'll understand if I don't trust Kane's intuition *too* far?'

Lestrade said, 'I am right? You appropriated the artworks of all nations and simply refused to give them back?'

'More or less,' Glass shrugged. 'For years I'd slogged my way through the army. I wasn't one of your chinless wonders, Lestrade, born to Eton and Sandhurst. My father was a circus trapeze-artist. I had to claw my way up. And always they were there, the hard-faced men with snobbery worn like a crown, above me, below me, suffocating me. So, I saw my chance. I pulled what strings I could and got put in charge of A.T. One.'

'Allied Transport,' Lestrade nodded.

'That was the cover, yes. Actually, it stood for Art Treasures International. The "I" became a "1" somewhere in the typing pool. We let it stand at the War Office. Our little "in" joke. My brief was to arrange for collection of certain choice pieces in case the beastly Hun overran various capitals. Pieces whose psychological value far outshone their actual worth. But I couldn't be doing with all that, Lestrade. Sod the psychology. Feel the worth.'

'The sword of St Louis.'

'Eighty thousand in the right quarter.'

'The Tsar's crown.'

'Seventy-five million. Want to make me an offer?'

'What did the Belgians volunteer?'

'It wasn't theirs anyway. Any more than the sword of St Louis belonged to the wogs. It was a hitherto unknown painting by da Vinci.'

'Measuring approximately eight inches by five.'

It was Glass's turn to be surprised. 'How did you know?'

'The mark below the nail in Fallabella Shaw's old house. You farmed the painting out to her, didn't you?'

'When bombing raids started in London, we thought it best to scatter what we could. Who would look for a priceless painting among the old clutter of a country cottage?'

'Hmm,' Lestrade nodded. 'Who indeed? So governments came looking for their national treasures?'

'When all the shouting had died down, yes. I was surprised it took them so long. After the War To End All Wars, the dust takes some settling I suppose. For as long as I could, I fobbed them off with excuses. Red tape. Postal charges. Insurance complications. Civil Service spoke unto Civil Service. After all, we've kept the Greeks' hands off the Elgin marbles for a century. In the end though, I had to get out. You remember the fire in Whitehall last year?'

'Vaguely,' said Lestrade. 'I was on a case elsewhere at the time.'

'In that fire, the treasures vanished. There were some red faces in the Cabinet, I can tell you. What could they tell the foreigners? There was no money in the kitty to cover the loss. We'd just fought a war for four years. It was time for Colonel Glass to go gaga. I'd always been something of a thespian – the circus in me, I suppose – I frothed at the mouth a bit and fell over a lot. Luckily, the War Office doctor is an army surgeon. He never noticed the difference.'

'But the foreigners came anyway?'

Glass nodded. 'It's a changing world, Lestrade. They'll be over here driving our buses soon, you mark my words, buying up chunks of Oxford Street. Harrods. They had to be stopped, of course.'

'But the fire . . .'

'I'd got away with it with my own masters. I couldn't risk any more snooping. Euperry came for the da Vinci. I'd dealt with

209

him in Belgium; knew his proclivities – they were abnormally large for such a little chap. I made him an offer he couldn't refuse – a rendezvous near the Serpentine well known to that fraternity – and shot him there. Made a devil of a splash. Still, it broke the ice.'

'And Varushkin?'

'Back to the beard again there. A naval one this time, not to mention the patch and the false teeth. I'd heard on the grapevine that the Ruskies were after their crown and the icon. I'd lost one in Archangel when I went out to make the negotiations. And I guessed the sneaky bastard had got it back. He was coming over to get mine and I wanted to get his.'

'And in the end?'

'In the end he got his. I didn't wait for him to come ashore. Unlike Euperry, Varushkin was a professional. He knew bugger all about art, but he was pretty good as spies go. As Commander Samson of Trinity House I got on board the *Motley* and killed him. I didn't have long.'

'You searched for the icon?'

'Yes. And while I was doing it I stashed him in his locker, in case anyone came in.'

'With his arm in the air?' Lestrade asked.

'Why, yes. How did you know?'

'It was still like that when we found him. Damned if I know why.'

Glass chuckled grimly. 'Perhaps he was pointing at me, Lestrade, do you think? Crossing the barrier of death?'

'Murder will out,' Lestrade nodded. 'But you couldn't find the icon?'

'No.'

'It was in his mattress.'

'Damn,' cursed Glass. 'It had to be something that simple. I chanced my arm that the coast was clear and dropped him over the side. Not as much of a splash as Euperry, oddly enough.'

'What of Al Haroun?'

'Ah, yes, the Arab. Not a difficult target, Lestrade. As you probably said yourself, there aren't many bedouins in London streets. I found him soon enough at the Savoy and sent him a cryptic message, in Arabic, of course.'

'Of course, Mr Zojaaj.'

'We met in Aqaba in '16. It was still held by the Turks then, so we had to be careful. It took quite a bit of haggling to get St Louis's sword out of old Feisal.'

'And Al Haroun responded to your message?'

'Like a lamb to the slaughter.'

'And the Frenchman, Vavasour?'

'Was after a particularly fetching necklace belonging to the Austrian woman, Marie Antoinette, which I had negotiated from Clemenceau himself on behalf of the British government. Another "Agent" as the French have it. The sly old bastard was posing as an historical adviser on a truly appalling film at Boreham Wood. So I did the same.'

Lestrade clicked his fingers. 'Mr Barnstaple!' he said.

'The Euphrates expert,' Glass bowed slightly, but not enough to take his concentration or his gun off Lestrade. 'It would have been risky to vanish myself as soon as the corpse was found, so I stayed on for a while, enjoying your rather melodramatic gropings.'

'And the murder of Colonel Glass, Colonel Glass?'

'Ah, yes. That mischievous little daughter of yours – she's quite a cracker, by the way – she'd sniffed around weak links like Archie le Fanu and got on to me. I had to put you off the scent. If you couldn't find me easily, you might be tempted to keep on looking. But if you found a vegetable, you might stop. The local home for vegetables was closed for redecoration. It was perfect. But to be a vegetable, I needed staff. And staff were a complication. So I rang some agency or other.'

'Hymie Ibizit,' said Lestrade. 'Using the cryptic alias of Shaw Dacres.'

'And he provided Philpotts – or San Marco, I believe he called himself. He was useless, but all he had to do was dribble a bit. In the end, I thought the wheelchair stole the show.'

'You made an admirable manservant, Mr Warmby, so loyal, so patient, so devoted.'

'Thank you, sir.' Glass fell into the role and out of it again. 'But Philpotts was one more loose end – the only one left, in fact. So I contacted him again, this time without his agent. The Karl Marx grave business was a bit theatrical, wasn't it? That

211

damned circus again. But I thought the Russian connection might possibly provide the odd red herring for you.'

'And Fallabella Shaw?' Lestrade sensed that Glass's finger might be a little tired on the trigger by now.

'Dear old Fal. She was a damn good secretary. Unfortunately she and Dacres began to suspect me. To this day I don't know how. Luckily, he was whisked away from A.T. One before he could say anything. Some hush-hush assignment back at the Front. But she was there, nosing, snooping, rummaging. She lived near me in Hertfordshire then. In pleasanter times I even suggested she made the move. I enjoyed her company, you see. One evening, I suddenly realized it wasn't safe to let her live. She had the da Vinci anyway and while she was taking it down from the wall, I put a bullet through her head. Pity, really.'

'Pity about Paul Dacres, too,' said Lestrade darkly.

'It was,' agreed Glass, 'he was a good man. Paul knew his art too – that's why he was chosen for the A.T. One job, of course. With him out of the way at the Front it was easy to bury Fallabella in the country somewhere and claim she'd been killed in an air raid – if anybody asked. There were lots of spare bodies lying around in the rubble; you'd be amazed. Then, Dacres came back.'

'Where had he been for three years?'

'Damned if I know. The papers said missing in action. That was good enough for me. Then – and this was the damnedest coincidence – I saw him one day from the top of a double-decker bus. I followed him to a hotel near Maida Vale. We had it out. He said he'd come back to denounce me as a thief and a traitor, because I'd stolen from our allies. Seemed particularly keen to get the Russian treasures back.'

'So you shot him and made it look like suicide?'

'That was my intention, yes. I suppose I misjudged you, ex-Superintendent. I remembered when Dacres and I worked together that he was engaged to your daughter. I didn't know how much trouble you'd be, so I went to his funeral, as Squadron Leader Leonard, don't you know! Just to see what you looked like at that stage. Wizarding my prang all over the place.' He gave the relevant salute.

212

'And my daughter,' Lestrade said. 'That was your first mistake, picking on the fiancé of Lestrade's daughter.'

'Well,' said Glass, 'I'm afraid now that story-time is over. Time for all retired policemen to be tucked up safe and cold in their coffins. Do I take the icon from your hand or from your dead body? As Professor Havelock Ellis, I promised you "Chummy" would commit one more murder – yours, Lestrade.'

Lestrade gingerly produced the linings of both pockets. 'I haven't got it,' he said.

Glass's smile vanished. 'What do you mean?' he snapped.

'The advertisement *was* a trick to flush you out, Colonel, as you surmised, but the joke's on you. I never had it to sell. So John Kane didn't tell you everything, then?'

'I suspected as much,' bluffed Glass. 'So who has it?'

'Mr Lestrade? I'm sorry it's so late. I let myself in.'

The strange voice shattered the moment. Glass's composure cracked and his finger jerked simultaneously. Lestrade was flung sideways, the shot ripping through his sleeve and shoulder. He threw himself behind the chair, pulling the lamp out of its socket as he rolled.

Pitch blackness. No one in the library breathed.

'Mr Lestrade?' the voice came again.

Another shot, followed by tinkling glass.

'Jesus!'

'Who the bloody hell are you?' Lestrade risked.

A third shot shattered one of Fanny's mother's porcelain poodles. It showered over Lestrade who realized anew that there must be a God after all.

'Er . . . Tom Hutchings. *Daily Mirror*. I'm doing an article on Nearly Famous Policemen and I've only just managed to find you. It's taken me four months. What is going on?'

'You'll be able to write an obituary in a minute, sonny,' Glass hissed, 'on Nearly Dead Policemen.'

Lestrade saw it first. A shadow in the hall, where the May moon dappled on the wall. The shadow of a gaunt old warrior stalking the night. The spirit of St Louis? But Lestrade had to give the warrior a target to hit. He stood up, his left arm dangling useless. He saw Glass's head and body come up, the deadly walking-stick level. He heard a roar and shielded his eyes from the flash as the colonel jerked backwards, the gun gone from his grasp, his chest a mass of torn flesh.

Lestrade plugged in the lamp and rose to survey the scene.

Uncle Gideon stood on the carpet, twirling his white moustache. 'Bloody Boer!' he rumbled. 'You all right, Sholto?'

'Never better, Uncle,' said Lestrade.

A quivering newspaperman emerged from behind the sofa. 'Er . . . I hope I haven't spoiled your evening,' he said.

Gideon crouched over his kill. 'What was he after, Sholto?' he asked.

'Everything, Gideon,' said Lestrade. 'He had it all already. Over seventy-five million pounds in his back pocket, but he just had to have a little bit more. That's what killed him.'

'Nonsense,' growled Gideon. 'A couple of Eley twelve bore cartridges up his jacksie – that's what killed him.'

'Mr Hutchings,' said Lestrade, 'would you be so kind as to call the police? We appear to have a body in the library.'

10

It was the next day that the Bandicoots arrived, as Lestrade knew they would. Fanny was appalled to hear the story of the night's events and upbraided Sholto in the way that women do, though both her eyes were strangely hot and wet. Uncle Gideon spent the day running a series of flag messages from his bedroom window to the effect that Kronje had surrendered and the whole bally thing was over bar the shouting.

It was far from over for Lestrade and Bandicoot, however. They left the ladies at home in case of a telephone message and to handle the official mopping up of operations by Kane and Macclesfield, and drove in the Lanchester through the darling buds of May.

It was the journey of a lifetime really. Had Lestrade been of the Islamic persuasion, he would have called it Mecca. Had he been of a Jewish bent, Jerusalem. As it was, it was plain old Scotland Yard. The Green Door.

They burst shoulder to shoulder through the entrance, batting aside Constable Greeno still carrying plants around. His startled cry mingled with that of Lestrade now that the door-frame had reminded him of his grazed arm. At the desk, the stalwart Sergeant Johnson hailed them.

"'Ere, you can't go up there!' he shouted.

Lestrade rounded on him, 'I was climbing stairs, Twenty-Twenty, when you were still filling your nappies. Now I feel sure there's some urgent typing you have to do, isn't there? Stolen gas meter, that sort of thing?'

Collapse of stout sergeant. He slunk off into a corner and reached for the wires-that-speak. A hand clasped over his own.

'You don't want to do that, Sergeant Johnson.' The willowy, kindly frame of Superintendent Wensley had appeared at his elbow.

'Er . . . no, sir, I just thought I'd order up some tea for Mr Lestrade, sir.'

Wensley looked wistfully up the wrought-iron staircase where the pair had fled. 'I don't think they have time at the moment,' he smiled. 'Now you cut along outside to see that no one's parked in Chief Inspector Dew's place again, there's a good lad. I'll watch the desk for you.'

'Very good, sir.'

They dashed past the Criminal Record Office, the Assistant Commissioner's enclave, Lost Property, with its sandwiches and lawn-mowers and Lestrade's old haunt, curiously empty now with Inspector Blevvins temporarily *persona non regatta*. Then they reached it – the Green Door.

Lestrade knew the code – three short knocks and a long one. Something that in code spelt out Save Our Special Branch. It opened a crack and the crack was immediately widened by Harry Bandicoot, whose boot held it fast. An astonished detective constable wrestled with it momentarily, then staggered back, his nose pouring blood from contact with Basher Bandicoot, who had once boxed for Eton and now boxed for justice.

'Good afternoon,' beamed Lestrade. 'Superintendent Quinn at home? No? Never mind. We'll see ourselves in,' and he marched through a typing-pool where papers flew in all directions. 'You don't spell counter-espionage like that, Constable,' he pointed out and kicked open the door of Sir Basil Thomson, Assistant Commissioner at the Branch.

'What the bloody hell . . .?' the bloodhound-faced man of the Maccassared hair leapt to his feet. So did the little, wiry grey-haired man with the rich, dark voice.

'Gentlemen,' Lestrade smiled. 'Sir Basil *and* Captain Kell. What a coo daytar. Harry, the door, if you please.'

The Old Etonian twisted the key in the lock and slid a filing cabinet into place against it. 'What about the window, Sholto?' he asked.

'We're six floors up, Harry,' Lestrade reminded him. 'Not even the levitationist D. D. Hume would try this one. The

216

gentlemen of the Branch will have to resort to crowbars if they want to get in here. Security is rather amiss this morning, isn't it? Thank your lucky stars, gentlemen, that Mr Bandicoot and I are not Irishmen. Just imagine if Paddy Quinn had barged his way in here.'

'What's the meaning of this, Lestrade?' Thomson barked.

'My daughter,' Lestrade told him. 'You have her. I want her back.'

'I haven't the faintest idea what you're talking about,' Thomson sat down, looking inscrutable.

Lestrade did the same. 'Some days ago, my daughter brought a letter from the Foreign Secretary to, I suspect, Captain Kell here. Since which time, she has not been seen. Which, in police jargon, Captain, means that you are the last person to have seen her.'

'I think it's time we came clean, Basil.' Kell produced a thin-stemmed pipe.

There was a sudden thump on the door.

'Send them away, Sir Basil,' Lestrade said. 'You see, if anything has happened to my daughter, I shall not hesitate to blow you both to oblivion,' and he snatched up the walking-stick he was carrying, pointed it at an appalling photograph of the appalling Lady Thomson and pulled the concealed trigger. Frame and lady shattered instantly.

'Are you all right, sir?' a voice called from outside.

'And whatever Sholto intends to do to you goes double for me,' Bandicoot promised, his jaw rigid, his back braced.

Thomson looked at the man's biceps and believed every word of it.

'It's all right,' he called to the men beyond the door, 'Captain Kell was just cleaning his gun. There's no cause for alarm.' Thomson was his old self again. 'Can I offer you crumpets, gentlemen?'

'We're not open to bribery,' Lestrade said. 'And we're both happily married. You were about to wash some linen in public, Captain, if I understood you aright a moment ago.'

Kell looked at Thomson who shrugged.

'Oh, I've got your man for you, by the way,' Lestrade said.

'What?' Thomson sat upright.

'The murderer of the foreigners and Fallabella Shaw and Paul Dacres, not to mention a rarely employed actor with a little part.'

'Who?' Kell and Thomson chorused.

'Bert Philpotts.'

Kell and Thomson looked nonplussed. 'Bert Philpotts is our murderer?' Thomson frowned.

'No, no,' Lestrade explained. 'Bert Philpotts is the actor. Colonel Glass, of Art Treasures International, is our murderer,' he told them.

There was a silence. 'So you know about that unit?'

'There's not much I don't know,' said Lestrade. 'Except the whereabouts of my daughter.'

'There's quite a bit you don't know,' Kell said, 'and perhaps it's time you did. You see, there's a legion that never was listed.'

'A legion of agents,' Lestrade nodded, 'including a man named Reilly – I wonder if Paddy Quinn's sure of him – and a man named Lockhart.'

'And a man named Dacres,' Kell said.

'Paul Dacres?'

'Known as Paul Dukes to our friends beyond the Urals.'

'The Duke!' Lestrade felt like a man who had found the last piece of a jigsaw.

'Rather flamboyant, wasn't it?' Kell said. 'I'm afraid in this dingy, rather sad little world of ours, we have to resort to childish games occasionally. It's all in a good cause, of course.'

'So why did Dacres disappear from the Front at Bapaume? And where was he for three years?'

Kell puffed on his pipe. 'Paul Dacres was in Military Intelligence – MO5 as it was then – before the War. Because of his knowledge of art he was a natural to become involved in the A.T. One establishment. He volunteered, like many other head-strong young men in 1914, for service with the Cavalry and then the Flying Corps, but he had a first-class brain and we couldn't waste him on the barbed wire. So we engineered his removal to return to the War Office.'

'Hence the fictitious foot wound,' Lestrade nodded.

'Quite. He was sent home with forged medical records and had to appear as though he had copped a Blighty. He was under strict instructions to tell no one, not even Emma Lestrade, his nearest and dearest. While supposedly recovering from his wound, he worked under Glass at the War Office. Then, in the January of 1917, things changed.'

'They did?' Lestrade had never been very hot on current affairs.

'The Tsar's regime was about to collapse. We knew it of course. It had been downhill all the way since Tannenberg. It was only a matter of time until he was overthrown. Reilly and Lockhart had worked with Dacres before. They caught the spy Karl Lody for us. We had him shot on Tower Green – didn't half give the ravens a fright, I can tell you. They also rumbled Trebitsch Lincoln – not, sadly, before he became Liberal MP for Darlington. Finally, the three of them sewed up Roger Casement good and proper. So they made a formidable trio and we sent Dacres back via France to join the other two who were in Russia already. The Germans had the Baltic and all ports watched, so he had to make it across land. He simply took off in a kite and vanished.'

'And in Russia?'

'Their first task was to help the Tsar in any way they could. By the time they got there, however, the old autocrat had been deposed and that was that. They failed.'

Not entirely, thought Lestrade, with a sad young lady in a darkened room in his mind. That little titbit he would not share with Captain Kell.

'Then, of course,' Kell said, 'the situation changed again. Kerensky and Co. of the Provisional Government which kicked out the Tsar were all in favour of fighting on against the Hun. But what if that will wavered? Worse, what if the Communists took over? The rest is history. That bald old Bolshevik, Lenin, took power in the October or was it November? They can't even sort out their calendar, these damned Ruskies. And he promptly pulled out of the War. What happened to our trio then, I've no idea. They all went underground. The next I heard of Dacres was the newspapers telling us that he'd shot himself in a London hotel. I couldn't believe it.'

'Neither could I,' said Lestrade. 'That's why I became involved.'

'Illegally,' grunted Thomson.

Lestrade smiled. 'Well,' he said, 'the only missing piece now is my daughter.'

'Ah, yes,' said Kell. 'That spineless old duffer Curzon sent a rather too-frank note by her. She, brave little girl that she is – I admire that in a woman, Lestrade – began asking all sorts of awkward questions. I got the impression that she knew too much already and the whole thing was too sensitive to let her walk away. Now that you have Glass, of course, the moment has passed. Superintendent Quinn has her. And you have my word that she is safe and well.'

'Where?'

'I can't tell you that. In what we call a safe-house. If you'll put that wretched walking-stick away and let me make a phone call, I'll have her waiting for you by the time you get home.' And he produced a little black book of telephone numbers; the book of Kell.

'Good enough,' said Lestrade.

'That's not your style, Lestrade,' Thomson commented.

'This?' Lestrade raised the stick. 'No, it's a souvenir belonging to Colonel Glass. One for the Black Museum, I think.' And he reversed it neatly for a man with only one and a half arms and left it on the table on his way out.

'Lestrade,' Thomson stopped him. 'Now that this little business is over, I don't want to see you this side of the Green Door again. Understand?'

The ex-Superintendent smiled. 'It would be my pleasure, Sir Basil,' he said.

'Or come to think of it, the other side either.'

The evening was almost as balmy as Uncle Gideon. The old man of that name was furthest from Lestrade's thoughts, however, as he leapt from the Lanchester under the evening stars. Harry Bandicoot was with him as the girl they both loved dashed across the lawn to meet them. She threw herself into their arms, hugging and kissing them both, while they muttered, 'Emma,' 'Emma,' over and over again.

It was when Lestrade pulled away that he saw them first –

shadowy men in trench coats and trilby hats, with ugly bulges under them both emerging from the bushes. He held the girl at his good arm's length and Bandicoot hid her with his bulk.

'Daddy . . .' she said, but he silenced her.

'I know,' he said. 'It's all right.'

'No, they . . .'

'Get her out of here, Harry,' Lestrade said quietly.

'But Daddy . . .'

'Listen to her, Sholto,' a jaunty Irish voice called.

He focused his eyes against the French windows and saw the silhouettes of Fanny and Letitia beyond. A rather ruffled Superintendent Sir Patrick Quinn, his collar where his hat should have been, stumbled down the path from the house.

'I see you brought her home for me, Paddy,' Lestrade said. 'Wonderful what a phone call can do, isn't it?'

'If this is your idea of a joke, Lestrade . . .' Quinn growled.

'Didn't Captain Kell telephone you?'

'Nobody telephoned me,' Quinn told him. 'I had a visit from the boys here.'

The jaunty Irish voice piped up again. 'Oh, his heart's in the right place. At least, it is for now.'

Michael Collins walked into the dying rays of the sun, resting the barrel of the Webley on his shoulder. 'I'm sorry,' he said to Lestrade, 'it took us a little longer than we thought. You've a fine girl there, Lestrade. Even has the look of a colleen, albeit a slightly Saxon one.'

'Thank you,' said Lestrade.

Collins smiled. 'By the by,' he took him by the shoulder, 'you've a fighting household here all right. Those two women inside put Padraic's lights out for a while, but I think he's all right now. Your butler chappie's a prisoner in the coal cellar; and as for that mad old bugger upstairs, well, I'm afraid we had to bind and gag him – for his own protection, you understand. We were only returning your daughter, after all. No harm meant.'

'And none done, I trust,' Lestrade said.

'Oh, Padraic'll be all right. Tell me, would you like us to wipe out Mr Quinn now we're here? We have the technology and a few minutes spare.'

'No,' Lestrade said, after too long a pause for Quinn's liking. 'No, I don't think so.'

'Ah, what a pity,' sighed Collins. 'Never mind. There'll be another time,' and he signalled his lads to go.

'Mr Collins,' Emma crossed to him, 'I don't approve of you or your methods or your cause, but I'm grateful that you returned me to my family.'

'Well now, miss,' Collins twinkled, 'if every Englishwoman was like you, we'd have no cause at all.' And he tipped his hat.

'By the way,' Lestrade saw him to his black limousine, parked surreptitiously behind the house, 'did you have any luck with the other icon? The pair to the one I gave you?'

'Curiously, no,' Collins said. 'But I did just happen to overhear your friend Inspector Kane tell his sergeant that the late Colonel Glass's treasures were stowed safely away in the Bank of England.'

'From where they'll be returned to their rightful owners,' Lestrade said.

'Ah,' said Collins, opening the car door and showing him the hilt of a beautiful medieval sword that glowed in the crimson of the evening, 'not exactly.' He produced from a sack a little known painting by da Vinci, the one Fallabella Shaw had died for, and an exquisite diamond necklace that had once adorned the neck, before they severed it, of a Queen of France; last, but by no means least, an Imperial crown, sparkling with diamonds, amethysts and rubies from the head, before he lost it, of the Father of All the Russias. 'It'll keep the fires of our cause burning for many a long year. Oddly, the other icon wasn't there. But we'll just have to manage, somehow,' and he winked at Lestrade and was gone, his boys melting into the darkness around them.

'Yes,' said Lestrade, 'it is odd, that, isn't it?' And he produced from his Donegal pocket a little pearl-and-silver Madonna, smiling at her Child. 'One at least is going back to its rightful owner,' he said. 'Rash of Colonel Glass to carry it with him on his visit the other night.'

*

The clock struck nine as Mr and Mrs Lestrade took breakfast. It was another day. Emma was visiting a certain sergeant of detectives named Norroy Macclesfield as it was his day off. They were to go later in the day to see a new film at the Palaceadium called *The Destruction of Sennacherib* and there was one part in it where Emma was going to insist that Macclesfield closed his eyes. Superintendent Patrick Quinn was back at his desk behind the Green Door, keeping very quiet about the previous night's events. Inspector John Kane was called in to investigate one of the most audacious crimes of the century – someone had broken into the vaults of the Bank of England, no less. And Constable Blevvins, uniformed Branch, was back where he started, counting horse troughs in 'H' Division and helping little old ladies across the road with the toe of his boot.

'Well,' said Lestrade, 'I've got to say it, Fanny. I've stood it long enough. What do you intend to do about your uncle?'

She put down her cup. 'Who?' she said.

'Gideon,' he told her.

'*My* uncle?' she said. 'But I thought he was *your* uncle!'

The subject of their conversation tottered down the stairs at that moment, suitcase in hand.

'Gideon?' Fanny got up from the table. 'Gideon, where are you going?'

'I've been a burden long enough, my dear,' he told her. 'I'm off to the St Ignatius Loyola Home For Only Partially Responsible Officers.'

'The . . .' Lestrade's mouth opened.

'Goodbye, General Buller,' Gideon shook his hand warmly. 'Can't say it's been a pleasure.' He stooped to kiss Fanny's hand. 'Lady Smith,' he said, catching his teeth just in time, 'may I congratulate you on your marvellous Peek Freans? Goodbye!' And he saluted briskly and was gone.

Lestrade *was* in the act of fetching him back when the telephone rang.

'Fred Wensley,' he said. 'Yes. Yes. Really? Are you sure? The Commissioner said that? Well, I don't know. Ha ha. Just like old times? God, I hope not. I don't know, Fred. I'll have to think about it. I mean, water under the bridge, you know. Bad memories. Leave something of an unpleasant taste. Yes. Yes, of course. No. I will think it over, honestly. Goodbye.'

Fanny had watched somebody else's uncle safely catch a bus at the garden gate.

'Do you think he'll be all right?' Lestrade asked. 'I've got a stiff left arm thanks to him. Without him, I'd have a missing head.'

'He's come through Spion Kop and God knows what else,' she smiled. 'Whoever he is, he'll be all right. Who was that on the phone?'

'Fred Wensley,' said Lestrade, reaching for his Donegal. 'They're forming a special unit at the Yard, called the Flying Squad. Apparently, the Commissioner wants me to run it.'

'But you resigned, Sholto,' she told him. 'You've retired.'

'Well, yes, in a manner of speaking,' he said. 'I mean, I'm not entirely convinced about it. Flying Squad. Flying Squad. Where would they put the the runways for instance? You might as well put bloody Lord Trenchard in charge of the police. No, I'm not sold on the idea. I told Fred I'd think it over.'

'But Sholto,' she fastened his top button, 'you're dressed, dear,' she said.

'Well, I . . . I just thought I'd pop over to the Yard and have a little chat with Fred. Oh, just for old times' sake, you know. I wonder if Walter Dew still makes a decent cup of tea?'

She patted his pocket for the brass knuckles and felt the icon instead. 'You'll be going the pretty way?' she said. 'Via Chertsey?'

He nodded.

'Well, then, Sholto Lestrade,' she said, 'I'll see you tonight. And mind how you go.'

A STEAL OF A DEAL

Order the next volume in the
Lestrade Mystery Series:
Volume XI: *Lestrade and the Dead Man's Hand*

Have **Lestrade and the Dead Man's Hand** sent directly to your home for a steal of a deal—20% off plus FREE shipping and handling.

The year is 1895 and a dead body is found on the last train to Liverpool Street in the London Underground Railway. Another corpse is found at the Elephant in the morning, wedged between the seats like an old suitcase. And another missed the late-night connection at Stockwell.

There is a maniac at large and Inspector Lestrade is detailed to work with the Railway Police. Will the London Transport System survive or will Lestrade run out of steam?

Volume XI in the Lestrade Mystery Series will be sent from the publisher—<u>via free expedited shipping</u>—directly to your home at a cost to you of **<u>only $15.95</u>**. That's a savings of nearly $10 over the actual retail price of the book and normal shipping and handling charges.

And, with the purchase of any book for $15.95, you may buy any of the first four volumes for just $9.95 each!

ALERT SCOTLAND YARD. IT'S A STEAL!

Call 1-888-219-4747 to get your
<u>Lestrade Steal of a Deal</u>!

❑ Yes, please send my copies from the Lestrade Mystery Series as indicated below.

Fax orders to 202-216-9183

❑ Enclosed is my check or money order.

or

❑ Charge my ❑ VISA ❑ MasterCard ❑ ⬤ ❑ NOVUS

Credit Card # _____Exp. date_____

Signature _____

Phone _____

Please indicate the address to which you would like your copies sent.

Name _____

Street _____

City _____State _____Zip _____

Mail this form to:

CALL 1-888-219-4747

Gateway Mysteries c/o Regnery Publishing
P.O. Box 97199 • Washington, D.C. 20090-7199

Qty.	Book	Code	Price	Total
	The Adventures of Inspector Lestrade	LST1	$9.95	
	Brigade: The Further Adventures of Lestrade	LST2	$9.95	
	Lestrade and the Hallowed House	LST3	$9.95	
	Lestrade and the Leviathan	LST4	$9.95	
	Lestrade and the Deadly Game	LST5	$15.95	
	Lestrade and the Ripper	LST6	$15.95	
	Lestrade and the Brother of Death	LST7	$15.95	
	Lestrade and the Guardian Angel	LST8	$15.95	
	Lestrade and the Gift of the Prince	LST9	$15.95	
	Lestrade and the Magpie	LST10	$15.95	
	Lestrade the Dead Man's Hand	LST11	$15.95	
		Shipping and Handling		FREE!
RSP233		Total		